She eyed him from under her lashes,
her gaze skimming over him from the
top of that dark head, down past those
arresting blue eyes, past those
high cheekbones and well-sculpted mouth,
past that strong jaw....

Goodness, he was a handsome man. She had only to look at
him and her cheeks were on fire!

Impersonating the princess had flung her deep into uncharted
waters. She was utterly out of her depth here in more ways
than one. Surely he could sense it? Her hand was shaking
so much she was likely to tip wine over her gown. *Does he
know that I am quaking inside? Does he suspect that I am
misleading him?*

Will I be safe if he learns the truth?

A new thought caught her by surprise. For the first time in an
age, Katerina was not sure she wanted to be safe.

* * *

Bound to the Barbarian
Harlequin® Historical #326—February 2012

Author Note

There is much that is known about the Byzantine Empire—the medieval Greek empire—and much that is unknown. It remains one of the most fascinating periods of history. It has glittering palaces, princesses, slaves, vaults filled with treasure, even handbooks on protocol. There is more than a little hint of the East and the exotic. Medieval Constantinople (Istanbul as it is today) was full of wonders. As with any period of history, there were horrors, too, but all in all, it is the wonders that prevail....

Stories about the Varangian Guard abound. They were the emperor's personal guard, elite mercenaries, and they had to swear an oath to serve the emperor until death. They were often Vikings or Anglo-Saxons. The particular inspiration behind this novel is one that concerns a rather strange right the Varangians won for themselves. It was a right given to no one else. At the time of the death of their emperor, the Varangians had the right to pillage the palace. The tradition was that they could keep whatever they could carry away. I may have stretched the point just a little in this story....

These books give insight into the times:

Byzantium, the Surprising Life of a Medieval Empire
by Judith Herrin

Byzantium
by Robin Cormack and Maria Vassilaki

Fourteen Byzantine Rulers
by Michael Psellus

The Alexiad of Anna Komnene
translated by E.R.A Sewter

BOUND *to the* BARBARIAN

CAROL TOWNEND

TORONTO NEW YORK LONDON
AMSTERDAM PARIS SYDNEY HAMBURG
STOCKHOLM ATHENS TOKYO MILAN MADRID
PRAGUE WARSAW BUDAPEST AUCKLAND

Recycling programs
for this product may
not exist in your area.

ISBN-13: 978-0-373-30635-0

BOUND TO THE BARBARIAN

Copyright © 2010 by Carol Townend

First North American Publication 2012

www.Harlequin.com

Printed in U.S.A.

Look for further novels
in Carol Townend's miniseries
Palace Brides
Coming soon from Harlequin® Historical

*Available from Harlequin® Historical and
CAROL TOWNEND in ebook format:*

**Praise for
Carol Townend**

THE NOVICE BRIDE
"*The Novice Bride* is sweet, tantalizing, frustrating,
seductively all-consuming, deliciously provocative…
I can't go on enough about this story's virtues.
Read this book. You'll fall in love a hundred times over."
—*Romance Junkies*

"From the very first words,
this story snatches the reader from present day,
willingly pulling hearts and minds back to the time of
the Norman conquest. Culture clash, merciless invaders,
innocence lost and freedom captured—all wonderfully
highlighted in this mesmerizing novel."
—*Romance Reader at Heart*

AN HONORABLE ROGUE
"Ms. Townend's impeccable attention to detail and lush,
vivid images bring this time period to life."
—*Romance Reader at Heart*

To my daughter, with all my love

Acknowledgments:

I should like to thank Professor Judith Herrin for her helpful answers to my questions on the male and female forms of Greek names, and on forms of address in medieval Byzantium. I have used Greek versions of names where possible, but in a couple of cases I have shortened the names of real people to avoid confusion.

CAROL TOWNEND

has been making up stories since she was a child. Whenever she comes across a tumbledown building, be it castle or cottage, she can't help conjuring up the lives of the people who once lived there. Her Yorkshire forebears were friendly with the Brontë sisters. Perhaps their influence lingers....

Carol's love of ancient and medieval history took her to London University where she read history, and her first novel (published by Harlequin Books) won the Romantic Novelists' Association's New Writers' Award. Currently, she lives near Kew Gardens with her husband and daughter. Visit her website, caroltownend.co.uk.

Chapter One

Ashfirth was unable to keep the shock from his voice. 'The Princess is in *here*?'

'Yes, Commander.'

Shooting a disbelieving glance at his captain, Ashfirth dismounted. He was careful to hide the twinge of pain in his leg. Lord, it felt no better, despite the rest he had given it. The ride from the port on the other side of the salt marshes had not been arduous, but his leg felt as though it was being gnawed by wolves. Surely broken bones mended more quickly than this? Removing his helmet, he hooked it over his saddle bow, surreptitiously easing his aching limb. He wanted his men to think he was fully recovered.

'What did you say this place was?' He shoved back his mail coif.

'It's a convent, sir.'

It didn't look much. The dome of the church was barely visible above the convent walls. It was cracked like a broken eggshell and someone had attempted to repair it. A botched job. Weeds had taken root in the rendering.

'I'll lay odds that roof leaks,' Ash said.

Captain Brand grinned and shook his head. 'Only a fool would take that bet on, Commander.'

Ash made a non-committal sound and completed his survey of the walls and buildings. Why on earth would the Princess take refuge in a minor convent outside Dyrrachion? To the military eye, the walls were also in dire need of repair. One section was little better than a tumble of stone; it was splotchy with yellow lichen and clearly had been that way for some time. Even as Ash looked, a bell tinkled and a brown-and-white goat leaped into view in the opening. The goat stood for a moment on top of the stones, its slanty eyes unearthly in the morning light. Then, the bell at its neck a-jangle, it leaped down and wandered into the scrub. Ash lifted a brow.

What the devil was Princess Theodora doing here? The answer flashed back in an instant. Tucked away at the northern edge of the Empire, this convent was to her mind probably ideal. The woman—Ash eased his leg again, he would strangle her when he finally got his hands on her— most likely thought this was the last place anyone would look.

'It *is* the last place,' Ash murmured, realising with a sense of surprise that he was closer to England, his home-land, than he'd been in years. The thought brought no pain, which was less of a surprise. Ashfirth had long ago come to terms with his new life, but come to terms he had, thank God.

'Sir?'

'If the Princess thinks *that* wall will keep us out, she can think again.'

Brand eyed the low wall and grinned again. 'Yes, sir.' The sunlight bounced off the razor-sharp edge of his battle-axe. Brand was a good captain, and an excellent scout. Once they had arrived in Dyrrachion, he had been quick to make contact with someone who had mentioned a nearby convent that offered shelter to ladies from all walks of life.

'Does this ruin have a name?'

'St Mary's.' Captain Brand cleared his throat, opened his mouth, appeared to think better of it and closed it again.

'There's more, isn't there? Come on, man, out with it.' Brand was struggling to keep a straight face. Like Ash, Brand was an Anglo-Saxon from England and Ash could read him as he might read a brother, particularly when, as now, they were speaking in English.

'Yes, sir. St Mary's is renowned hereabouts.'

'St Mary's doesn't look as though it would be renowned for anything except the wretched state of its masonry.'

'It takes in women, sir…women who choose to leave the world because they repent of their former way of life.'

Ash raised an eyebrow. 'The Princess has taken refuge in a convent for fallen women?'

'Yes, sir.'

'The Princess must be desperate.'

'Sir?'

'Why else run to Dyrrachion, to a convent for fallen women—she really doesn't want to marry Duke Nikolaos, does she?' Briefly, Ash spared a thought for the woman they had tracked to this remote outpost.

'Why should marriage to the Duke of Larissa be so repellent, sir?'

'Lord knows.' Ash had never met Duke Nikolaos, he knew him only by repute. Accounts spoke of a fine soldier, a brilliant commander. A man of honour. 'The Duke of Larissa's holding is at the heart of the Empire; he is of the old elite, the military aristocracy. She could hardly hope to do better—her reservations about marrying him are odd, to say the least.'

'Wasn't Princess Theodora's first betrothal to an outsider?'

'Yes, she was betrothed to one of the Rascian princes. The rumour is that she grew fond of him—that must explain her reluctance to marry Duke Nikolaos.' Ash grimaced. 'But the Rascian prince is dead, she has to forget him.'

Brand rubbed his chin. 'That may be easier said than done, sir.'

'Nevertheless, she must forget him.' Ash knew that Greek princesses usually viewed marriages made outside the boundaries of the Empire as something of a penance. He also knew that Greek princesses were highly sought after all over Christendom, possibly because such contracts rarely took place. 'Prince Peter was only a minor prince. Her new fiancé, Duke Nikolaos of Larissa, is of a different order altogether—he is one of the most powerful men in the Empire. The Emperor considers this marriage important, Princess Theodora will not be allowed to wriggle out of it.'

Ashfirth glanced at the convent. The Princess might be reluctant to return home, but his priorities were clear. As Commander of the Varangian Guard, Ashfirth answered to the Emperor and to no one else.

Back in the Great Palace in Constantinople, the ageing Emperor had summoned Ash to a private audience in an apartment where the walls glittered with golden mosaics from floor to ceiling.

The Emperor, arguably the most powerful man in Christendom, had slumped in his throne like a man sapped of strength. There he had sat, much withered by age, seemingly diminished by the trappings of power that surrounded him. There was the double-headed eagle on the Imperial standard; there were the Imperial robes. It had struck Ash that never had that standard looked more forlorn. And as for the robes, it seemed that they were wearing the man.

Surely it ought to be the other way around, surely the man should wear the robes?

The voice was creaking and tired. 'Commander, the Rascian prince who was betrothed to my niece the Princess Theodora is dead,' Emperor Nikephoros had told him. 'You are to bring her home.'

Strictly speaking, Princess Theodora was not the Emperor's niece; in truth, she was the niece of the *previous* Emperor, Michael Doukas. But it would not have been tactful for Ash to have pointed this out because the new Emperor—despite his advanced years—had married Emperor Michael's young and beautiful wife. This made the question of Princess Theodora's relationship to him a moot point.

'My niece has been living among barbarians for too long,' Emperor Nikephoros had gone on to say. 'In the Palace she may reacquaint herself with more civilised ways and prepare herself to meet her new betrothed, Duke Nikolaos.'

Which was how Ash came to be thousands of miles away from his quarters in the Boukoleon Palace, and now found himself near the port of Dyrrachion, staring at the gate of this out-of-the-way convent.

A convent for fallen women.

The gate looked sturdier than the walls; it was made of seasoned oak bleached by many summers. A small barred window had been cut into it at eye level. At present it was shuttered fast, but a bell-pull hung alongside it.

Unstrapping his battle-axe, Ash hung it over his pommel alongside his helmet. He caught Brand's eye. 'You, too, Brand—there is no sense in frightening the ladies.'

Unless we have to. Frightening the ladies might be the only way to get the Princess to accept his escort back to Constantinople.

'Yes, sir.'

While Brand disarmed himself, Ash gave a final glance at the lichen-splotched walls and approached the gate. The walls would not present much of an obstacle if the Princess balked at going with them; in truth, his men would likely relish a minor challenge after being cooped up on board ship. But he must start with a diplomatic approach; she was a member of the Imperial family.

Brand was watching him, reading his mind. He eyed the walls. 'We could get in that way easily, sir.'

'Save that thought, we might need it later.' Ash gestured at the gate. 'In the meantime, see if you get someone's attention, the place appears to be deserted.'

Brand grinned. 'Perhaps they ran out of fallen women.'

'With the city and port so close?' Ash gave a short laugh. 'Not likely. The Princess and her entourage are in there, I am sure of it. All we have to do is extract her, then we may be back at the Palace by Easter.'

Nodding agreement, Brand heaved on the bell-pull.

Ash shifted, taking the weight off his bad leg. Lord, but it ached—the Princess had better hurry; the thought of a massage from his body-servant Hrodric was becoming more attractive by the moment.

The shutter in the gate clicked open. Ash squared his shoulders.

Princess Theodora might have had him chasing all over the Empire, but finally he had found her. He might feel like wringing her neck, but since she was the Emperor's niece and a member of the powerful Doukas family, it was probably treason even to think such a thought. So, when a pair of brown eyes—very beautiful brown eyes—came into view on the other side of the grille, Ash had a smile ready.

'Good day,' he said, switching effortlessly to Greek. 'I should like to speak to Princess Theodora.'

The eyes widened. *Doe's eyes.*

Ash thought he heard a woman's voice, and for a moment those doe's eyes slid sideways. Someone standing next to her was speaking to her. Then the dark eyes met his, directly. A visceral jolt went through him. He frowned.

'Your name, sir?' Her voice was light and clear. Courteous.

'Ashfirth Saxon, Commander of the Varangian Guard. The Emperor has charged me with escorting Princess Theodora back to the Great Pal—'

The eyes withdrew, the shutter closed with a snap.

Gritting his teeth, Ashfirth exchanged glances with his captain. As one, they turned to look at the crumbling wall.

'I'll give her half an hour,' Ash said.

Brand's face brightened.

Yes, the men are definitely in need of exercise.

On the other side of the gate, the Princess was standing at Katerina's side. Her violet veil was trembling.

'Is he there, Katerina? Has the Duke come in person?'

'*Despoina?* My lady?'

'Is the Duke outside?'

Katerina pressed her nose to the grille and peered through a crack in the shutter. 'I do not know if those are his men, my lady. What does Duke Nikolaos look like?' Katerina's gaze was caught by the taller of the two warriors standing at the entrance. 'There is a man here who calls himself Ashfirth Saxon. He wants speech with you.'

'Ashfirth Saxon?' Princess Theodora's tone was scornful, but Katerina heard the quiver in it and pitied her. Her mistress really did not wish to marry Duke Nikolaos. 'Who is this Ashfirth Saxon?'

*He's tall and fierce-looking. He has wind-burned skin.
His hair gleams like jet and his eyes—Heavens!—how did
a man with such dark hair come by eyes so blue?* Katerina's
gut clenched as she inched the shutter open, the better to
study him. Ashfirth Saxon had eyes that were almost as
turquoise as the stones set in the cover of Princess Theodora's book of psalms. They made a disturbing contrast
with the jet-black hair.

'He says he is Commander of the Varangian Guard
and—'

'The Varangians? Holy Mother, don't tell me the Emper-
or has sent his personal guard!' The Princess tugged at the
sleeve of Katerina's gown, bracelets chinking. 'Are you
certain? Can you see battle-axes?'

'Yes, *despoina*. My lady, the men on horseback all have
axes and—'

'They are mounted?' The Princess's voice calmed.
'Varangian guards usually fight on foot.'

'Not all are mounted, my lady.'

'Are they dressed for battle?'

'They are wearing coats of mail, certainly.'

The Princess swore, using an oath that Katerina was certain ought never to be uttered within the walls of a convent.

'Princess!'

'Don't be such a prude, Katerina. You know where most
of these nuns have come from—they will have heard far
worse, I am sure.'

Katerina doubted it, but she held her tongue. She should
not have spoken up, it was not her place to criticise.

The Princess poked her in the ribs. 'Are you sure you
can see no sign of the Duke? His standard, perhaps?'

Peering past the iron bars, Katerina twisted her head
from side to side, hoping to see the rest of the soldiers, but
her view was limited. It was blocked by Ashfirth Saxon and

his companion. *So tall. Handsome devil, too. Except that he looks so angry.* Ashfirth Saxon's mouth was no longer smiling, it was set in a thin line. And those startling turquoise eyes might be looking at her past thick dark lashes, but they looked cold. Dispassionate. What did she expect? If this man was Commander of the Varangian Guard, the personal bodyguard to the Emperor, he would likely be more hard and ruthless than the rest.

Katerina cleared her throat. A guardsman's battle-axe flashed in the sun. 'I can see no standard, but they are very well armed. If I were you, I do not think I would want to keep this Ashfirth Saxon waiting.'

'If you were me?' Princess Theodora's voice became sharp. 'You are insolent today, *slave.*'

Hurt sliced through Katerina like a blade. *Slave.* Well, that was what she had been until the Princess had rescued her—a slave. She had been one for so many years, it was a wonder the word had kept the power to wound, but wound it did. Particularly when it came from the lips of her princess, the princess who had freed her from the torture that her life as a slave had become. That Princess Theodora had sunk to remind Katerina of her past merely emphasised how repugnant she found the thought of marrying the Duke of Larissa.

Shooting the Princess a bleak glance—she was chewing her lip—Katerina's heart softened. Her mistress was not by nature vindictive, as Katerina herself had good reason to know, it was simply that she was under too much strain. Duke Nikolaos terrified her. She knew it was not just slave girls who found themselves at the mercy of their menfolk.

Not even a princess can escape what men have planned for her!

The next moment a gentle hand reached for hers. 'Katerina, forgive me?'

Katerina looked into the Princess's eyes. Princess Theodora had eyes that Katerina had been assured mirrored her own almost exactly. They were, according to Lady Sophia, one of Princess Theodora's ladies-in-waiting, the same shade of brown. Their eyes, Lady Sophia had said, had the same shape—they even had the same eyebrows. And the Princess's mirror had confirmed it.

'For what? You spoke the truth, *despoina*. Until you freed me, I was a slave.'

For a moment the old bitterness welled up and Katerina felt her heart harden. Her bitterness was not directed towards the princess who had bought and freed her, rather it was directed towards the man who had sold her into slavery. Her father.

Towards the Princess, Katerina felt only gratitude. She longed to be able to repay her for her generosity in offering Katerina—a peasant girl—a place in her aristocratic entourage and training her. But what could she—a maid-servant—possibly have that a princess might desire?

A thoughtful expression came over Princess Theodora's face. She leaned forwards and a beringed hand lifted to close the wooden shutter. From the other side of the gate, came the jangle of a bell and the bleat of a goat. A man laughed.

'Katerina?'

'My lady?'

'Accompany me to the church. There is something I wish to meditate upon.'

'Yes, *despoina*.'

When Princess Theodora, golden bracelets chinking in the light, linked arms with her, Katerina was unsurprised. This was more like the mistress she knew. Princess Theodora, niece of the Emperor himself, was a warm-hearted, even-handed woman who—while knowing of Katerina's humble background—unfailingly treated her in the same way she treated her high-born ladies-in-waiting. Since taking Katerina under her wing, the Princess had taught Katerina the ways of the Court. She had taught her how to speak in a more refined manner—she had even taught her how to read.

Not many high-born ladies would even notice when a slave was being maltreated, but back in Rascia the Princess had noticed. Not many high-born ladies would then be willing to buy that slave to prevent her from further harm, but the Princess had done exactly that. And it was a rare woman indeed who would then go on to free the slave and offer her a position among her ladies.

If only there were some way of repaying her...

Lady Sophia and Lady Zoë made to follow them, but the Princess waved them away. 'Leave us. I wish to offer up a few personal prayers, Katerina's company will suffice.'

The church was cool and dark after the bright sunlight. Princess Theodora led Katerina to an alcove overlooked by a gaudily painted and earthy-looking statue of Saint Mary. Mary Magdalene, Katerina thought, lips twisting, the saint of fallen women everywhere. She shot her mistress a sidelong glance. *Of course, how apt.*

A couple of tallow candles lit the alcove and two nuns were kneeling before the statue. Reformed sinners? Perhaps. As the Princess and Katerina approached, the nuns glanced up, crossed themselves and scurried into the main church.

'Katerina, I have a favour to ask and, out of all my ladies, you are the only one who might undertake it.'

'Princess, from the moment you bought me in Rascia and gave me my freedom, I have been searching for a suitable way of thanking you. I would do anything for you!'

'Anything? Be careful what you promise, Katerina.' The Princess's smile was strained. 'You do not know what I may ask. It might be—' she bit her lip '—somewhat dangerous.'

Katerina gripped her mistress's hand. 'I would do *anything*! I mean it, how could you think otherwise? What must I do? Tell me!'

'No.' Princess Theodora jerked her head away to stare at the cross on the altar. 'It is too risky, I cannot ask it of you.'

'Princess…' Katerina moved closer. 'I want to help you. Let me help you.'

Brown eyes looked steadily into brown. 'If it were not for my…the baby…I would not think about asking. If only the Commander had not found us so soon.' Her chest heaved. 'Still, we cannot alter that, not now. We shall have to take it one step at a time.'

And then, to Katerina's astonishment, the Princess's hands went to the pins of her violet veil. 'First, we shall see how this suits you.' Then, gaze flickering towards the main church to ensure they were not overlooked, the Princess kicked off her jewelled sandals and nudged them towards Katerina. 'And these, I want you to try these on for size.' There was a flutter of silk as the veil was removed.

Katerina's eyes went wide. *'My lady?'*

The Princess was looking her up and down, like a seamstress measuring someone for a new gown. 'You are a little smaller than I, but we are almost of a height. Good. And it is most fortunate that our eyes are a match.'

A cold shiver ran down Katerina's spine. She found herself staring at the jewelled sandals on the church flagstones.

'Well? Try them on, Katerina. If they fit, you are going to meet with Commander Ashfirth to see what he has to say.'

Katerina swallowed. 'That is how I am to repay you?'

The Princess, busily shaking out her veil, would not meet her gaze. 'Perhaps. Now be quiet while I think, and put this on.'

Some minutes later, the snap of the shutter drew Ashfirth's gaze back to the convent gate. He straightened and strode across.

Doe Eyes was back.

He knew her at once, even though this second time she was so heavily veiled that her eyes were barely visible. The soft fall of her veil had the look of fine silk, it was violet in colour and shot through with gold threads.

'Commander Ashfirth!'

Her voice was still light and clear, but something about it had changed. Ashfirth was unable to put his finger on what that change was. Was it more forceful? More confident?

'The Princess will see me?'

Behind the bars, Doe Eyes withdrew slightly. 'Commander—' her voice was cool '—it would please the Princess to know exactly why you are here.'

It would please the Princess. Ashfirth narrowed his eyes. *This is a delaying tactic, she knows why I am here.* 'Am I addressing the Princess?'

He couldn't read her, not without seeing her whole face—that damned veil hid too much. Everything but a slight flicker in the brown eyes.

'Answer my question, if you please, Commander.'

At this moment, she certainly had the tone of a princess. Lofty. Calm. A gold thread winked in the light. This must be the Princess. Most likely she was irritated that he had caught her unprepared when he had first knocked. It didn't escape him that she had ignored his question. He would be brief.

'His Imperial Majesty the Emperor Nikephoros has commanded me to escort Princess Theodora back to the Great Palace at Constantinople.'

There was a pause, and again the doe's eyes flickered. Her head turned to one side and Ashfirth caught a faint mutter of voices. If Doe Eyes was the Princess, and Ashfirth strongly suspected that she was, someone behind the gate was certainly advising her.

The brown eyes met his. 'Is Duke Nikolaos with you?'

Ashfirth shook his head. 'Duke Nikolaos will join you once you have reached Constantinople. The Emperor wishes you to reacquaint yourself with…' Ashfirth paused to search for the right words, the diplomatic words. Peter, the Rascian princeling who had been her fiancé, was in the eyes of many Greeks a barbarian. The Imperial Court had been astonished when word had reached them that the Princess had allowed herself to become enamoured of him. 'The Emperor wishes you to reacquaint yourself with life at the Palace.'

When Peter of Rascia had been killed in a petty border skirmish at the edge of his territory, the Emperor had been swift to arrange a second betrothal. Byzantine Princesses were valuable commodities, and as a member of a powerful family, this young woman would have been brought up on the idea. Her person could be traded according to the political needs of the time.

Ten years ago Emperor Michael had found it politically expedient to betroth her to the vassal ruler of Rascia. Had the Prince lived, the contract would have been honoured, but his death altered everything.

Today, it was less important to placate a minor kingdom at the far reaches of the Empire. A different Emperor occupied the throne, one who needed to look closer to home for support. The military aristocracy was crying out for change and Emperor Nikephoros needed every ally he could lay his hands on.

In offering the Duke of Larissa this well-born Princess for his bride, the Emperor hoped to placate him. Marriage with the Princess would, he hoped, ensure the Duke's loyalty should the conflict among his generals come to a head.

The brown eyes stared into his. *What is she thinking?* Ashfirth was fully conscious that Princess Theodora would likely peg him for a barbarian in much the same way that the Imperial Court had thought her Rascian prince a barbarian. Ash was an Anglo-Saxon, a dispossessed Anglo-Saxon in charge of the Varangian Guard. The Court only tolerated him because of his loyalty to the Emperor and his skills as a leader and warrior. The citizens of Constantinople never forgot that the men of the Varangian Guard were mercenaries, barbarian mercenaries.

The woman behind the grille had her head tilted slightly to one side. She was obviously listening to her advisor, but those brown eyes were fixed on him. While the low muttering continued, Ashfirth was able to watch her quite openly. Something was telling him that this woman, princess or otherwise, had her secrets. He had not given up on trying to read her, but when the long eyelashes swept down, he had learned nothing.

'Constantinople is a long sea journey away,' she said, in that cool, carefully modulated voice. 'You cannot expect a princess to be ready at the snap of your fingers. Be so good as to return on the morrow.'

Ashfirth felt a frown forming, he held it back. *'Tomorrow?* The Princess must have received the Emperor's summons, she must know how…eager he is for her return to Court.'

He paused, gritting his teeth. The Princess had to have known someone was coming to escort her back to the capital! Ash had been informed that several letters had been sent. Not that a reply had ever been received. The Emperor had given her the benefit of the doubt; he had assumed her replies had been lost *en route*. Ashfirth was not so sure. Had she replied? Surely the Princess would not do the Emperor the discourtesy of simply ignoring his letters?

However, those doe's eyes were looking steadily back at him, giving nothing away. And she was right, blast her. The journey was likely to take some time and there was no sense starting off on the wrong foot by naming her a liar. Especially if this was the Princess.

Keep it simple. Non-confrontational.

'Our ship leaves this afternoon,' he said.

Doe Eyes tipped her head to one side and listened to her counsellor.

'Two hours,' she said. 'Come back in two hours.'

'The Princess will be ready to leave?'

'Yes.'

Nodding curtly, Ashfirth turned away. A light click informed him that the shutter had closed.

Two hours?

Make that four. The woman has not been born who can keep proper time. And this one is a princess who not only leaves the Emperor's letters unanswered, but attempts to evade his summons to Court.

Catching Brand's eyes on him, Ashfirth spread his hands. 'Two hours, Captain. Tell half the men they have two hours before reporting back for duty. Something tells me that Princess Theodora won't be too punctual.'

'Two hours? Right, Commander.'

The Princess reached in front of Katerina to slide back the shutter and the tall, dark commander was cut off from sight.

'Oh!' Katerina said.

'What?'

'He has a limp.'

Princess Theodora looked blankly at her. 'Who?'

'Commander Ashfirth.' The Princess's dark eyes searched hers and Katerina felt her cheeks warm. 'Yes, he's limping. I didn't notice at first, it is only a slight limp, but…'

When her mistress lifted an eyebrow at her, Katerina trailed to a halt—the Princess wasn't remotely interested in Commander Ashfirth. Worse, she was looking at Katerina as though she had never seen her before, a slow smile dawning.

Inside the convent, the baby began to cry. The Princess smothered a small groan.

Katerina's stomach clenched with foreboding. Hastily, she snatched at the pins of the violet veil and made to hand it back.

The Princess brushed it aside, and Katerina caught the glitter of tears.

'*Despoina*, what is it?'

'Katerina, I am sorry…' Princess Theodora's voice broke. She gave a weak smile 'But I fear I am going to have to ask for your help after all.'

Katerina swallowed. 'Are you?'

The Princess nodded. 'Yes. I would not do so if I did not have to, you do understand?'

'*Despoina?*'

The baby had stopped crying, but nevertheless the Princess took Katerina's arm and set off in the direction of the convent guest house. 'I do not wish to marry Duke Nikolaos, and you say you wish to return the favour I once did you.'

The Princess pushed through the guest-house door, her eyes going straight to the tiny child in Lady Sophia's arms.

'I have her, *despoina*, she is all right,' Lady Sophia said, bending back over the infant. 'Aren't you, my dove?'

'What do you want me to do, my lady?' Katerina looked at the Princess, at the baby Lady Sophia was cooing over, and then back at the Princess. She was beginning to feel distinctly uneasy.

'It is simple. I should like you, Katerina,' Princess Theodora said, 'to pretend to be me.'

Chapter Two

'I must pretend to be you?' Katerina's jaw dropped. 'My lady, you are not serious!'

'I regret to say that I am.' Princess Theodora glanced pointedly at the infant in Lady Sophia's lap. The Princess's tone intensified, the words tumbling out. 'My time with my daughter is likely to be short. You must forgive me, Katerina, but I am desperate to be with her as long as I may.'

Hurrying to one of the travelling chests, the Princess pushed back the lid and leaned it against the wall. She reached inside and sent a stream of silks and satins flying towards her pallet: first came her favourite pink gown, the one with the silver embroidery at the neck and hem; next came the blue one made from finest English wool; then the brown silk, which shimmered with silver threads when she walked; the cream one with green acanthus leaves embroidered at the hem; the delicate green with pearl-encrusted cuffs…

Several veils floated through the air and settled on the gowns: the deep purple one that was reserved for important ceremonies because only members of the Imperial family were entitled to wear purple; the cream; the grey; the yellow...

'Despoina?'

The Princess whirled and grabbed Katerina's hand. 'Here, these will suit you. What a blessing we are similar in height and build. Do you like them?'

Do you like them?

Katerina's insides turned to water. *The Princess means this! The Princess really means this!*

Princess Theodora's eyes were bright and intense, her jaw was set. She looked so determined, she seemed not to have noticed that Katerina had reservations, that sheer terror was a breath away. That, or she was choosing to ignore it. The Princess wanted more time with her baby daughter, which was perfectly natural. Princess Theodora was not the first princess to anticipate her wedding night; she was not the first princess to bear a child before she was married. Unfortunately, it seemed likely that little Martina would be taken from her the moment she set foot in Constantinople.

In preparation for her forthcoming marriage, all evidence of Princess Theodora's transgression would be swept away.

Heart full, helpless in the face of the Princess's pain, Katerina watched her mistress turn to another of the iron-bound chests and dip into that. A pair of kid shoes landed on the bed; some short riding boots; sandals; purple slippers...

Katerina's heart sank when she saw the purple slippers. 'Despoina?'

'Mmm?'

Katerina extracted the purple veil and matching slippers from the rapidly growing pile and held them out. 'I can *never* wear these. You know it is forbidden. Ordinary

people just *cannot* wear purple! I was not born in the Great
Palace. I am not remotely related to the Emperor. What
would happen to a slave who did such a thing?'

'I gave you your freedom some time ago, Katerina.'

'That does not alter the fact that I am just a poor girl from
one of the islands. Surely any offence would be compounded if someone like me committed it? I could be beheaded—'

'Nonsense!' Princess Theodora drew herself up, her eyes
looked haughty even while her mouth was trembling. 'I
will see that no harm comes to you. I cannot force you, you
are a free woman now. But if you do consent to take my
place, Katerina, I will write a letter exonerating you from
all blame. It will be made quite clear that you are acting
under orders, my orders.'

A shadow fell over them, Lady Anna was standing in
the doorway.

'Not now, Anna.' The Princess waved her away.

Lady Anna ducked back outside and the light strengthened.

Princess Theodora drew in a breath and took the purple
slippers and veil. Pointedly, she replaced them on the pile.
'Katerina, you said you wished to repay me for releasing
you from servitude. Here is your chance.'

'Yes, but…but…to *impersonate* you! *Despoina*, I could
never carry it off!'

'Of course you could.' The Princess turned Katerina's
hands palm up. 'When I bought you, your hands were work-
worn, your nails broken. See how they have healed, you
have the hands of a lady now.'

'But—'

'Think. You have learned our ways. I taught you to read.
You can even write—'

Katerina let out a short laugh. 'Only my name!'

'That is enough to convince, particularly since most

ladies cannot even read.' The Princess glanced at her sleeping daughter. 'Besides, if you agree to help me, I can offer you real freedom.'

'Real freedom?'

'I will give you a grant of land in...where did you say you came from?'

'Crete.' There was a lump in Katerina's throat. She swallowed hard. She was not certain she wanted to set eyes on Crete again and had opened her mouth to say as much, but the Princess was unstoppable...

'Crete it is then. I shall give you a grant of land in Crete. And gold. And since your time with us has turned you into a lady in all but name, I will also find you a noble husband, if you so wish. Katerina, I know it is no light thing that I ask of you.' She gave a great sigh. 'But perhaps you have changed your mind about wishing to help me.'

'No...but...'

The Princess fell to her knees.

Katerina blinked. Lady Sophia stared. Princess Theodora, niece to the Emperor, was on her knees before her body-servant.

'Katerina, I beg you, I *implore* you! Take my place, let Commander Ash...what was his name?'

'Ashfirth Saxon.'

'Let him escort you to Constantinople. Give me a month, pretend to be me for a month or two, that is all that I ask. I will try to wean her...and...and another couple of months will give me more time to get used to the thought of losing her. Please, Katerina?'

'*Despoina*, do you really think matters will be easier two months from now? I am afraid you are merely delaying the inevitable.'

'I need more time with her! Please, Katerina, if you had

a child, you would understand. Go with the Commander. Please.'

For a moment Katerina could feel the penetrating blue eyes of Commander Ashfirth boring into her. 'But…but he is a barbarian!'

The Princess's expression softened. 'Not all barbarians are cast in the same mould as Vukan, Katerina.'

'Yes, I understand that. But the Commander will soon realise that I am no princess. My speech…it…it is not that of a lady.'

Her mistress shook her head. 'It may not have been when you joined us, but it is now. Besides, he mistook you at the gate.'

'It is one thing to mistake someone who is speaking through a grille and quite another to embark on a journey with them and not discover their true nature. The Commander will find me out and…and…'

'He is a foreigner, as you have pointed out. A barbarian's ear will not be finely tuned to the nuances of our language. He will not find you out.' Rising, Princess Theodora shook out her skirts. 'You have a quick mind. If you think about it, you will realise that you already know how to be me.' Her eyes grew warm. 'You have been my servant for…how long?'

'Two years, my lady.'

'That is quite long enough for you to have learned my mannerisms. As I said, we are similar in looks and colouring.'

'But…but—he said you are summoned to the Great Palace in Constantinople, I have never set foot there! If by some miracle I were to reach it undiscovered, it would become obvious at once that the Palace is unknown to me.'

Princess Theodora frowned. 'Ye…es, I see, that is a good point.' Her brow cleared. 'I know! You shall take several of my ladies with you. No one will think twice about the Princess travelling with her ladies-in-waiting, indeed, it will be expected. I shall make certain that Lady Anna is among them—she knows the Palace better than anyone. On the journey, she can describe it to you. She knows whom you will be likely to meet, she knows palace protocols, and—'

Palace protocols. Katerina was beginning to feel more than a little queasy. She wanted to help the Princess, but this…!

She shook her head. 'My lady, it won't do. What if I were summoned to meet the Emperor? He would know at once that I am an impostor.'

Her mistress gave a sad smile. 'My real uncle, if you remember, was supplanted and put in a monastery. This Emperor has never met me.'

'But didn't he marry Emperor Michael's wife? Surely she will realise—'

The Princess made a dismissive gesture. 'Katerina, it is *ten years* since I was last at the palace, I was a child. No one will know that you are not me, I promise you.' She smiled and clasped her hands together. 'I would not ask you to do this if I thought there was any danger for you. I am sure Commander Ashfirth will treat you courteously, everything will be fine. A few weeks, Katerina, that is all I ask, a few weeks. Martina will be stronger then. And think, you will have riches and a grant of land.'

'If I survive. Surely it must be dangerous?'

'As I said, you shall carry letters, which will exonerate you if this turns out badly. I have grown fond of you, you must know I would not have you suffer.' She looked towards the doorway, and raised her voice. 'Anna, are you out there?'

The doorway darkened. *'Despoina?'*

'See if there is a scribe to be found in the convent. If not, find me ink and parchment.'

'Yes, my lady.'

Princess Theodora looked intently at her. 'Don't worry, Katerina. You shall take your orders with you. And we have a good two hours to transform you into a princess.'

Two hours. Katerina stared at the purple slippers and then at baby Martina. Her palms felt sticky. It was all very well for the Princess to assume that her letters would be taken as gospel, but in Katerina's experience men who were deceived did not take kindly to those who deceived them. A pair of penetrating blue eyes flashed into her mind. And the first person she would have to convince was none other than the Commander of the Varangian Guard. *Saint Titus, help me.*

'Katerina, I am relying on you. A few weeks, once you have reached the Palace. That is all that I ask, just a few weeks.'

While he waited for the two hours to pass, Ashfirth walked with Brand to the top of the hill. His leg had had enough of riding, instinct was telling him that it needed this different form of exercise or it would stiffen up, perhaps permanently. They had spent too long at sea.

They stopped just short of the summit. A little way below them lay the convent with its crumbling walls and vegetable garden. Next to it, a small orchard was bursting into life, there were green shoots everywhere. The wind ruffled Ashfirth's hair; it had broken up the clouds and was pushing them across the sky—white sails scudding across blue. A gust caught the fruit trees and the branches waved.

Past the convent and orchard, the hillside sloped more steeply, it was thickly covered in bushes and scrub as it ran down to the sea. The sea was choppy, the waves flecked with foam. In the deeper waters, a striped red-and-white sail was slowly progressing from west to east in the same direction their ship would follow.

'Brand, is that a Greek vessel?'

'Can't say at this distance, sir. It might be, but it could just as easily be Norman.'

'That is my fear.' Ashfirth heaved a sigh. There seemed to be rather too much Norman activity in these waters—the Emperor's rule here was definitely under threat. He must make a report to that effect when they returned. 'We will have to be circumspect.'

The port—and their own ships—lay at the end of a promontory that was bordered on one side by sea and on the other by salt marshes.

'Do you think the Princess will make difficulties, sir?'

Those soft brown eyes came into Ashfirth's mind and he shook his head. 'She will know she cannot run for ever. By the time the month turns, Princess Theodora will be safely where she belongs, in the women's quarters of the Great Palace.'

Brand gave him a straight look. 'Before we left, people were muttering—taxes, rising prices. Are you expecting trouble when we get back, Commander?'

Ashfirth hesitated. His loyalty was to the Emperor, but he did not believe in keeping his men in the dark. And Brand spoke no less than the truth—when they left Constantinople, several disturbing rumours had been doing the rounds.

'Rising prices are the least of it,' he said. 'There are those in the army talking of acclaiming a rival emperor.'

'General Alexios Komnenos?'

'The same.' In Ashfirth's private opinion, General Alexios would make a far better emperor than Nikephoros, who had grown old overnight and who seemed to have given up on government. The Empire needed a firm hand, particularly—Ash scowled at the red-and-white sails across the water—with so many Normans nibbling away at the boundaries…

'General Alexios is not the only pretender to the throne,' Brand said.

'Apparently not. One way or another, a storm is looming.'

'Yes, sir.' Brand considered. 'Rioting?'

Ashfirth grimaced. 'It is possible.' The price of wheat in the city had risen to such an extent that many were unable to afford it. Time was when the Emperor had handed out bread free to those who had need of it, but that had been years ago. The current Emperor, shut up in his palace, was blind to the needs of his citizens and his unpopularity was growing by the day. 'Whatever happens our duty is clear. We are not there to control the populace, we serve the Emperor.'

And pray that he heeds the contents of my report. Ash wanted no repetition of the shocking incident that had taken place a couple of years ago, when a band of infuriated Varangians had actually attacked the Emperor they were meant to be protecting. It had happened before Ash's promotion, and he was determined there would be no repetition, not while he was Commander. But he was aware there were rumblings of discontent even within the Guard.

'Yes, Commander. We obey the Emperor, our loyalty is only to him.'

Ash nodded, but in truth he longed to serve a man who commanded more respect. It was something of a surprise that Emperor Nikephoros had clung to power for so long. Particularly when there were others in the army who were far more able. Ash had to admit that General Alexios headed the list.

Alexios Komnenos came from the military aristocracy. At twenty-four, the General had already done ten years'

service in the army. His record was impeccable, he had
never lost a battle. What an Emperor General Alexios might
make!

Abruptly, Ashfirth shook his head to clear it of such a
disloyal thought. The Commander of the Varangian Guard
must serve the Emperor he was sworn to. And Ashfirth had
taken an oath to protect Emperor Nikephoros.

*Hell, trouble is coming and I am sworn to a man who
does not command my respect. A man who has yet to heed
my advice.* Ashfirth gazed bleakly at the cross on the dome
of the church. He had sworn a holy oath and he would not
break it. Come what may, he was the Emperor's man.

'Brand, the sooner we get Princess Theodora to the Great
Palace, the better.'

A couple of hours later, Ashfirth and Brand were sitting on a low wall opposite the convent gate, a loaf and a
wineskin between them.

Eyeing the position of the sun, Ash tossed his bread
aside. For this meeting with the Princess he had thought
it polite to remove the trappings of a warrior and don the
clothes of a courtier. He had put aside his mailcoat and
leather gambeson and was wearing a blue linen tunic. His
cross-gartered chausses were tucked into his riding boots.

The gate creaked and slowly opened. Ash exchanged
startled glances with his captain.

*Surely this could not be the Princess already? Heavens!
A woman who is only a few minutes late? And she...a princess...how extraordinary.*

He strode over, brushing crumbs from his tunic.

She was standing in the midst of her ladies-in-waiting.
*Doe Eyes. Lord, so many ladies, a grand woman. She is
not going to like being commanded.*

She was not tall, the top of her head barely reached

his shoulder. Close to, her brown eyes were flecked with green lights. Ashfirth blinked. Something had changed. Her eyes were starkly outlined with some sort of black paint or cosmetic, he was confident they had not been before. The eyeliner made those beautiful eyes more noticeable. Oddly, the cosmetics had the effect of changing his perception of her. Before, he had received a fleeting impression of softness and vulnerability. It was not there now.

He was puzzling it out when those long lashes swept down. She had darkened her eyelashes, too, they appeared thicker and longer than when she had spoken to him through the convent grille. It was baffling how the cosmetics defined her eyes and drew his gaze, while at the same time they seemed to hide her. She looked mysterious and other worldly. Earlier, he had been conversing with a pretty young woman. Did she usually face the world from behind a painted mask?

Shame. I prefered the pretty woman.

But this, Ashfirth must remember, was the Princess, his opinion of her was irrelevant.

For her departure from St Mary's, the rest of Princess Theodora's face was almost entirely swathed in her veil. Her body was lost beneath the folds of a green silk cloak. She was slender, as far as he could judge, tiny and delicate. Gold glittered at her throat, in the threads of her veil, at her fingers and wrists.

'Princess Theodora?' Aware that he had been staring, Ashfirth bowed. Behind him, he could hear the men saluting, their coats of mail clinking.

'Commander.'

He held out his hand. She would not like what he had to say. Ashfirth might have set aside his mailcoat, but he was painfully aware that he was no courtier to win her over with clever words. He would simply have to do his best.

Slim fingers lightly touched his. When he attempted to lead her away from her ladies, she pointedly withdrew her hand from his. It was not quite a snub, but it was close.

'*Despoina*, will you walk this way? There are matters I would discuss with you.'

She gestured haughtily at one of the women. 'Lady Anna, please attend me.'

Ashfirth cleared his throat. 'My apologies, my lady, but what I have to say is for your ears alone.'

An arched brow lifted, the brown eyes searched his.

Ash found himself holding his breath. He was praying that she was not going to prove troublesome. He had his orders and he had hoped to execute them with courtesy— she *was* a princess—but after receiving a disturbing report in Dyrrachion this morning, he realised he might no longer have that luxury. If Princess Theodora became awkward, he might have to resort to force.

When she nodded, Ash breathed again.

'Very well, Commander.'

She allowed him to lead her to one of the apple trees at the edge of the orchard. Her ladies remained by the convent gates, their silk veils fluttering in the breeze: pink, green, bronze. Bright as butterflies. One of the goats must have got into the convent again, Ashfirth could hear it bleating from over the wall. It sounded rather like a baby crying. The Princess must have heard it, too, because for a moment her attention wandered from him.

She sighed and then those dark, outlined eyes were looking expectantly at him. 'Commander?'

'*Despoina*, if you will forgive me, I must be blunt.'

'Please, say what you must.'

Be courteous, she is a princess. Be tactful. Do not question her about her failure to respond to the Emperor's letters.

'When we arrived in Dyrrachion,' Ash kept his voice

low, confidential, 'one of my troopers overheard a conversation in Norman French.' He paused; she must be aware there had been Frankish incursions into Imperial territory in Apulia. She had been out of the Empire for some years, but surely even in Rascia word must have reached her about losses in Apulia?

She frowned, eyes bright and alert. Clever. She had heard. 'You think they are spies, that the Normans have designs on Dyrrachion? How many were there?'

'My men saw only two, my lady. We do not know what they are planning, but their presence here does concern me. Several Frankish ships have been sighted in these waters. It is vital we leave without fanfare, and because our Varangian galleys are so distinctive, I have reserved a Venetian merchantman for your use.'

Rings flashing, she waved at her entourage, at the pile of trunks and travelling chests that had been deposited next to her ladies-in-waiting. Brand was in their midst. Ash had asked him to discover which of the trunks belonged to the Princess so that they might be extracted from the rest, the baggage mules were waiting.

'As you see, we are ready, Commander,' she said, voice aloof.

Ashfirth cleared his throat and resisted the desire to shift the weight from his healing leg. 'I am sorry to say this, my lady, but with your uncle's enemies nearby, it is vital we leave as unobtrusively as possible.'

An immaculately plucked eyebrow rose.

'It would not do—' Ash pressed doggedly on '—for word to reach the Normans that the Emperor's niece was seen boarding a ship bound for the capital.'

'What are you saying?'

'Your entourage is too large. So many ladies are bound to attract attention.'

'Commander, my ladies-in-waiting accompany me *everywhere*. Surely you are not telling me I cannot take my ladies...that...that I must travel *alone* with you?' Her voice was high, incredulous.

Spoilt, of course. Used to getting her own way. A pang of something that felt surprisingly like disappointment shot through him. *Spoilt.* Ash held down a sigh and reminded himself that he was dealing with a member of the Imperial family. This woman had spent much of her life in a foreign court where a Greek princess was bound to have been seen as a rare treasure. Her every whim would have been granted. It had probably been years since she had been denied anything.

And Ash did not like the tone in which she had asked if she must travel alone with him—as though he were some kind of monster...

'I am not saying that your ladies may not travel to Constantinople, *despoina*. All I am saying is that they may not travel on your ship. I would suggest that they follow us in the Varangian galley in a couple of days' time. My captain, Brand, will accompany them. You need not concern yourself about their safety—Brand is my best man.'

Her chin inched up and her veil slipped to reveal a pretty mouth; it was set in a very determined line. 'It is not their safety that concerns me.'

In the face of such arrogance, Ash could only stare. 'My lady—'

'I do not travel alone.'

The veil slipped a little further, and she drew it back over her face. It was then that he noticed her hand was trembling.

The Princess was nervous? When she glanced sideways at his men, Ash realised he was right—Princess Theodora was nervous.

He looked down at her dispassionately. Did his men

frighten her? The Varangian Guard were famed the world over for being ruthless warriors, but she must know they would never harm her.

Hell, we came for her in full battle regalia. He had had no choice. To do otherwise, when Normans were hanging around the nearby port, would have been foolhardy in the extreme.

Ash became conscious of an unsettled feeling in his core and realised he was weakening towards her. It was likely that this woman never took a step without her ladies. Was he asking too much?

It was also becoming painfully clear that he was not as well equipped for executing this commission as he had hoped. His experience in dealing with princesses was non-existent. This was the first time he had addressed one face-to-face—if face-to-face was the right way to describe a conversation with someone so heavily veiled that most of her features were hidden. Be that as it may, he clearly could not expect her to travel alone with him. 'You may choose *one* lady-in-waiting to come with you on the merchantman,' he said.

Relief sprang into her eyes, the darkened lashes lowered. There was a pause, then...

'Thank you.'

Then her lashes lifted and Ash felt a distinct jolt. He was taken by a most inappropriate urge to examine that pretty, determined mouth; it was a struggle to keep his eyes politely on hers.

'And you say you plan to accompany me in the merchant-man, Commander?'

'Yes.'

'As for my other ladies—can you assure me that they will follow in the Varangian galley?'

'Indeed.' Ash smiled, and offered her his arm. It was a

relief when she laid her fingers on his sleeve. 'From now on, we shall have to be careful how we address you.'

'Oh?'

'It is important that no one realises who you are.'

For some reason her eyes widened and she bit her lip. 'I see.'

'So with your permission, my lady, from this moment I shall refer to you simply as Lady Theodora. Will that be agreeable?'

'I...yes.'

'Which of your ladies will you choose to take with you?'

'Lady Anna, I should like Lady Anna to accompany me.'

Ashfirth nodded and looked her up and down. 'My lady, there is another matter I feel we should discuss before we leave. Your clothing.'

'My clothing?' A small hand stroked down her silken skirt. 'What is wrong with my clothing?'

'Can you ride in that gown? In that veil? Are they not too fine?'

Her doe eyes went wide. *'Ride?'* She swallowed. 'Commander, I...I do not ride.'

Ashfirth went stock-still. Behind that veil she had definitely lost colour. *She cannot ride? Whoever heard of a princess who could not ride? Was she afraid of horses? And why the devil had no one thought fit to inform him of that fact?* 'You don't ride?'

She glanced briefly towards her ladies, as though searching for help. Her chin inched up. 'No, Commander, I do not.'

Swallowing a curse, Ash fought to keep his expression neutral and his tone polite. 'I see. And what about Lady Anna—does Lady Anna ride?'

'Yes, she has her own horse.'

'But you do not.'

'No.'

'My lady, I do not wish to cause you undue alarm, but we ought to set out as soon as possible. And since the path down to the bridge is too precipitate to accommodate a cart or wagon, you will have to ride with me.'

She lifted her fingers from his arm, gold bracelets flashed. 'You brought no litter?'

'No. My lady, I do apologise, but you will have to ride with me.'

Chapter Three

The beginning of the ride to the port was a nightmare. She was practically in his lap, shaking from head to toe. *Has he noticed?*

Commander Ashfirth had said the path to the bridge was steep and he had not lied—on one side the land fell sharply to the sea. Spiky rocks were poking up through the water like the claws of some titanic monster fighting free of Poseidon's net. And Katerina was sitting precariously on a horse. *A horse.* Her pulse raced.

Horses terrified her and from the outset her mind only had room for fear. Ever since Katerina had been a child, horses had worried her, and her fear had been compounded by her experiences on the slave-ship. For much of that most terrible of voyages she had been chained close to the slavers' horses. There had been a storm and…

She did not like to remember. For years she had kept her memories locked away. But now, for the first time in her life, here she was *on* a horse herself.

On a horse in the arms of Commander Ashfirth, to be precise. The horse was black, like his hair. A stallion. She had heard him call it Caesar. It was huge. Unfortunately, being forced to ride this great black beast had brought back memories she would rather forget.

Darkness. Flashes of lightning. Waves crashing down on her. Thunder. The taste of salt on her tongue. The thirst. Men screaming; ropes straining, cracking like whips. Flailing hoofs. Blood...a dead slave...

Katerina forced herself to take slow, calming breaths.

Forget about Caesar. Commander Ashfirth knows how to handle him. This horse will not get out of control like those on the slave-ship. Caesar will not kick out, or rear up, or...

Forget about being on a horse.

It wasn't easy. The path was narrow, little more than a goat-run. On the one side there were those jagged rocks in the water, and on the other the scree-covered hill that sloped up to St Mary's. If Katerina shifted, ever so slightly, she could see the last of the convent walls, the trees in the orchard, the goats...

Even though she had scarcely moved, the Commander's grip on her tightened. He had one arm round her waist, the other held the reins. Casually. As though it were nothing to him to have her up before him while he controlled the great stallion.

Behind them Lady Anna was on her grey mare, Zephyr. Lady Anna was a competent rider; like the Commander, she was entirely at ease, smiling, tossing back the odd remark to Commander Ashfirth's manservant. The thin track was forcing them to ride in single file, and Hrodric—the Commander's manservant—was immediately behind Lady Anna. He had one of the pack animals on a leading rein.

Lady Anna was actually laughing. *Laughing.* It didn't seem to have occurred to her that if she fell, those boulders on the hillside would cut her to ribbons. Katerina hardly dared move. Still, it was a relief to see Lady Anna smile. Lady Anna was not in the habit of confiding in Katerina, but Katerina had received the distinct impression that Lady Anna shared Princess Theodora's reluctance to return to Constantinople—she had heard her mutter something about not wanting to see her father. Now *that* was an emotion Katerina could understand.

One of Caesar's hoofs sent a stone rattling down the hill. Katerina stifled a moan. *I must remember my dignity at all times, I am meant to be the Princess.*

But oh, everything was going horribly wrong. Already.

Several ladies were meant to be travelling with her, all of whom had sworn to help her, to cover up when she made a mistake. But *he* was insistent that the other ladies—and that included the Princess—were to travel on the Varangian galley.

What could she do? She had not been born to command, and this man had his reasons for insisting she travelled separately from the entourage. In any case, whatever she said, it was unlikely he would listen.

Katerina's fingers dug into the front edge of the saddle; she was gripping it so hard the white of her bones could be seen. It was bad enough that she should have to impersonate the Princess when the whole entourage was on hand to help her, but to be made to travel with just one lady! *Holy Mother, help me...*

She could feel him at her back. Warm. Strong. He had removed his body armour for the ride back to the port because he wanted no one to realise he was a Varangian. They were to travel under false colours.

If only he knew.

Nevertheless, the fact that he had removed his body armour was a mercy, otherwise that coat of chainmail would have torn Princess Theodora's silk gown to shreds.

Her mistress had generously given it to her. Katerina had hoped that, in a few weeks, when she had carried out her orders and had truly earned it, the gown would still be in one piece. She had never worn such a delicate gown, had never dreamed it might be hers.

Below, the rocks were still clawing their way out of the sea. Katerina's heart thumped. She looked swiftly away and forced her mind elsewhere.

Who could have imagined that repaying her debt to the Princess would become so complicated so soon? *I must remember that if all goes well I will have wealth as well as land of my own. When this is over, I must ask the Princess if the land can be somewhere other than Crete, I have no wish to return home. Dear Lord, for the Princess's sake, let me succeed. Do not let the Commander find me out.*

The Princess had ordered her to act as though she were a princess. And on the voyage to Constantinople, Ashfirth Saxon wanted her to play the part of a princess pretending to be a noblewoman. And if that were not enough, she must not forget that as far as the sailors were concerned, Ashfirth Saxon was a rich merchant.

'My lady,' he had said. 'From this moment you cannot address me as "Commander". I am Ashfirth Saxon.'

What a nightmare! By the end of the voyage, I will surely be insane...

A seagull screeched past a foot above their heads. The stallion snorted and tossed his black mane.

A whimper escaped. *I am doing this for the Princess, for baby Martina...*

Commander Ashfirth's hand came to rest on hers.

'My lady, you are quite safe.'

Safe? I am in your arms, how can I be safe? You are a man; you are Commander of the Varangian Guard; you are not Greek, you were not even born in the Empire. You are a barbarian.

Relax. He believes you to be the Princess, you will be safe.

Katerina shot another look towards the sea and the pointy rocks, and almost moaned aloud. Quickly, she brought her gaze level with the path, and hung on for dear life.

Her veil fluttered, it had to be blowing in his face.

'Excuse me, my lady.' Releasing her, Commander Ashfirth reached out and caught at the fabric. There was a slight pull on her scalp as he matter of factly twisted it into a rope and pushed it over her shoulder. She said nothing. Since she wasn't about to let go of the edge of the saddle, it was an intimacy she must forgive him. His arm came back round her, her body was pulled snug against his.

'Too steep,' she muttered, 'it is too steep here.' *And you are too close.*

Commander Ashfirth's saddle had clearly not been designed with two people in mind, but to give him his due, he had attempted to cushion it for her. He had called for a thick woollen blanket, but the wool was coarse and her thighs itched.

My legs are showing. It is not very dignified. He must realise I am not the Princess, he must...

Another sideways glance at the sea below had panic bubble up inside.

'Relax, my lady,' his deep voice murmured. 'The path levels off shortly, the marshes are only a little way ahead and it is flat there.'

His thighs were enclosing hers. As she glanced at them, her sense of panic intensified. Before she had been trembling, now she was rigid. Old terrors. She had feared this might happen.

Distract yourself. He is a barbarian, but he will not hurt you. You are the Princess.

His chausses were grey, made from linen of a particularly fine and even weave. The best quality. The muscles of his thighs were taut and firm. Quickly, she looked away.

The horse swayed on down the path. Katerina had no stirrups, there was nothing except the Commander to prevent her from slipping sideways. What if she fell? Would he think the less of her if she grabbed hold of his knee?

Talk to him, distract yourself. Remember your dignity.

Katerina cleared her throat and said the first thing that came into her head.

'Command—' hastily she corrected herself '—sir, I did not realise Varangians possessed horses.'

'Not all of us do. As you are aware, we are primarily foot soldiers, but those of us who can afford it keep horses.'

When he spoke, it was with the easy confidence of a man sure of his place in the world. Through the fabric of her twisted-up veil, his breath was warm on the back of her head. 'I see. Sir, there is something I would like you to explain.'

'My lady, I am entirely at your service.'

'You said that we are in a hurry because Normans have been seen in Dyrrachion?'

'Yes. I suspect they are scouting for weaknesses in the city defences, but I cannot be certain. However, Normans are opportunists and I am determined they must have no inkling of who you are.'

'You fear they are spies, sir?'

She felt him nod. 'It seems likely.'

'And this is why you must spirit me away with a reduced escort?'

Another nod. 'Exactly. The ship I have reserved for you is less ostentatious than our galley. My hope is that the world will see us as prosperous traders. That is why I am taking only half of my men on the first boat. We shall, of course, conceal our arms and uniforms. Captain Brand and the other men will escort your ladies, and they will be prominently armed, as befitting the escort of a princess.'

'Can I not persuade you to let more of my entourage travel with me?' Katerina did not like to beg, but it would bolster her confidence to have more of the ladies about her.

'I am afraid not. Captain Brand has been ordered to make much fanfare when your women and their servants embark on the galley. What with their baggage and so forth, I am in hopes that he will spin it out for a couple of days.'

'Thus distracting attention from us?'

'Exactly. With the size of your entourage, there will be no doubt that someone of great importance is setting out for the capital. Captain Brand's ship will be taken for the Imperial galley and in the meantime ours will have slipped away unnoticed.'

A cold sweat broke out on Katerina's brow. *Saint Titus, help me, Commander Ashfirth intends to use the second ship as a decoy! But it will be no decoy, not with the real Princess on board!*

Think, Katerina, think. If the Norman scouts in Dyrrachion are truly the Emperor's enemies, and they hear that the Princess is on that second ship, what might they do?

Would they try to capture her and demand a ransom? Would they dare?

She kept her voice light, admiring. 'How clever. In making a decoy of your galley, no one will notice ours.'

'That is my hope.'

Heart like lead, Katerina stared between the stallion's ears. The track had levelled off to a little above sea level, they were approaching the bridge across the marshes.

What would the Commander think if he knew that his

strategy, far from ensuring the safety of the Princess, was actually putting her in the path of danger?

The Princess! Somehow I must warn her.

'Sir, when will our vessel cast off?'

'As soon as Captain Brand and your entourage arrive at the port. Within the hour.'

Within the hour.

Lord, no sooner had she begun to repay her debt to the Princess than she was in such a tangle she could scarcely unravel it. Somehow, before the hour was up, Katerina must get a message to her.

Princess Theodora must be warned of these new dangers.

The chance didn't come until after Commander Ashfirth had escorted Katerina and Lady Anna onto the trader.

Katerina had not been in a ship since the slavers had dragged her, with chains clanking at her wrists and feet, on to theirs. The contrast between the courteous way the Commander handed her aboard this time, and the way the slavers had treated her four years ago couldn't have been more marked. Nevertheless, that hated memory was hard to dispel. Her mouth was dry, her heartbeat erratic. And yet she must pretend all was well, she must present a calm face to the world.

And above all, I must get a message to my mistress.

As she gazed about the deck, she felt his eyes on her. He watched her constantly, or one of his men did. *Was he suspicious? Please, Lord, let him accept me as the Princess.*

An awning was rigged up near the stern and a giant of a guardsman directed her to it. Another barbarian from outside the Empire, the man's Viking ancestry was obvious. Long blond hair was tied back in a sheepskin ribbon, his beard was ruddy. The arms revealed by his sleeveless leather tunic were scarred and roped with enough muscle to wrestle a lion and win. This Hercules of a man might have discarded his mailcoat, his axe might be secreted away, but Katerina had no doubt that the sword thrust into his belt was razor sharp. His eyes were at odds with his scarred, brawler's body; they were a gentle grey.

'Lady Theodora, since the weather is set fair, you may use this as your quarters,' the blond Hercules said. His Greek was not as fluent as the Commander's, but it was adequate. And clearly he had been briefed as to how to address her. He bowed her in under the awning. 'Unless you would prefer to go below decks?'

Katerina shook her head. 'Below? My thanks, but I much prefer to be up here. This will suit me very well.'

'Co...Ashfirth asked me to tell you that in here you may be assured of your privacy.'

'Thank you.' She looked warily at him. In recent years Katerina had kept men at a distance, but this Viking's eyes told her she need have no fear of him. 'What is your name?'

'Toki, my lady. Toki Fairhead.' He leaned towards her and lowered his voice conspiratorially. 'I am a sergeant.'

'Thank you, Toki.'

When the sergeant continued to hover in the doorway, it dawned on her that he was watching for her reaction. She made a show of looking about her. It was shady under the awning, and protected from the breeze. There were flaps on either side of the opening that could be released and tied shut, like a door. When they were closed it would be like living in a tent, a spacious pavilion of a tent.

Some effort had been expended to make her quarters comfortable. A pallet was made up with creamy linens, and the travelling chest that the Princess had given her was already in place, pushed to one side. A goatskin rug had been spread on the boards, and a brass ewer and jug rested in a corner.

'Thank you, Toki, this is most satisfactory.' As she spoke, the Commander's manservant shouldered his way in with another pallet, doubtless for Lady Anna.

'It won't be what you are used to,' the sergeant said gruffly, 'but it will only be for a short time.'

Katerina smiled. Princess Theodora had been the most considerate of mistresses. Since being freed by the Princess and offered the choice of becoming her maidservant, Katerina had never had to sleep on the floor, she had always had a pallet. But space for herself and just one other? Privacy such as this? Never.

'Toki, these quarters are perfect. Where is Lady Anna?'

'With the horses.'

She managed not to grimace. 'When she has finished there, would you please send her to me?'

Sergeant Toki bowed himself out, and it was not long before Lady Anna ducked through the opening.

'You wanted to speak to me?' Lady Anna's voice was tight, Katerina hoped she did not resent being summoned. It was possible.

Not only does Lady Anna regret being sent home, but she is a noblewoman. Every time she looks at me, she sees a Cretan villager who was once a slave. Is she affronted by being asked to treat me as if I were the Princess? I shall have to tread carefully, if I am not to alienate her.

'Lady Anna—'

'Ashfirth Saxon's man, Hrodric, explained matters to me. You had best call me Anna, as the Princess did,' Lady Anna said, taking a seat on one of the pallets. 'And I suppose I had better get used to calling you "my lady".'

Katerina gave a swift headshake. 'I don't think that will be necessary. Ashfirth Saxon may know that you and the Princess are on the best of terms. I have often heard you call her Theodora, perhaps you should call me that for the time being—it will seem more natural.'

Lady Anna lifted her shoulders. 'As you wish. When we are being informal, Theodora it shall be.' Her eyes were shrewd. 'Was that all you wanted to say? I have to tell you that I am doing this for Theodora, for the *real* Theodora. If you think to use this as an excuse to order me about, you can think again.'

'That is far from my mind,' Katerina said, firmly. *Saints, my task will be impossible if Lady Anna decides to take against me.* However, back at the convent there hadn't been time to think of everything; she must make the best of it. 'Like you, I wish to help the Princess.'

'The Princess was generous, I hear she gave you a casket of jewels. Is it true she has also promised you land?'

'Yes, it's true, but even without these gifts I want to repay the Princess for her kindness to me. That is why I called for you a moment ago—I would not have done so were it not important.'

Lady Anna nodded. 'Hurry up then, I want to get back to Zephyr. What did you have to say?'

'Can you write?'

Lady Anna blinked. 'Write?'

'We have to get a message to the Princess, and I think it best if Ashfirth Saxon is kept in the dark.'

Lady Anna's haughtiness fell away, her eyes widened. She touched Katerina's hand. 'A secret message? Why, what on earth has happened?'

'*Anna, can you write?* I can read, but my name is the only thing I can write.'

'Yes, I can write. Tell me, Ka-Theodora, tell me! *What has happened?*'

As soon as Anna understood what was happening and that Princess Theodora—the *real* Princess Theodora—

might be in danger should she sail in the other ship; as soon as she understood that Commander Ashfirth intended using the Varangian galley as a decoy for their merchantman, it took moments for her to unearth a quill and ink and letter a carefully worded message.

'How do we get it to her?' Anna asked, waving the parchment in the air to dry it.

Lifting the canvas flap, Katerina peered outside. As she suspected, the Commander stood nearby. He and his sergeant, Toki, were looking up at the mast. She bit her lip. Those turquoise eyes missed nothing. 'I can scarcely march through the port with it myself, our…guard is bound to notice. And we cannot ask any of his men. Perhaps one of the sailors might be persuaded to take it. I don't think they answer to him.'

Anna nodded. 'I'll do it.' Tucking the roll of parchment out of sight beneath her veil, she went out on to the deck.

Some half an hour later, Katerina was leaning against the ship's guardrail, ostensibly watching crates of Venetian glass being offloaded. In truth, she was gazing at the Varangian galley moored in the deeper water on the next quay. With the Varangians' shields mounted along the gunwale, it was unquestionably a ship of war. Katerina looked at the barbaric shields and shuddered. Dragons and wolves snarled at each other from the brightly painted limewood; rams clashed with bulls; ravens flew over whales…

As the Commander had planned, every eye in the port was on that Varangian galley.

And this was the vessel in which the Princess must sail!

The message had been sent. Lady Anna had bribed one of the sailors with a gold coin Katerina had unearthed from a purse at the bottom of the Princess's trunk.

Yes, matters were apparently proceeding exactly as

Commander Ashfirth had ordered. The second party had arrived from the convent some minutes ago, Katerina could see the Imperial entourage milling about on the Varangian ship.

They hadn't needed heralds to announce them. If there were Norman spies in Dyrrachion, they wouldn't be able to miss them. Rich gowns bellied out in the breeze, laughter rang out above the gulls as the sea breeze blew veils out like pennons. Fishermen stared, porters goggled. Against the mailcoats and leather jerkins of their escort, against the drab sun-bleached clothes of the sailors, the silk gowns of the ladies-in-waiting looked as bright as poppies waving delicately at the edge of a field.

Katerina felt as though she had swallowed a stone. It was too late to regret taking part in this scheme, but the Princess would put it right, the Princess would know what to do. She had to!

Much as the Princess wanted to delay her marriage to Duke Nikolaos, surely when she read the letter she must realise their plan had become unworkable? Even now—Katerina cast a surreptitious glance in Commander Ashfirth's direction—it was not too late to confess all. If the Princess were to board this ship and admit to the truth, Commander Ashfirth must accept it.

He was standing amidships. He chose that moment to glance across and as their eyes met, Katerina's stomach clenched. It was odd how her body reacted when she looked at him; she felt a tightening in her stomach, a shiver of… what? It must be the old fear, but she was no longer certain.

Was this fear? It must be. And yet…he had held her in his arms on the ride from the convent and, though she had been wary of him, he had behaved impeccably. Of course, he would not hurt her, not while he believed her to be the Princess. She had thought his touch would distress her, but it had not; when he had looped back her veil she had felt perfectly safe.

A lock of his dark hair lifted in the breeze; his eyes seemed to bore right into her. Out of his body armour, Commander Ashfirth was startlingly attractive. His shoulders were wide, his waist narrow. Commander Ashfirth had none of the bulk of Sergeant Toki, but she suspected he had all of the strength. It was there in his confident stance, in the alertness of his gaze, in the way his men jumped to his command. When a dark eyebrow lifted, Katerina realised she had been staring.

Flushing, she nodded to him and returned to her contemplation of the Varangian galley. *Please, Princess, please. If you will not put an end to this, at the least let me know that the message has reached you, that you know to take care...*

'Theodora?' Lady Anna had torn herself away from the horses and had come to stand at her elbow.

'Anna?'

'I am sorry,' Lady Anna's voice was so low Katerina could barely hear it above the rumble of cartwheels on the dockside. 'That Viking...oh, Lord...he spotted our sailor and...' Her voice trailed off and she jerked her head in the direction of the quay where the Varangian galley was moored.

Katerina's stomach gave a sick lurch. Sergeant Toki was stalking towards their ship, the parchment crushed in his fist. Some straw from one of the packing cases was wafting across the dock; he strode straight through it.

Oh, no!

And there stood Princess Theodora amidst the bright, sparkling flutter that was her ladies. The Princess was affecting carelessness as baby Martina, snug in Lady

Sophia's arms, was being clucked over by an enormous Varangian with legs like tree trunks.

Had the message been intercepted before or after it had been delivered?

Katerina bit her lip. Commander Ashfirth was by the handrail, head tipped to one side as he watched his sergeant's approach. No more than curious yet.

Holy Virgin, this was not good.

Katerina's heartbeat quickened; she wanted to wave at the Princess, to jump up and down and catch her eye. *Had she read the letter before it was intercepted?* Katerina had to know.

With a frown, Commander Ashfirth pushed away from the handrail and went to meet his sergeant. His eyebrows became a black line. The sergeant pointed, first at the galley, then at Katerina. There was a brief exchange of words and the parchment exchanged hands. And then Commander Ashfirth was striding towards her, the heels of his boots loud on the deck.

'Lady Theodora?'

Katerina stood tall. The look in those turquoise eyes alarmed her, the set of his mouth was unyielding. She cleared her throat. Her mouth was dry with fear, but she would die before he knew it. 'Sir?'

His jaw clenched as he took her arm above the elbow. It was not a gentle grip.

Heart banging like fury, Katerina lifted a brow. She glanced loftily down at the hand on her elbow, as though startled that he had dared to touch her. *React as a real princess would react.*

'Really, sir!' She was pleased with the way her voice came out. Shocked. Indignant. With a small hint of outrage.

It had no effect. The Commander's fingers tightened like steel, and she was swivelled towards the canvas shelter.

Anna made a movement as though to come to her aid. Hastily, Katerina shook her head.

'This way, my lady,' Commander Ashfirth spoke through gritted teeth.

Strong fingers bit into her as she was hauled towards the pavilion and unceremoniously bundled inside.

Chapter Four

He paused in the entrance, and for a brief moment the glare of light from the deck made a silhouette of him. Time seemed to stop, and for a heart-stopping moment he was stripped of his individuality. This was not Ashfirth Saxon, Commander of the Varangian Guard, but a broad-shouldered, powerful man such as she had seen striding across the side of an antique vase. A man with no face. He was invincible, one of the heroes of myth, and she was entirely in his power...

Katerina's hands began to shake. *No, no, no. Not now. I am no longer a slave forced to do every man's bidding.*

Bile rushed to her mouth and she was swept back in time to the moment when Vukan—a fellow slave—had pushed her into a storeroom and issued her with an ultimatum.

'Bed with me,' Vukan had said, 'and I will keep you safe from the others. No one else will come near you.'

Outside, the gulls were screeching in Dyrrachion's harbour.

I am no longer in Rascia. Think about the gulls scrabbling for leftovers from a fisherman's haul; think about anything, but do not let the old fears take hold. You must act at all times as though you are the Princess.

Ashfirth Saxon stepped towards her and the instant the light fell on his face—proving beyond doubt that this was the Commander—the blind terror left her. Her pulse remained jumpy, she was still afraid, but this was a different type of fear; she had battled with it before and had survived. This was the fear of a woman when confronted by a strong man. Thank God, she had kept her head high, she did not think he had noticed her moment of abject terror.

'Really, sir! How dare you manhandle me in such a way? And how dare you come in here? Toki assured me this shelter was for my personal use.' Her voice did not tremble, the blind fear was entirely gone.

He towers over me, but then he would tower over most men. He cannot hurt me, I am the Princess.

Ashfirth Saxon was furious. It had been there in the hard grip of his fingers and it was still there in the set of those wide shoulders. Katerina put her chin up. It was most strange though, because even though she knew this man was angry her terror had quite gone. Men, yes, she remained wary of men in general, but not this particular one. It was incredible. Was it because she had finally met one who could control himself? She had begun to think no such man existed.

Don't be a fool! The only reason this man will not harm you is because he believes you to be the Princess.

With an impatient noise, he turned away to close the tent-flaps. The shadows deepened, and Katerina was alone with a man as she had not been since the dark days of her slavery.

And the abject terror did not return, though her heart thudded like a drum.

'My lady, explain yourself, if you please.' His voice was strained, his fist clenched and unclenched on the parchment.

He is angry but he will not hurt me. He is not Vukan. He will not demand sexual submission as the price of his protection. If she repeated this to herself often enough, she would believe it. *He will not hurt me, he is not Vukan...*

'What do you mean by sending this frivolous piece of nonsense—' he waved the letter under her nose '—to the other ship?'

'*Frivolous nonsense?* Sir, I do not care for your tone.' A glint in his eyes warned her that she was testing his patience. She gave a careless shrug. 'Some of my belongings were packed in the wrong coffer. I asked one of my women to bring them over.'

'You were missing some belongings? Oh, dear, Lady Theodora, that will not do.'

His tone was blistering; she squirmed inside.

Unrolling the parchment, he started to read. Holy Virgin, the man could read Greek! '"To Katerina, my body servant. Greetings," it says. "I have discovered my favourite ivory comb is not with me, the one engraved with Celtic patterns. It is in the holly-wood box, along with my silver hairpins and tortoise-shell comb. I need those too. Anna says we will need them to dress my hair properly. Please be so good as to find them. I order you to bring them to my ship at once. I cannot sail without them."' His lip curled. '"*A comb... hairpins...I cannot sail without them.*" Lord, my lady, I thought I made it plain. *We cannot be seen to communicate with the other ship.*' His blue eyes burned like flame. 'It was not a light request. This is no palace game. Your person—' a long finger stabbed at her breastbone '—is at risk here, your person.'

Again his hand came towards her, but before he touched

her a second time, his fingers curled and the hand was lowered. It came to her that he had not intended to touch her and that he had startled himself by so doing. He glared at her. 'Do you understand, my lady?'

'Thank you, sir, you have made your views plain. I shall not attempt a second communication with my woman.'

'No, my lady, you will not. I have seen to that.'

At her puzzled expression, Ashfirth Saxon lifted an eyebrow. Opening the canvas door-flap, he pointed outside.

They were moving! Their ship was sliding slowly by the large vessel, indeed, it had almost reached the edge of the dock. She saw the bright flash of silk, a burst of female laughter, the flash of a silver bangle. Close to hand, a rope creaked; a sailor shouted an order. A deckhand ran past the entrance to the pavilion. Another shout. The ship gave a slight jolt.

'We have cast off!'

'Yes, we are underway. That should put paid to any further attempts to communicate with the other ship.' He leaned towards her. 'Tell my, my lady, do you usually ignore advice when it is offered? Or only when it suits you?'

'Sir?'

He spoke through clenched teeth. 'I am the Emperor's right hand. His sword arm. When I command you, it is your Emperor who commands you. Is that clear?'

Katerina tried to look down her nose at him which, given his height, proved impossible. 'Perfectly.'

'Good. I am going to give you some more advice, and this time you are going to heed it.'

'Oh?'

'You are remain in this tent for the rest of the day. Sergeant Toki will be posted outside.'

She drew in a breath. 'You would confine a princess?'

'Until I know she will do as she is told, yes. As I said,

this is no game. I have my orders. I shall send Lady Anna to join you, and you will both remain in here until all chances of bribing one of the sailors is past.' He let the tent-flap fall back into place and the shadows closed in again, creating an illusion of intimacy. He sighed. 'I am sorry if you consider that I have violated your privacy, my lady, but we could hardly have this conversation out on the deck. With the exception of the captain, the sailors of this ship believe you to be a Greek noblewoman returning to Constantinople. Only my men know the truth. My main concern, my *only* concern, is to ensure your safety. And to that end I am prepared to sacrifice anything.' He tucked the parchment into his belt and made a sound of exasperation. 'I thought you were intelligent, I thought you could be relied upon to understand the gravity of your situation. I seem to have misjudged you. Hairpins, indeed! I will not make that mistake again, I can assure you.'

So tall and assured. With every moment spent in his company, the conviction was growing that Ashfirth Saxon was a rarity in Katerina's world, a dependable man. The Princess had insisted that such men existed and that Katerina was a fool if she let her experiences blind her to them.

He might confine me, but I really do not think he will hurt me.

Determination shone in those turquoise eyes. This man appeared to mean it when he said he was prepared to sacrifice anything for her. She was the Princess and he had been ordered to see to her safety. Many men would pay lip service to their orders, but if she could trust her instincts, this one was a rarity. He would carry out his orders with ruthless thoroughness, he would ensure her safety, he would die for her.

He thinks you are the Princess. If he knew your real identity, he would toss you overboard sooner than breathe.

Katerina thought quickly. *Was Ashfirth Saxon dependable enough to be trusted with the truth? With matters as they stood, the real princess was in danger!*

No, she could say nothing, it was not her truth to tell. She must remember her place—she was but a maidservant carrying out her mistress's orders. It was not up to her to reveal Princess Theodora's deception. *I do not like lying to this man, but I have no choice.* What an irony! The one time in her life she needed a man who was not dependable, and the Emperor sent this one! She could have done with someone like Commander Ashfirth years ago; God mocked her to send him now.

His eyes had darkened. He cleared his throat and shifted back a pace. 'My lady, I will send Lady Anna to you.'

Katerina's pulse quickened. *Is he attracted to me? Yes, I think he is. He is watching my mouth, his fingers are digging into his palm, and...*

The realisation that Ashfirth Saxon might be attracted to her sent panicky thoughts flying this way and that. Her stomach clenched; she could not cope with this!

Remain calm. Concentrate. This man is not driven by his baser instincts, he does not expect sexual favours from you, nor will he force compliance on you even if he desires you.

Indeed, there appeared to be a steadiness in his character that was at odds with what little Katerina knew of his comrades in the Varangian Guard. They were known to be wild, fierce fighters who fought to the death. Mercenary barbarians. If they had a fault, it was loyalty. No, they had another fault, Varangians had something of a reputation for drinking themselves insensible. It was hard to visualise this man doing such a thing, Commander Ashfirth was all control; anyone could see that.

Unfortunately, as far as she was concerned, this presented something of a challenge.

What if something happened to the Varangian galley while she was masquerading as her mistress? She would never forgive herself if the Princess and her baby came to harm...

What could she do? She was following the orders of her mistress. It would help if she knew more about Ashfirth Saxon's background and nature. Perhaps he was not quite as honourable as she imagined. If she could only question him without raising his suspicions, she might discover another way to get word back to the Princess. But he was so angry with her! She must try to make amends...

He tipped his head, his attention caught by one of her earrings...that is, by one of the earrings Princess Theodora had given her. It was a gold filigree butterfly, Katerina had been told it came from somewhere in the East, somewhere beyond the land of the Turks.

'Thank you, sir—' she kept her expression carefully neutral '—I should enjoy Lady Anna's company, but I do have some questions.'

His gaze shifted from the butterfly. 'My lady?'

'Will we make landfall this evening?'

'No, tonight we will anchor offshore.'

'Shall we be dining on board?'

'Yes...but I should warn you, my lady, you will have to accustom yourself to simple fare. You and Lady Anna will be served here in the pavilion.'

'I understand. It is Lent, I was not expecting a banquet.' She smiled. 'Sir, I have a favour to ask.'

A dark eyebrow lifted, his eyes were fixed on hers.

'Since you have seen fit to deprive me of the company of my other ladies, and since you have confined me in here, I would be grateful if you would join us for the evening meal.'

His eyes were briefly lit by what looked like surprise. And was that a disarming hint of uncertainty? Yes, it was uncertainty; she had wrong-footed him with her invitation to dine. The tension lifted a little.

Then he bowed and shielded his eyes. 'Thank you, my lady, I would be honoured.'

With a slight smile, he ducked out onto the deck, the parchment still in his belt.

Katerina stared at the swinging tent-flap.

Good, she would use tonight to learn as much as she could about Commander Ashfirth. She would test him. Subtly, of course. She would begin by seeing if he was one of the men who had helped the Varangians earn their hard-drinking reputation; she would try loosening his tongue with wine.

It was vital to find out exactly who she was dealing with, and not only for the Princess's sake. If the unthinkable happened and the Princess did come to harm, the letter exonerating Katerina from blame might prove worthless, not to mention the promise of land and the gift of jewels. And as for that other precious document that was hidden in the jewel chest—the document of manumission that proved she was no longer a slave—that would become irrelevant. Would it weigh in her favour that Katerina had been obeying orders? She certainly hoped so, but she could not be sure...

Commander Ashfirth might appear to be able to control his temper, he might appear to be dependable, but he was a man. When he discovered how Katerina had deceived him, even he must be roused to anger. And men, as she had so painfully learned, became vicious when angry.

How confusing it was! She put her hand to her aching forehead. For years Katerina had longed to meet a reliable, temperate man, and now she thought she had found one, she felt as though she was stumbling about in a blindfold. But one thing she could see—their ship might be on its way to the capital, but that need not prevent her from helping the Princess.

The pretence must go on, she thought, as the ship's bow lifted on a wind-blown wave.

The sun had set some time ago. The huge red-and-white striped mainsail had been furled, and above the mast the heavens were velvet black and patterned with stars. They were anchored in a secluded bay off the coast of Epirus. No Normans had been sighted this far south, but even though it was known to be a safe area, Ash had taken the precaution of putting extra men on watch.

He made sure to present himself outside the Princess's quarters in plenty of time. It wasn't polite to keep a member of the Imperial family waiting. His lips twisted. Princess Theodora might not be entertaining him in the Great Palace, but he felt he owed her this courtesy. She had taken the loss of her ladies and his punishment for attempting to summon her body-servant far better than he had anticipated. Her invitation to dine had surprised him.

A horn lantern swung gently from a pole set outside the pavilion. The light from a lamp inside was filtering through the canvas, like a full moon shining through cloud.

He straightened his belt and shoved his hand through his hair. In honour of the occasion—dining alone with a princess was not something Ash had done before—he was wearing a blackberry-coloured silk tunic, one that up until this moment had seemed fine enough. By rights Ash should be wearing his dress uniform, but the necessity for secrecy had made that impossible. The crew had no idea who he was, any more than they knew that the lady they were returning to Constantinople was in truth a princess.

He straightened his tunic. *Why the devil do I feel so ill at ease?* The tunic had been an extravagance; it was banded with metallic embroidery at the neck and hem. Tonight it did not seem nearly fine enough. At his wrist there was a dull gleam of gold—his father's arm-ring. The arm-ring was the only tangible reminder of his former life in England. Conscious that the Greeks must view Anglo-Saxon adornments as barbaric, Ash usually kept it out of sight beneath his sleeve. Tonight, on a rare impulse, he had left it showing.

He cleared his throat. 'Ladies, it is I, Ashfirth Saxon.'

The flap lifted back, Lady Anna gestured him inside.

'Come in, sir.'

In the past few years, Ash had made it his business to learn Court protocols. The Great Palace was ordered by rules, and soon after he had arrived he had realised that, if he were to succeed in his new life, he had best learn them.

However, this situation was unlike any he had encountered. He was dining with a princess who had but a single lady-in-waiting in attendance. He doubted there were protocols for a situation such as this.

'Good evening, Lady Anna.'

Princess Theodora's bed had been made up to resemble a couch and she was lying on her side, propped up on her elbow in the Roman style. Cushions with great silken tassels had appeared; she was surrounded by furs and richly coloured rugs. In a flowing green gown and diaphanous veil, she could have been an Empress of the old Empire. Her headband glittered with gemstones.

Out of the corner of his eye he saw that Lady Anna's bed had been made up in the same way; there was a camping stool and…

An emerald ring flashed as a small hand was extended from the furs. Her doe's eyes glowed in the lamplight. 'Good evening, sir.'

Ash side-stepped a glass hanging lamp that had not been there earlier and bowed over her hand.

Scent. She is wearing scent. The tent was filled with a sensual blend of roses and musk and some other spicy ingredient Ash did not recognise. Cinnamon? She had not been wearing it earlier. Nor the ring with the emerald in it. It must be worth several kings' ransoms. He must remind her not to dress so ostentatiously, it might attract unwanted attention. They did not want anyone asking questions about her.

He kissed her fingertips and made a point of eyeing the glass lamp swinging above them—the colours and swirls had a definite Venetian cast to them. His gaze took in the leather camping stool, the heap of cushions, yet more furs. 'Where, may I ask, did all this come from?'

Her fingers slid from his and she waved him towards the stool. 'Toki found them for me.'

'He did what? He was ordered to guard you.'

'To keep me confined, don't you mean?'

Ash looked at her. Those dark-lashed eyes were so wide, her skin was so clear. The Princess was quite the loveliest woman he had seen in an age. She was so lovely, she had probably wound Toki round her little finger in a trice. In truth, it was very hard to chastise her when she looked up at a man in that way—that tentative smile with its fascinating suggestion of shyness was irresistible…

'Sir, I swear I did not leave this tent.'

Ash shook his head. 'I shall have to have words with

Toki. He must have breached the ship's cargo, the merchant who owns them will be most displeased.'

'Please, sir—' her voice was husky '—do not chastise Toki. When he heard you were coming to dine, he offered to help.'

Ash gave her a sceptical look.

'Wine, sir?'

Anna was proffering a goblet, absently, Ash took it. 'My thanks.'

Princess Theodora's face drew his gaze. As he sipped his wine and the Princess gestured for Anna to serve them their meal, he was able to observe her.

Pretty, *very* pretty. Princess Theodora had the dark delicate features that had always appealed to him. Fine, arched eyebrows, a clear brow. Those soft brown eyes, those thick black eyelashes. Her complexion was unblemished and a long and glossy strand of hair had slipped free of her veil— it was a rich brown in colour.

Her veil was less all-enveloping this evening, less like a nun's. She shifted and the furs fell away to reveal a green gown that fitted more closely than the one she had travelled in. As Ash had suspected, she was tiny. A gem-studded belt accentuated a slender waist. Her breasts were clearly visible under the green silk; they were small and finely shaped, like the rest of her.

Ash felt a stirring in his groin. *I want her. Heaven help me, I want the Princess!*

She was watching Anna as she bustled in and out with plates and serving dishes. Vaguely Ash was conscious of Hrodric assisting; he too must have volunteered to help. Covers were lifted off dishes. Chicken—he could smell the chicken and herb sauce he had ordered. It had been cooked in the port that morning; someone on board had managed to heat it for them.

The Princess turned towards him, one elegant brow lifted. 'Chicken, sir, in Lent?'

Ash shrugged, somewhat dazed by the power of what was a most unexpected and extremely inconvenient flash of desire. 'I thought you might like it.'

'Thank you, I do. The convent fare was somewhat... spartan.'

'We will not eat so well every day,' he warned.

'So it will be soldiers' rations tomorrow?' She smiled and for a brief moment, she was not the Emperor's niece, but simply a pretty girl who had caught his interest.

His heart squeezed. Such entanglements were not for him. Even if she were not the Princess, it was a point of honour for Ashfirth that he never allowed himself to become fond of a woman. That way, he would never again have to endure the pain of losing someone he loved. It had taken him years to recover from the blows that the Norman invaders had dealt him when they had stolen his family and his life in England. The experience had taught him a harsh lesson. *Guard your emotions, always.*

Why the hell had she asked him to dine with her? He was no courtier. What did he have to say that could possibly interest this woman?

My men are happier on the battlefield, my lady. They see this commission as something of an insult. Or—and this was perhaps even worse—my men serve your uncle honourably, but they look to the day when a better man occupies his throne.

Lord, I had best eat quickly and leave.

His leg throbbed. Surreptitiously, he eased it.

The wine slid down easily; Lady Anna refilled his goblet.

The chicken was fragrant with thyme and bay; Lady

Anna ladled it into wooden bowls. There was dark rye bread to mop up the sauce.

Hrodric set dishes of honey pastries flecked with almonds on one of the travelling chests; bowls of dried fruits were set next to them—apricots, figs, plums. He bowed himself out.

The food appeared to be exactly as Ashfirth had ordered. Not knowing what she was used to, he had warned her it would be simple fare, but he had done his best to see that the supplies taken on board were fine enough to suit the palate of a princess. He bent over his bowl, the chicken was cooked to perfection, thank God.

Ash was conscious of those dark eyes resting on him from time to time. Him—entertain Princess Theodora? Impossible. But he *was* hungry. And the wine was easing the ache in his leg. Absently, Ash rubbed it.

'Your leg pains you, sir? Were you hurt in the service of the…my uncle?'

'No, it was a stupid accident.'

'Oh?'

Those eyes were so sympathetic, Ash found himself adding, 'Happened in the Hippodrome.'

Her eyes were blank. 'Sir?'

'My lady, you remember the Hippodrome? The arena outside the Palace?'

She nodded awkwardly. 'Naturally—but I was just a child. Please continue.'

'My horse threw me in a race and I broke my leg. It is healing, but more slowly than I would wish.'

'Your horse threw you?' She grimaced. 'I am not surprised you were hurt, if you fell off that monster. He is *huge.*'

'Huge? Caesar?' Ash laughed, shaking his head. 'You call Caesar huge?'

The doe eyes watched him. He was struck by a ridiculous longing to find the green flecks in them, but he was not close enough to see them.

'He seems huge to me, sir.'

'He is not a destrier such as a Norman knight would have. He is too fine-boned. Caesar was created for speed, he loves polo.'

'Polo? Oh, yes.'

She smiled as though she knew exactly what he was talking about, but something was definitely wrong here. Ash was struck by a ridiculous thought. *That mention of polo has disconcerted her and she does not want me to know it.*

Thoughtfully, he rubbed his chin. Was her smile a little too bright? She *must* know what he was talking about; everyone knew that polo was played in the Hippodrome.

How very strange.

'Caesar seems very large to me,' she murmured.

'My lady, that is only because you have a hatred of horses.'

Her gaze was downcast, she made a jerky movement. 'It is not a hatred exactly, but—' when her eyelashes lifted, his chest squeezed '—I confess it, sir, I do fear them.'

'Were you not you given riding lessons as a child?'

'I…I…' She took a deep breath, her cheeks flushed like a rose. It was distractingly attractive. 'Let us simply say that I did not take to it.'

'You must have been poorly tutored. There are horses from every corner of the Empire in the imperial stables. I cannot believe they could not find one to suit you. My lady, if you would allow, when we reach the palace, I will pick you out a horse and—'

She drew her head back. 'You would teach me to ride?'

'My lady, I would be honoured.'

'Thank you, sir, you are more than kind.' An odd, secretive smile was playing about her lips. 'You do not realise what you are offering, but I thank you for the thought.'

The Venetian lantern swayed as the boat rocked, the shadows shifted. As he stared at her, Ash was filled with an uncertainty that was foreign to his nature. Had he actually offered to teach the Princess to ride when they reached the palace? Madness. And had or had she not accepted his offer? And—more madness—what was it to him whether she accepted or not?

Firmly he closed his mouth, it seemed he must guard his tongue with this woman. The little Princess certainly had a charm about her, he must take care to keep a safe distance between them. He was here to fulfil his commission, no more than that.

He reached for a dried fruit. When she held out her goblet, he refilled it. She was still toying with her chicken; clearly, it was far too early for him to make his excuses and leave. He would simply have to allow himself the pleasure of conversation with a beautiful and intelligent woman. It should be easy to keep his opinions of her uncle to himself. And why on earth had he offered to teach her to ride? He frowned at the wine, it did not seem particularly potent...

Her veil had slipped. She hadn't noticed and Ash wasn't about to draw her attention to it, not when the lamplight brought out the burnished brightness in her hair. Lady Anna must have piled it up beneath her veil, but a brown tress had escaped the hairpins and worked its way free. It was perfectly straight. It was a pity the Princess wore so many cosmetics, but at least this evening he could see something of her face.

It was a face worth seeing. When she smiled, she had the sweetest expression. What a waste to hide it behind veils and paint. Doe Eyes—she would probably have him thrown out of the Guard if she knew his secret name for her—-was prettier than any princess had a right to be.

'Apricot, my lady?'

As she set her chicken aside and leaned towards him to take a fruit, the scent of musk reached him, together with that other exotic fragrance he could not name.

'Thank you, sir.' Those beautiful brown eyes fastened on his.

She smiled and sank back against the silk cushions. Her mouth was tempting, too tempting for a woman who was beyond his reach. It was dark with the wine and looked faintly moist. Perhaps she had darkened it with lip-rouge, the ladies of the court were known to use it. It made her look as though she had been kissing, which was probably deliberate.

Ash usually avoided the high-born ladies of the court. A number of them had taken to choosing lovers from among the Varangian Guard. Despite various offers, Ash had never succumbed. He knew what was said about the stamina of his men, and he found the idea of being taken to bed simply because he was thought to be a barbarian with good staying power distasteful.

But tonight, here he was, to all intents and purposes alone with Princess Theodora. He glanced uncertainly towards Lady Anna. She had finished her meal and was lying back on her pillowed couch. Ash heard a distinct snore. Lord, she had fallen sleep—ought he to waken her? How would Emperor Nikephoros react if word reached him that Commander Ashfirth had dined in such intimacy with his niece? What would her new fiancé, the Duke of Larissa, have to say?

This cosy meal with the Princess was probably breaking a thousand unwritten rules. But Ash was here by her express invitation and it was clear she thought him honour-bound to entertain her. She was still smiling that shy smile, beneath the come-hither rouge. Her mouth was like the rest of her, neat and prettily shaped.

One kiss, I would like one kiss. Would her kiss be prim? Shocked? Would she slap me in the face for my effrontery?

When his blood rushed to his braies, Ash knew he was in real trouble.

Chapter Five

Shocked at the direction his thoughts had taken, Ash shifted on his stool and reached blindly for a piece of bread he did not want. What was the matter with him? He should not be thinking of kissing the Princess, however much she smiled at him. Nor should he find the thought of arousing her anger so…stimulating.

Princess Theodora had invited him here because she was not used to her own company, she was afraid of becoming bored on ship. It was even possible—he shot her a suspicious look and was met with another bland smile—that she was deliberately taunting him because she was angry at being separated from her ladies and wanted revenge for being confined in the pavilion for the day.

Ash cleared his throat. The devil of it was that he was genuinely attracted to her. *Forget it, you can never act upon it.* Lord, for the sake of his peace of mind, the voyage couldn't end too soon. The ship lifted gently in the swell and a bell sounded, they were virtually alone on a calm, dark sea.

Another snore drifted from the figure slumped on the

pallet. Despite himself, his mouth twitched and he found himself exchanging amused glances with the Princess. 'Does she do that every night?'

'I believe so.'

'You must long to escape.'

'Indeed I do, but my...rank holds me prisoner.'

What an extraordinary remark. 'You, a prisoner? Ah, you must be referring to your confinement this afternoon?'

Shaking her head, she gave him a wry smile. 'No, I was not referring to that, sir. However, it has occurred to me that a...a princess who has no choice about whom she marries is a prisoner to her duty just as much as a slave is to her master.'

Thoughtfully, he watched her over the rim of his goblet. 'You would compare yourself to a slave?'

She lifted her shoulders, the gems in her headband glittered. 'Neither the princess nor the slave has much choice in the course of their lives. Both must obey without question, both must go where they are directed.'

'That is true up to a point, my lady, but everyone has their duty. It is not for me, for example, to question the will of the Emperor when he asks me to bring you home,' Ash said.

'Nor for me to question your orders, it would seem.'

He lifted his cup to her. 'Quite so. I am glad we have come to an understanding, on that matter at least.'

How interesting, Katerina thought. When she had smiled at him a few moments ago, the man had actually blushed, he really did like her. The thought had her muscles go tight as a bowstring; chilling memories were never far away. She forced herself to relax.

He likes you? Do not delude yourself. He does not know you. He likes your looks; in short, he lusts after you. Katerina had enough experience of that particularly sin to recognise it when it was staring her in the face. Commander Ashfirth would not act on his feelings, though. *As long as he believes me to be the Princess Theodora I am safe.*

What if I cannot convince him? What will he do? He confined me here in the pavilion for trying to send that letter—how might he react if he sees through my pretence?

She eyed him from under her lashes, gaze skimming over him from the top of that dark head, down past those arresting blue eyes, past those high cheekbones and well-sculpted mouth, past that strong jaw… Sweet Mary, he was a handsome man. She had only to look at him and her cheeks were on fire!

Impersonating the Princess had flung her deep into uncharted waters, she was utterly out of her depth here in more ways than one. Surely he could sense it? Her hand was shaking so much she was likely to tip wine over her gown. *Does he know that I am quaking inside? Does he suspect that I am misleading him?*

She gripped the stem of her goblet. *He must not see my nervousness. And I must not let my fear of being caught out betray me. I am safe with this man as long as he believes me to be the princess.*

Will I be safe if he learns the truth?

A new thought caught her by surprise. For the first time in an age, Katerina was not sure she wanted to be safe. He was all lean power, was the Commander, but it was a power that he appeared to control. The fingers that cradled his wine goblet were slender and attractive. And he was not, rather to her surprise, indulging in the wine as much as she had expected.

He fascinated her. Was it possible that her misgivings were in part caused by proximity to a man who attracted her?

Her gaze was caught by a gleam of gold at his wrist. 'Is that an Anglo-Saxon arm-ring, sir?'

Nodding, he extended his arm so she could examine it. 'It was my father's.'

It was an unusual piece of work, similar to one Katerina had seen on a Viking trader who had come to her village before she had been enslaved. Determined to hide her nervousness, she made herself reach out and touch it. It was fashioned like a twist of rope, and looked solid, heavy. It had to be worth a fortune!

I am the Princess, a solid gold arm-ring is nothing to me.

The turquoise eyes had darkened, and not for the first time she saw them drop to her mouth and move quickly away. Her heart fluttered, the surface of the wine in her goblet trembled.

The Commander is a barbarian, remember the lesson that Vukan taught you: barbarians are ruthless, they are only out for themselves.

And yet…it was heady to see that powerful frame folded up on a leather stool not two feet away and know that Ashfirth Saxon had been ordered to do her bidding. All that handsome, masculine strength was entirely at her disposal. It was heady realising that he was attracted to her and that he would not act unless she crooked her finger at him. Not that she would do that, of course—she had no wish to find herself even more out of her depth!

It dawned on her that as far as men were concerned, Katerina had always been in the position of weakness. No longer. The moment she had agreed to step into Princess Theodora's shoes, this man had become hers to command—provided she heeded his advice.

For the first time in my life I have a measure of power.

Ashfirth Saxon wanted her. She had seen that brief look he had directed towards her breasts, he had been measuring her with his eyes. It was the kind of look she had seen many times before, the kind of look Vukan had given her in the days before he had given her his ultimatum, just before he had said, 'Bed me, and I will keep you safe from the others.' It had made her skin crawl when Vukan had looked at her in that way, but her skin was not crawling at this moment...

The Commander was wondering about the shape of her, he was wondering what it might be like to touch her. He lusted for her, but he would not touch her. Heavens, it would seem that tonight was a night for novelties, the knowledge that Ashfirth Saxon wanted her brought no fear, none whatsoever. He could look at her and her skin did not crawl. There was a slight tension in her belly, but it was really rather pleasurable, it was almost as if...almost as if she *wanted* him to touch her.

But he is a barbarian! He is dangerous...

Katerina cleared her throat. His eyes lifted. They were very dark, that bright blue had almost vanished into the black. She took a sip of wine, using it to moisten her lips. When the ship tilted, she leaned towards him, allowing herself to move closer to him than was strictly warranted by the sway of the ship. She could feel the heat from his body.

Anna slept on. On the other side of the canvas one seaman muttered to another. The timbers creaked.

Commander Ashfirth looked steadily at her, nostrils flaring.

'Ashfirth,' she murmured, and made another discovery. His name lent itself to being murmured. 'I may call you that, may I not?'

His brow creased, that puzzled look was back. 'If you wish, my lady.'

Katerina's pulse jumped, she had wrong-footed him again and she rather liked it. In truth, she liked it *a lot* when she wrong-footed him. Ashfirth Saxon was so confident in the place he had won for himself, so proud of his honour, so certain of his duty. He was the Commander of the Varangian Guard, and he had been bidden by the Emperor to escort his niece safely to the palace.

The Commander had not hesitated to punish her when she had tried to send that message to the Varangian galley— he had punished *her*! It was so confusing—as Princess Theodora, surely she ought to be in the position of strength? How could she command a man who punished her?

On the other hand, he seemed drawn to her and that must give her power over him. Could she use that power? Dare she? Or would she be bringing even more trouble on herself?

Katerina might find herself between a rock and a hard place, but that didn't mean she shouldn't seize the opportunities that came her way. She gave what she hoped would pass for a teasing smile and watched with some satisfaction as his cheeks darkened.

Oh, yes. Impersonating the Princess might have its dangers, it was certainly not to be taken lightly, but with this man as her guard, there were some compensations…the question was, dare she make the most of them?

When Katerina came out on deck the next morning, the ship had weighed anchor and the striped sails were filled with wind. They were heading east, pointing towards the sun. A fine spray filled the air, she could taste the salt. Overhead, the ropes were pulled taut, trimming the great sail. Every inch of the black rigging groaned with the strain. It was exhilarating.

Commander Ashfirth was at the handrail with the ship's Captain, his gaze fixed on a tiny flotilla of ships on the southern horizon.

'What would you say, about two dozen?' the Captain said.

The Commander's expression was thoughtful. 'It's hard

to make out precisely, but that's a fair guess. They *must* be Norman. Do you think they are headed for Ba—?' Seeing Katerina, he broke off abruptly and gave her a bow. 'Good morning, my lady.'

'Good morning, sir.' The sails of the distant flotilla were little more than dots; Katerina was unable to judge which direction they were sailing in, they might even be at anchor.

The Commander offered her his arm and led her across the deck away from the Captain. On this side of the ship, the coast of the Empire was slipping by. They were close enough to see sheep grazing on hills that rose to the sky; there was a fishing village hugging a natural harbour; a chapel on a rocky promontory…

'Please, sir, there is no need to interrupt your conversation on my account.' What had they been talking about? It had looked important.

He put his hand on hers. 'I trust you slept well, my lady?'

'Yes, thank you.' Katerina was startled at the way his hand continued to cover hers, it felt very warm. This man threatened her composure and she did not want him to realise it. Under that sleeve, the forearm that was steadying her was strong. She glanced up at him, confused by the strangest of thoughts. He made her feel safe, she had slept deeply, better than she had slept in years. Even after the Princess had taken her out of slavery, she had never slept so well—and while she found him…unsettling, she had awoken eager to see him.

But should the Commander be touching her in this way? Did this mean he was beginning to suspect her identity? Surely he would not touch the Princess in so…familiar a fashion?

He did not answer my question, either. What were they talking about?

Disengaging herself, Katerina reached for the guardrail

and took in a lungful of fresh salty air. Last evening he had told her that he himself would be taking his turn on watch outside her shelter. Knowing that must have helped her sleep. She could not afford to make a slip when in this man's company, but apparently her instincts had already judged him and found him trustworthy.

A gust of wind teased the edge of her veil. The Commander was scowling at the far horizon with its flotilla of ships. Behind the flotilla, a blur of grey marked the coast of some foreign land that must lie far outside the Empire.

She cleared her throat, and nodded towards the dark line beyond the ships. 'What land is that, sir?'

His eyes widened. 'That's Apulia, my lady.' His tone was shocked.

Apulia!

Katerina's heart sank and she cursed herself. *Stupid, stupid.* She fixed her gaze on the distant blur and fought to keep her expression blank and unconcerned. *I should have known, the Princess would have known. And I should have remembered.*

Until very recently, Apulia had been part of the Empire. Now it was in Norman hands and, as niece to the Emperor, she really should know that.

'So that's Apulia,' she said, as though coming to a sudden realisation. 'I had forgotten we were so close.' She waved a languid hand. 'Our Empire is so large, it is sometimes a struggle to remember the exact whereabouts of the more far-flung outposts.'

Katerina held her breath for the Commander's reaction. In truth, Princess Theodora, the real Princess Theodora, would have died before making such a mistake. Princesses of the Greek Empire were well tutored, some might say learned. Over her head, she saw the Commander exchange glances with Captain Leo. With luck they would put her slip down to carelessness, or arrogance.

Captain Leo stepped towards them. 'I have observed that ladies do not always have a strong sense of direction,' he said, smiling.

Ashfirth's lips twitched, but he said nothing.

Katerina kept her head up, she was very aware of two pairs of male eyes watching her. *Waiting for me to make another slip?*

It gave her a jolt when she realised they were deferring to her and she, the Princess, must take the lead. Releasing her breath on a sigh, she gave them what she hoped passed for a gracious smile. 'Please, do not stand on ceremony on my account, you may continue with your discussion. You were speculating about those ships, I believe?'

Another exchange of glances took place between the Commander and the Captain.

Captain Leo waved at the nearby coast. 'Ashfirth was asking why our course takes us so close to the coast…'

The coast? Katerina's brow puckered. That was non-sense, she was certain they had been talking about Normans…and Apulia…and those vessels on the distant horizon.

They are hiding something from me! But what? She glanced swiftly from one to the other. Her next thought was not a pleasant one.

Could it be that Commander Ashfirth and Captain Leo were contemplating rebellion? Commander Ashfirth was a mercenary, after all.

No, no! *He commands the Emperor's personal guard. The Varangian Guard are loyal to the core; in truth, they are more loyal than many generals in the Imperial army…*

Katerina's knowledge of politics was weak; when she had been enslaved such matters had not touched on her life, her one thought had been for survival. During her time at the Rascian court, however, scarcely a day had gone by without news of some attempted coup against the Emperor reaching them. There had been so many rebellions, she had given up counting.

What do you really know about Commander Ashfirth? You assume that he is honourable, but better men than he have plotted against the Emperor—generals, admirals, courtiers. Princess Theodora's new uncle is a weak ruler, he is not universally accepted. And Ashfirth Saxon is a mercenary, a hired warrior...

She smiled steadily at the Commander. 'You were discussing our course, sir?'

Commander Ashfirth nodded. 'I was under the impression that we would make more headway if we sailed farther out from the shore. There will be more in the way of wind, and less twisting and turning as we follow the land. Our passage back to the capital should be swifter.'

'Yes, of course. Deeper water, fewer rocks,' Katerina said, recalling the ride from the convent and trying to sound knowledgeable. She would follow Ashfirth's lead even though she was certain that he and the Captain had *not* been talking about their course. They had been discussing the Norman fleet.

Why mislead her? It could only be that they were hiding some secret purpose. Katerina's heart sank and she found herself wishing that she was not mistaken in her earlier assessment of Commander Ashfirth. Her role as the Princess might be a temporary one, and she did not understand this, but it mattered, it mattered a great deal, that her instincts about him as a man were sound. Commander Ashfirth *must* be an honourable man.

'Quite so, my lady.' The Captain was smiling at her.

Politely, she smiled back.

'Hugging the coast has its problems,' Captain Leo continued, 'and it undoubtedly takes longer. But in this case there are advantages.'

'And those are?'

'These past few months pirates have been operating out there in the deeper waters.'

The bottom fell out of Katerina's stomach. 'Pirates? Here?'

In a heartbeat her head was filled with images of the slave ship—the smell, the fear. Heavy chains were chafing at her wrists and ankles, her throat was parched, and her ears were full of the whimpering of the other slaves, of screams. Knees weakening, she gripped the ship's rail.

She tried to swallow and could not. 'Pirates? Do you think they might be slavers?'

The Commander gave the Captain an irritated glance. 'Not slavers, we trust, but pirates do sometimes operate off this coast.'

'In truth,' Captain Leo continued, 'it makes little odds whether they be pirates or slavers, I would not want to encounter either.'

Katerina was beginning to shake. *Pirates!* Memory was a terrified cramping in her stomach, and she knew she had lost colour. Had Commander Ashfirth noticed? Releasing the ship's rail, she backed away, somewhat surprised to find her legs still supported her. *Pirates! Here?*

With an effort, she found her voice. 'I trust that we are in capable hands, Captain.' Nodding a dismissal at them, she dived towards the pavilion.

Had she given herself away? Did Commander Ashfirth suspect?

Oh, Lord. Not only had she blundered by revealing a complete ignorance of Imperial affairs—that dark splotch on the horizon was Apulia and she should have known!—but then mention of the word 'pirate' had her all but swooning.

Had he noticed? Sweet Virgin…that blue gaze noticed everything. As Katerina stumbled across the deck, she could feel it boring into her shoulder blades.

Take care, Katerina, walk more slowly, keep your head up. Remember, you are the Princess. You are Princess Theodora…

Somehow she reached the pavilion and pushed inside.

'Ka—Theodora!' Lady Anna took one look at her, dropped the gown she had been folding, and hurried over. 'Whatever's the matter?'

'P…pirates,' Katerina managed. 'The Captain says there are pirates in these waters. He and Ashfirth Saxon are discussing our route, hoping to evade them.'

Anna took her hand. Her eyes were kind and full of concern. 'There are pirates in most waters, Theodora. It is only to be expected that they might be found here, where Imperial power is at its weakest.'

All Princess Theodora's ladies knew Katerina's story, or most of it. They knew that she had been saved from a life of drudgery and abuse when the Princess had bought her, but this was the first time one of the ladies had shown overt understanding of her plight.

Awkwardly, Lady Anna patted her hand. 'I suspect you are thinking about the time your father sold you to the slavers…'

Eyes filling, Katerina nodded; this unexpected sympathy was almost her undoing. She swallowed hard.

Anna was shaking her head. 'Theodora, you must not concern yourself.' She lowered her voice. 'Commander Ashfirth was hand-picked by your uncle, he will have everything in hand.'

'I hope so,' Katerina managed. 'I confess it is the thought

of slavers that upsets me.' She was fighting to keep her wits, there was an ominous prickling at the back of her eyes. *I must not dissolve into hysterics, someone might hear. The Princess Theodora does not dissolve into hysterics.*

Anna turned back to the gown she had been folding, and stowed it carefully in its coffer. As Katerina watched the reverence with which Anna handled the fine silk, an idea began to take shape in her mind.

Yesterday, that gown had belonged to the Princess; today it was hers. As were the many other beautiful things that the Princess had given her for carrying out this pretence.

Moving to another coffer, Katerina pushed back the lid and drew out a veil. Even though the light in the pavilion was weak, it shimmered like a rainbow.

She lowered her voice to a whisper. 'Are these things truly mine, Anna?'

'Yes, they have all been gifted to you.'

Katerina looked thoughtfully at the Princess's lady-in-waiting. *Are they truly mine? What will Lady Anna do when I announce that I am considering selling them?*

'Anna?'

'My lady?'

Heart beating hard, Katerina settled herself on a couch and folded her hands in her lap. 'I should like us to conduct an inventory of the things that I have brought with me. The things—' she looked hard at Anna '—that have most recently been gifted to me.'

Anna's gaze was bright, intelligent. 'All these things?' Her wave took in the travelling chests Princess Theodora had pressed upon her.

Thanking God for Lady Anna's quick wits, Katerina nodded. 'Exactly. My most recent…acquisitions.' With a glance towards the pavilion entrance, she cleared her throat and lifted her voice. 'We forgot my ivory comb in the rush to leave, let us see what else we might have forgotten.'

Soon the two couches were lost beneath heaps of green silks and red damasks; beneath purple slippers and shoes; beneath belts studded with cornelian and lapis lazuli; beneath psalters with gems set into the covers. Finally, Anna unearthed the Princess's enamelled jewel casket that up until this moment had been in her keeping. She unlocked it, and passed it over.

It was so heavy, Katerina almost dropped it. It was made from gold and had dozens of bright enamelled animals running across its surfaces. Her mouth fell open. 'She gave me this too?'

Anna nodded. 'Open it.'

Breathless with surprise, Katerina did so. Fingers unsteady, she drew out a gold diadem embellished with lapis lazuli. There was a miniature icon painted in gold and studded with mother-of-pearl; a dagger with a huge emerald set into its silver hilt...

Katerina shook her head. 'Dazzling,' she managed, extracting a filigree collar from a heap of jewels, it hung from her fingers like a golden cobweb. But the golden collar was not the finest piece. There were bracelets set with rubies and sapphires; there was a silver necklace set with amethysts...

She was stunned. 'Anna, I had not realised she had given me so much—I cannot possibly keep these!'

Anna leaned close, running her fingers over an amethyst cloak fastener that went with the silver necklace. Imperial purple, a colour Katerina would *never* wear! 'She wants you to have them.'

'The friend who gave me these,' Katerina said carefully, ever mindful of the possibility of listening ears 'has a generous heart.'

'Yes.'

Someone coughed outside. 'My lady, may I come in?' Commander Ashfirth pushed back the door-flap, and Katerina forced herself not to leap up. *You are the Princess,* she reminded herself.

Remaining firmly on the edge of the couch, she waved him in. 'Please do.'

Ashfirth entered, stopping dead when he saw the turmoil.

What was she up to?

Princess Theodora's pavilion had been reduced to chaos. There was scarcely anywhere for a man to put his feet, and there was certainly nowhere to sit, except the corner of the couch that she was perched on.

'You are setting up a market stall, my lady?' he asked, face as blank as he could make it.

It certainly looked like one, albeit a market stall that was being ransacked by the Vikings. Gowns spilled over the couch and on to the wooden deck, like a silken waterfall. Jewels winked; gold gleamed—a king's ransom in gold.

Her cheeks took colour and her nose inched up, assuredly, she resented his question. What was she doing? 'You are concerned that pirates may find your jewels, my lady?'

'It had crossed my mind.' Her voice strengthened. 'Anna and I have been checking through the few trifles I have been allowed to bring with me.' She picked up a silver headdress, turning it in her hands and examining it as though she had never seen it before. 'We are sorting out the more valuable of my things, and were wondering how best they might be secured in the event of an attack. There is a particular reason I should like to be certain they reach Constantinople. Can you advise me?'

'About the pirates, my lady, I very much regret that Captain Leo mentioned them. I have no wish for you to be alarmed and came to reassure you that we are taking the safer coastal route. I am fully expecting to avoid trouble.'

Ashfirth blinked at a bracelet studded with amethysts the size of pigeon's eggs, at a dagger with a gold hilt, at a heap of golden coins. Even he had never seen such an ostentatious display of personal wealth in his entire life, though he had, of course, seen the Imperial Treasury with his own eyes.

The Imperial Treasury was hidden below the Great Palace, in a labyrinth of underground tunnels and vaults. Ashfirth was one of a select few who had seen inside it. Shortly after enlisting as a Varangian officer, Ashfirth had taken his turn at guarding the assembled valuables of seven hundred years of absolute power. It was true that the Imperial coffers were not as full as they had once been, but the rumours that they were empty were unfounded. However— his gaze ranged over the silken cloaks, the damask gowns, the jewels—never had he seen so much outside the Palace.

What is she doing—gloating over her wealth? Ashfirth's spirits sank, the thought was distasteful, and—how ridiculous—it was disappointing. *So what? The Princess is avaricious.*

Nonetheless, disappointment sat cold and tight in his guts. He looked down at her, a small, beautiful, brown-eyed girl, a woman he was strongly attracted to, or he would be if it were not for the gulf between them. A woman he might like if she were not so obsessed, so gloating. Ashfirth tightened his jaw. She sat so demurely on that couch, trying on an earring here, a bracelet there—surrounded by the trappings of enough wealth to launch a thousand pirate ships.

If she were not the Princess, I would snatch her out of that pool of silks and shake some sense into her, I would kiss her and...

He set his jaw. *He would kiss her?* This must stop! If he were not careful, he was in danger of being bewitched—an indulgence Ash had sworn never to allow himself. When he had come into manhood in an alien land, he had made a firm decision. Never would he allow a woman that power, particularly if she was a lady of the Court.

Over the years, Ashfirth's decision had been vindicated many times—he had witnessed more than one man fall when his noble lady tired of him. Vladimir, a Varangian captain, had had to flee the City after several suspicious bouts of food poisoning. And there had been young Sergeant Drogo, who had become all but suicidal when his lady passed him over for a more powerful lover with close connections to the throne. Money, power, prestige—these things were prized by Court ladies.

Sadly, Princess Theodora was no different from the rest. She was looking thoughtfully at him, and those gut-wrenchingly beautiful eyes gave no hint of what was really going on in her mind. She was worrying about her jewels. *Money, power, prestige...*

'Sir?'

'My lady?'

'I have made a new resolve and I should like your advice because I do not know how to proceed.'

'Yes?'

'When we reach Constantinople I am going to try to do something for the slaves there. Slavery is unchristian and barbaric, human beings should not be treated like so much cargo.'

'You wish to help slaves, my lady?' Ashfirth managed to keep the surprise out of his voice.

'Indeed. When we reach the Palace, I shall need your advice.'

'What is it you want to do, set up a hospice?'

She shook her head. 'I want to free them, sir.'

'What, all of them?' He held down a laugh.

'I would if I could.'

Her intensity surprised him, but the Princess couldn't be serious. But even if she was, Ash did not have to be a soothsayer to know how matters would proceed—court ladies were all the same.

This would be yet another in a long line of charitable ventures that was abandoned even before it had begun.

Chapter Six

Mindful of the need for tact, Ash chose his words with care. 'My lady, you cannot free all the slaves—slavery is part of the fabric of the Empire. Too many people have made fortunes by trading in human flesh, they will not take kindly to your interference.'

The Princess lifted her nose. 'You refuse to help me?'

'No, of course not. I am simply saying it will not be easy.'

'I appreciate that, but I would be glad of your help.'

'You might be best to discuss this with your uncle, the support of His Imperial Majesty would undoubtedly help far more than mine.'

'Ask my uncle?' Her eyes widened, her fingers clenched on the gold filigree collar. 'Oh, no, I am sure the Emperor has enough on his mind without my importuning him.' Her gaze lifted. 'But perhaps you might accompany me to the slave market?'

Ash bowed his head. 'If that is your wish.' It was easy enough to agree, this was but a whim, it would be forgotten before they made landfall.

'My thanks.' She tipped her head on to one side. 'Sir, you came here with something particular to say, I think?'

'I came to ask if, until we reach friendlier waters, you might prefer to make your quarters below.'

A plucked brow rose. 'You would put me in storage with the Venetian glass?'

Ashfirth spread his hands. 'It is safer below, my lady. You could sleep near my men and—'

'I will not go below decks.'

Holding down a sigh, Ashfirth gestured at the filigree collar and gorgeously enamelled box. 'Well your most precious jewels would be better secured there. We could put them in a strongbox and bolt it to the hull, if you wish.'

'Sir, the—' her voice wavered '—the thought of being confined in any way, even below deck, is abhorrent to me. I cannot…I cannot…"'

Impatience was a breath away, but those brown eyes were holding his, as though she were pleading with him. The Princess? Pleading with the officer sent to guard her? What a tangle of contradictions she was.

'My lady, in my view this ship will be safe if we keep to the coast. But if you are concerned about your valuables, I strongly advise you that you let me have them stowed below in secret. It would be safer for you if you were out of sight below decks too.' A wave of his hand took in the pavilion. 'Rudimentary though this shelter is, I admit we may have made a mistake in putting it up—it draws attention to you. And I am not speaking of the pirates here. Until I saw that little fleet, I had no idea that Frankish units were quite so…active in these waters. But you can rest assured that my men are at your disposal. If you were threatened, they would fight as vigorously for you as they would for the Emperor.'

How does one impose one's will over a spoiled princess?

In all probability her slightest whim has been catered to since she left the cradle. 'They should have sent a courtier,' Ash murmured, lifting a brow at her lady-in-waiting.

'A courtier?'

Ashfirth shook his head, there was nothing more he could say. This commission was turning out to be far more complicated than he had anticipated. Not only was he concerned, very concerned, about the Norman fleet that was gathering off the Apulian coast, but it was becoming painfully clear that he was not the best man to deal with the Emperor's niece.

He was a warrior and he relished his calling, particularly the sheer physicality of it. There was little to match the triumph at finding that extra ounce of strength. In battle, the fighting might be bloody, but in the throes of an engagement it came down to one thing, kill or be killed. It was simple, it was uncomplicated. Strategy, too, he could deal with, he enjoyed wrangling over tactics with his junior officers. But persuading a spoilt princess to take a prudent course of action? That was another matter entirely.

'I do not have the pretty words to persuade you, my lady. You must trust me, I have your welfare at heart.'

She tipped her head to one side and toyed absently with the filigree collar. Ash tried not to look too obviously at her mouth. Hell, this really was not the job for him. He found her far too appealing. He ought not to be wondering whether she had darkened her mouth with one of her cosmetics this morning, or whether that was its natural colour. It ought to be a sin to possess a mouth like that. It distracted a man, it made him long to sin…worse, it made him long with sin *with her*.

Holy Virgin, he was attracted to the little Princess, to the spoilt little Princess, in the most carnal way possible!

Those lips had to be rouged—did she realise the effect they had on a man?

The warmth in his groin was back. Ashfirth gritted his teeth. *This is the Emperor's niece.*

And here was another contradiction—for all her sophistication, the Emperor's niece had a peculiar air of innocence…no, not innocence…unworldiness.

'Surely it is very cramped down below?' the Emperor's niece was saying. 'And filled with crates and such like?'

'She is not heavily laden. What there is can easily be shifted.'

Her forehead creased. 'Won't the glass be damaged?'

Now she was concerned for the ship's cargo? Truly, she was a mystery, Ashfirth couldn't make her out.

'Not if we shift it with care. It won't matter even if some of it has to be secured on deck—sea water can't damage glass. In any case, if there were breakages, the merchant would be compensated.' Ashfirth's exasperation was growing.

'I see. And where will your men sleep? I was under the impression you and your men sleep outside, up on the deck.'

'My men bed down where they are ordered.' Ashfirth kept his voice reassuring. 'My lady, this ship is not as large as many of the Venetian traders because it was built for speed and the area below deck is correspondingly small. And while, as I have said, I do not believe we are in any immediate danger, it would clearly be safer for you if you were out of sight and we dismantled the pavilion.'

The brown eyes gazed at him. She nodded and pushed the enamelled casket towards her lady-in-waiting. 'Very well. Anna, please tidy the…my jewels away, so they may be placed in the strongbox. We shall be removing below decks, if—' the brown eyes held his '—and only if, you yourself, sir, will undertake to guard us.'

Relieved by her acquiescence, Ashfirth could only bow. 'My lady, I am entirely at your command.' As he looked into those dark brown eyes, it seemed that those polite words—*I am entirely at your command*—words that he uttered every day as an empty formality were, when uttered to the little Princess, becoming no less than the truth.

He waited while Lady Anna tidied away her jewels. Clearly, it had been too long since Ash had bought himself some of the gentler pleasures of life. If they put into a decent port in the next couple of days, he would make haste to the nearest bathhouse, and see what the local girls had to offer.

This is the Emperor's niece.

'I will send Hrodric to carry your chests below,' he said.

'Thank you, sir, you are most kind.'

Ash waited until Lady Anna had locked the enamelled jewel chest and handed it to him, and then he was out of the pavilion like a man with a thousand demons on his tail.

Below deck, Ashfirth ducked his head to avoid cracking it on a beam. The Princess was overseeing the establishment of her new quarters and she had made it clear that she wanted him close. Given his growing attraction for her, that was likely to prove a very mixed blessing.

The hammocks of the merchant and his crew had been unhooked and part of the glass cargo had been evicted.

Princess Theodora seemed very edgy, Ash watched her almost leap out of her skin when Hrodric came up behind her. Was she afraid of his men? He saw her send a shy smile to Toki as the sergeant roped her couch to iron staples driven into the ship's ribs so she could rest securely.

Not for her a hammock, the niece of the Emperor must have a couch.

'My thanks, Toki,' she said, when Toki had tied the last

knot. She seated herself, skirts billowing in a stray draught. The hold was full of shadows, but her expression when she gazed upon his sergeant was calm. Sergeant Toki was one of Ashfirth's toughest men. Built like Odin, he was as formidable in a fight as he was in appearance, but he seemed to have won her confidence. If she was afraid, it was not of his sergeant, but something was disturbing her.

While she directed her lady and the sergeant in the placing of her things, he studied her. The mysterious Princess.

She must have a nervous disposition. She had been nervous when she had emerged from the convent and the reason for that was easy to divine—she hadn't wanted to travel without her entourage. She was used to having a whole flock of fluttering women at her beck and call…to dress her, to entertain her, to serve her meals…

Was that the reason for her particular jumpiness now? Her hands—she was hiding them in the folds of her skirt— were trembling. Why? Had it been Leo's unguarded mention of pirates?

She had mentioned wanting to help slaves—had the thought of slaving ships upset her? No, it could not be that—what experience could Princess Theodora have of slavers? Besides, if slavers were to take her captive, they would never enslave her, never—a Greek princess would be ransomed.

So why the devil was she so damned nervous?

Ashfirth Saxon's men are efficient.

A piece of sacking had been rigged up to form a crude screen. Having led Katerina to her couch behind it, the Commander seemed to have decided his duty was done. He gave her a curt nod and vanished through the makeshift curtain, leaving Katerina and Anna alone in a shadowed space scarcely larger than a nun's cell.

As soon as his footsteps faded, Katerina looked at Anna. 'Anna, while we finish sorting our things, I should like you to describe the City and the Great Palace. When we get there, I must have some idea of which building is which.'

'Yes, I was forgetting that you have not been there. What did Theodora tell you?'

Katerina lowered her voice so it was little more than a sigh. 'Next to nothing, time was short. And in any case, the Princess has not been there herself in some years. She was a child of ten when she left for Rascia—the Palace must have changed since then.'

'It has, but not so much, I think.'

And so, as Katerina went through the fine linens and silks that she had been given, and as she marvelled at the gold and jewellery—the Princess had been so generous!—she learned about the Palace. Every now and then she would glance at the sacking, lest Commander Ashfirth returned.

'The Great Palace is built near the end of the peninsula—'

'Like Dyrrachion?'

'Yes, except there is no marsh. Constantinople is surrounded by sea on three sides. The Boukoleon Palace—that is most likely where we shall be taken, because the women's quarters are in the Boukoleon—is almost on the shore. In the Palace, when you look out of the great windows, you might be on a ship.' Anna shot Katerina a sly glance. 'The Varangian Guard are billeted in the Boukoleon, so you will not be far from your officer should you need him.'

'My officer?' Katerina struggled to hold down a blush, and pretended to examine a length of pink silk.

'He is…interested in you. Don't think I didn't notice. Last night at supper his eyes never left you.' Anna's gaze became speculative. 'And from what I could see, he was not the only one to be…interested.'

'What would you know? You went to sleep!'

'Let me have that, you're crumpling it.' Anna took the silk from Katerina with a knowing smile. 'I wasn't asleep all the time, I know what I saw.'

Katerina brought her brows together. 'The Palace, Anna, you are meant to be helping me, so I don't make any more blunders.'

'Any *more* blunders? Heavens, what happened?'

Sheepishly, Katerina gestured in a southerly direction. 'I forgot something the Princess would never have forgotten. I forgot that it is Apulia that we are sailing past!'

Anna winced. 'That is a pity. Do you think that he—?'

'Anna, you *must* describe the Palace! He may return at any moment.'

'My apologies. Where were we?'

'Entering the Boukoleon Palace by the way of the harbour…'

'Oh, yes. Kat—' Anna flung a guilty look at the curtain '—Theodora, you won't believe it when you see it. The Palace is a city in itself—there are gardens and fountains, there are orchards, there are halls with walls and ceilings covered with gold—'

'Walls covered with gold?' Katerina sent her a sceptical look. 'You are teasing me…'

Eyes bright, Anna shook her head. 'No, I am telling the truth, you will have to hide your amazement when we get there. The Great Palace is the most luxurious palace in Christendom, there is gold *everywhere*. And not just in the Great Palace, why, one of the city gates to the east… well, never mind, I think I had best stick to the Palace.'

'Please.'

'There are beautiful, beautiful tiled floors. Some of the walls are covered with thousands of coloured mosaics, others with paintings and frescoes. It is as though the people who lived in the Palace when the Empire was young still haunt it. The passage that leads from the Palace to the Emperor's box in the Hippodrome has hunting scenes on it. There's another that takes you straight from the Palace into Hagia Sophia, the great church where the Emperor hears Mass. It must be the biggest building ever made, it is like a mountain.' Anna touched her hand and her voice became a dramatic whisper. 'I have also been told there is a labyrinth of tunnels deep beneath the Palace.'

'A labyrinth? Surely you exaggerate?' Snatches of stories from Katerina's childhood shot through her memory. Stories of another sprawling palace, from a time before time, of a maze of underground corridors, of a monster crouching in the darkness of a central chamber...

Shivering, she dragged a silk shawl about her shoulders.

'I have never seen it, but I believe it exists. That is where the Imperial Treasury lies—deep beneath the Palace. They say that in good years when the revenues pour in from the provinces, they have to dig extra tunnels to make more vaults.' Anna lifted an eyebrow. 'Ask Ashfirth Saxon if you don't believe me. He would know because of his right to pillage.'

'His right to pillage?' Katerina's head was beginning to throb with the effort of imagining everything. *Walls lined with gold? A labyrinth? Underground vaults?*

Anna's expression was nothing if not mischievous. 'Hasn't he told you about Varangian pillaging rights?'

Katerina rubbed her brow and shook her head. 'We are hardly on intimate terms, Anna.'

'The Varangian Guard won this right thanks to their unswerving loyalty to their Emperor. They are barbarians, but once they have sworn their oath, they remain loyal until death.'

'They are honourable men.' Katerina bit her lip, she was

beginning to dislike the way Anna referred to the Commander and his comrades as barbarians, even though it was true that he was Anglo-Saxon and not Greek.

'Yes, I believe they are. But once their Emperor has died, their duty is done until they swear their oath to the next one. At that point they tend to run wild. It has become their right to enter the Treasury and take as much as they can carry. They call it palace pillaging.'

Katerina snorted. 'Now you *are* making fun of me.'

'I swear it's the truth! They may take what they can carry. It has become a tradition, but it only happens on the death of their Emperor.'

'Death must invalidate their oath.'

'Exactly. And after they have made their oath to the new Emperor they once again become the most loyal and trusted soldiers in the Empire. Ask Ashfirth Saxon, if you do not believe me.'

Days passed.

As the days extended into weeks, Katerina forgot all about the pillaging rights of the Varangian Guard, although she did spend much time gleaning what she could about life in the Great Palace—the rituals, the banquets, the ceremonies. She wanted to know how long the voyage might take, but Anna could not tell her, and Katerina was afraid of asking the Commander something that Princess Theodora would certainly have known.

Part of her—the cowardly part—hoped they never reached Constantinople and might stay for ever at sea.

One morning, Katerina was alone in her quarters as the merchantman rose and fell on a gentle swell. The sackcloth curtain was looped back, she was studying a finely painted image of St Mark in Princess Theodora's jewel-studded psalter.

'Princess?'

She looked up as Ashfirth Saxon came lightly down the stairway and bowed before her. Resplendent in the red dress uniform of the Varangian Guard, he was every inch the Commander. His dark hair was windswept, his blue eyes bright.

'Sir?' Katerina frowned. 'I thought we agreed that you should not use my title on board ship.'

'We have entered the Sea of Marmara, Constantinople is in sight. And since we shall be docking in the Palace Harbour rather than in the Golden Horn, it was time to tell the crew who has been voyaging with them. Your uncle's standard has been raised and the look-out will have seen it. Doubtless there will be a reception party waiting to greet you.'

The bottom fell out of Katerina's stomach. *A reception party! Dear Lord, the true test is about to begin. Let me not fail.*

The Commander crooked an arm at her, his smile offered reassurance. 'We are in home waters, the danger is over. I came to see if you would care to catch a glimpse of the city as we approach?'

'My thanks, I would.' Carefully, Katerina set Princess Theodora's psalter aside and took up her cloak. She found herself fussing with her hair, straightening her veil. *Am I grand enough? Do I look the part? Ought I to change?*

But Ashfirth Saxon was eager to be back on deck. 'Come, my lady.'

As she tucked her arm into his, an ache in her chest told her that this was one familiarity she would miss when Ashfirth Saxon learned her true identity.

Up on deck, he led her to the handrail, and even if he had

not warned her that the crew had been told of her supposed identity, she would have known it. Heads swivelled in her direction. Some men bowed, others simply stared. A few smiled and nodded.

'I saw her uncle once,' she heard a seaman mutter to his neighbour. 'Her real uncle, the one who retired to a monastery.'

Katerina smiled and nodded back, it seemed the right thing to do. Then she turned and looked towards the city.

Constantinople!

Her breath left her. Even though Anna had warned her, it took all her will to hold her jaw in place.

Above the restless shimmer of the sea, the city walls gleamed like an endless white ribbon. Katerina had never seen their like, but it did not end there. Piled up behind the walls, seemingly crowded against them, were dozens of buildings of every shape and size. There were towers, a thousand windows, and the light was bouncing off an extraordinary golden column. A vast dome pushed up through a cluster of other, smaller, domes. One vast cliff of a building had rows of windows overlooking the sea, with terrace upon terrace and gilded balconies. In the fresh breeze, flags and pennons streamed out from several roof-tops. This must be the Great Palace.

The deck shifted beneath her feet. Katerina had been warned that Constantinople was magnificent, but she had not been prepared for the sheer scale of it. For an instant it felt as though the city crouched on the edge of the sea was alive, and it was sailing towards them rather than the other way around.

She stared at the largest of the domes rising up from behind the sea walls. 'Hagia Sophia,' she murmured, deter-mined to hang on to what she had been told.

'It must feel very strange,' Commander Ashfirth said.

She froze. 'Commander?'

'Coming home after so long, it must feel very strange.'

'Yes, it does feel strange.' *More strange that you could know.* She forced herself to meet that watchful gaze. *Have I roused his suspicions? I ought to distract him.* 'And you, Commander, has our city won your heart? Or do you still think of England?'

A shadow fell over him. 'England is ever in my thoughts.' He shrugged the shadow away. 'But Constantinople has become my home.'

A seagull swooped past.

'You are certain you will never return?'

'Not while a Norman sits on the English throne.'

'Where in England were you born, Commander?'

Ashfirth's gaze returned to the city on the horizon. Her question had caught him off-guard, but rather to his surprise the answer came easily. 'Ringmer.'

That clear brow wrinkled. 'Ringmer? Where is that?'

'It is a village in the south of England, I am a South Saxon.'

And then, Ashfirth had no clear idea of how she did it, save that she was gently, quietly persistent, he found himself describing the death of Anglo-Saxon England as they sailed towards the Palace. It was not his habit to talk about his past, but he could not see the harm. Once he had escorted her to her quarters, she was not likely to see him again, and talking about England was certainly safer than discussing her uncle and risking revealing his true feelings about his suitability as Emperor.

As the sea hissed past the side of the ship, Ash explained how his father had, with the other South Saxon thanes, rallied to the call to arms and had gone to fight for King Harold. He told her about the long march they had made to the north to defeat the Norwegian King, Harald Hardrada.

He told her about the long march back. About how the Anglo-Saxons had to fight the Norman forces before they had fully rested. About Hastings. And she hung on to his every word, or so it seemed.

'My father never returned home,' he said, when the tale was finally done.

She was leaning towards him, her veil was a silken swirl in the wind, and those beautiful brown eyes were still fastened intently on his.

The Princess…her eyes, they were so large…

'Your father was killed in the battle with the Franks?'

'We assume so.' Ash cleared his throat. 'My mother waited and waited, but no news came until the summons for her to ride to Lewes for her remarriage. To a Norman.'

'What were your parents called?'

'My father was Aiken, Thane Aiken of Ringmer. My mother's name is, if she is still alive, Mildryth.'

'Did your mother love your father?'

'Yes.'

'Poor woman. When did this take place, sir?'

'1066.'

Her persistent questioning struck him as strange, but perhaps it could be explained; Normans had invaded England, and now they were eyeing up her uncle's western territories.

'And what happened then? After the Franks had come and their King was crowned?'

A series of images paraded through Ashfirth's memory, as vivid as freshly painted icons. There was his mother, red-eyed with weeping as she was forced to dress for her second wedding; there was his brother's body, floating in the mill-pond with not a mark on it; there was the stick his stepfather had used whenever Ash had 'misbehaved'. And the last, darkest image, in which his mother handed him a bundle containing one of his father's arm-rings as she thrust him out of the hall…

He swallowed. 'I was sent away.'

She gave a swift intake of breath. 'Why?'

'My mother feared for my life.'

'How old were you?'

'Ten.'

Those sympathetic eyes held his for a moment before she glanced at the approaching city walls. She had lost colour and her hands were white on the guardrail. She sighed. 'Your early life was harsh, like m—' she bit her lip '—like many. But you have done well since then, I think.'

Ashfirth shrugged. 'I survived.'

'You did more than that.' Her gaze had sharpened, she was frowning at the lighthouse tower in the Palace grounds. 'Your Captain Brand, he came with you from England?'

'Yes, he's from my village, but how did you…?'

Her mouth relaxed. 'At St Mary's, I observed the way you spoke to one another. There is an ease between you that speaks of long friendship.'

Her perceptiveness startled him, perhaps it should not, but what was even more startling was the ease with which she had led him to unburden himself of his most painful memories. As a princess, Theodora would have been trained to put men at their ease, to draw them out and observe them. From childhood, she would have been expected to win a man's confidence, and after so many years at the Rascian court, gaining the confidence of a barbarian must be second nature to her.

But it is not my nature to unburden myself to a woman. The fact that he had done so was unsettling. Notwithstanding the differences in their station, the Princess had qualities that drew him. Qualities in addition to the obvious physical ones that usually attracted a man to a woman.

She tore her gaze from the lighthouse and her smile was warm. 'I am glad you have found your place here.'

Ash nodded. 'I am sure you will understand the lure of Constantinople—there is nowhere like it. You must have missed it.'

'I...yes.'

Ashfirth Saxon had a strong profile. As his dark hair lifted in the breeze, Katerina found herself studying him, wondering what he had been like as a boy when his mother had told him to leave England. He had a smooth brow, it was high and unlined. His nose had a slight bump in it, but the bump in no way detracted from his looks. And he had eyelashes long enough and dark enough for a woman to envy—one might almost believe he had been using the Princess's cosmetics! Her surreptitious glances—Katerina did not want him to notice her looking at him—reminded her of what she already knew. His mouth was finely shaped, attractive. His whole person was attractive. She did not need to look at him to know this, she knew it already, but she liked looking at him.

There was a strength in Ashfirth Saxon that went far beyond those wide warrior's shoulders, that assured Commander's stance. She could not define it precisely, but there was...

His head turned, and in a heartbeat Katerina's eyes had fastened on the gleaming golden column in the approaching city. 'I was young when I left, my memories have faded,' she said, thankful that the wind was cooling her cheeks.

'They will return once you are ashore, *despoina*, the layout of the Palace will not have changed that much.'

'So Anna assures me.'

With a sinking feeling in the pit of her stomach, Katerina continued to study the city rising from the waters. There was so much of it! Anna's description had not prepared her for the reality, she must be crazed to think that she, Katerina, could carry this off!

As the white walls grew ever nearer, ever larger, Katerina found herself feverishly attempting to identify the various landmarks, trying to work out which building was which.

Hagia Sophia—the great dome made that one easy. And that break in the walls—could that be the entrance to the Palace Harbour? Yes, that must be the harbour, because that monumental building behind it could only be the Boukoleon Palace. But that… Katerina's brow wrinkled as she stared at a tower to one side of the Boukoleon. *What on earth is that tower? I ought to know.*

'Are you all right, my lady? You look concerned.' A warm hand touched her elbow.

One small question cannot hurt. 'That tower, sir, is it manned?'

'The lighthouse? Yes, of course. Surely you remember the lighthouse?'

'Yes, yes, I remember it.' She swallowed. Anna had made no mention of a lighthouse! She gave him a lofty look. 'I was meaning, is it manned during the day?'

'My men use it as a watch point in the day.'

She nodded. Yes, that break in the walls had to be the entrance to the Boukoleon Harbour. It was flanked by towers, with sentries on top. There were seven flags on the Palace roof, the large one in the centre was instantly recognisable—it was the Imperial standard with the double-headed eagle.

Her heart began to thud.

I am expected. They think I am the Princess.

She began to pray. *Dear Lord, please do not let the Emperor and his wife come to greet me. Let me creep in quietly and find somewhere to hide. Dear Lord…*

The sail was furled, several men took up oars. Their ship glided slowly, inexorably, between the two towers and entered the Imperial harbour.

They had arrived at the Great Palace, and her true test was about to begin.

Chapter Seven

Katerina's wits had frozen along with the rest of her, she did not think that she could move. It was as though she had turned into a mosaic figure on a church wall. Dimly, she became aware of the Commander speaking.

'*Despoina*, you will remember the lions, I am sure,' he was saying, smiling.

'L-lions?' With an effort, she blinked and came back to herself. The quays were marble—*marble!*—and lined with statues of fearsome beasts, he was gesturing at a lion. There was an ox, then another lion, and another…they looked as though they were waiting to pounce.

'How could one forget the lions, Commander?' Katerina forced a smile. Her heart bumped, her cheeks burned. She couldn't meet his gaze.

The windows of the Boukoleon Palace looked down on them like eyes, so many eyes. At the top of the building, a row of steel helmets winked in the sun; there must be a walkway high on the roof—a guard post. Nearer to hand, dozens of battle-axes flashed, the marble quays were under the watchful gaze of a contingent of Varangians, like the Commander, they were in red dress uniforms. More eyes.

The sentries had done their duty, word had spread of her arrival. The wharves were thronged with courtiers and ladies-in-waiting. The entire Palace, or so it seemed, was looking at their ship.

Katerina's fingers dug into the handrail. *I cannot do this! So many people are watching!* Her slightest false step would be noticed, someone would surely denounce her as an impostor…

'My lady? Are you well?'

She kept her voice steady. 'I confess it, Commander, I feel slightly…apprehensive. It has been so long…I am no longer accustomed to great ceremony, there was much less formality in the Rascian Court.'

The urge to hide was overpowering. She had to get away! Was this what life at the Palace was going to be like? *I simply cannot bear it. All those eyes!*

Katerina looked at Commander Ashfirth, but he would not help her; of all the eyes that were fixed on her, his blue ones seemed especially watchful. A moment more and she would betray herself utterly. She put a hand to her forehead, rubbing it as though it were paining her. If only the wretched man would *go away*.

'Commander, have you seen Lady Anna?'

He waved down the deck. 'I believe she is overseeing the offloading of your belongings.'

'Would you be so good as to send her to me?'

He leaned closer, a slight crease between his eyebrows. He was so close she could see the dark stubble of his growing beard and the length of his eyelashes. 'My lady, you have lost colour.'

'I feel a little dizzy,' she admitted, gripping the handrail.

'And since I cannot be getting sea-sick at this late stage in the voyage, it must be all those courtiers staring at me...'

'You had better get used to it.' His tone was sharp. 'There is nowhere like Miklagard, but there will be...expectations of you here and if you do not meet them, well, gossip flies around Miklagard as well as any city.'

'M-miklagard?' His eyes were searching, far too searching. If only she could get rid of him, she might manage to compose herself.

'Princess, you *must* recall. Miklagard is the Norse name for Constantinople, it is seen as a mythical city, full of many wonders and great riches.'

'It had...slipped my mind.'

'My lady, you will have to accustom yourself to being the centre of attention. Your arrival has been long looked for, people are bound to be curious.' A smile took the edge off his words and he touched her sleeve in a fleeting gesture of support.

His fingers were long, and his touch, light though it was, seemed to release her from some of her fear. She became aware of a small glow in her belly. His nails were clean and cut straight across. A scar running across his thumb and forefinger said this was a warrior's hand, but other than that it had the shapely elegance of a courtier's. She lifted her eyes to his. *Does he suspect?*

He gave her arm a gentle squeeze and lifted his hand away. 'It is understandable you are anxious, *despoina*. Even though you belong here, I can appreciate all this—' he indicated the marble wharves and the courtiers and soldiers that filled them '—must be overwhelming after Rascia.'

Ashfirth Saxon would not take the hint.

Katerina had hoped that he would leave her in peace once he had summoned Anna, but he did no such thing. He brought Anna to her and then hovered at her elbow, with a solicitous air that did nothing to calm her mind. *Does he suspect?*

She tried ignoring him. 'Anna, look at that tower, I had forgotten how tall it is.'

'The lighthouse? Yes, my lady, it soars into the sky.' Anna launched into a commentary about the Palace and the people on the quays. 'Look, my lady, the Empress has sent her ladies to greet you! There is Lady Pulcheria and Lady Maria and...'

Anna, bless her, was doing her best to let her know the lie of the land.

Why did the Commander not go away? He must suspect...

'You will enjoy being back in civilisation, Princess,' Anna burbled on. 'We shall hear Mass in Hagia Sophia. And I can't wait to see the horses in the Palace stables. If you recall, the Hippodrome lies just beyond the Palace, it must be slightly to the left of where we are now, while the Senate and Palace Gardens will be on the right.'

A crease formed on Commander Ashfirth's brow. *He must suspect.* And if he did not, Anna's well-meaning recitation of the layout of the Great Palace was certainly giving him pause.

Distract him.

'Thank you, Anna.' Katerina turned towards the Commander. 'Sir, there is something I have been meaning to ask you.'

'My lady?'

'It is about those Norman ships we sighted off Apulia.'

Ashfirth looked down at her. The little Princess was clearly troubled, and he wanted to help her. She was white as a sheet. Still pretty, of course, she would always be pretty, but her expression could only be described as terrified. Far too terrified for someone who was returning home. He had been aware of her reluctance to return, but once he had got her safely on board he had dismissed it, telling himself that it was perfectly understandable. As he understood it, she had grown fond of her Rascian prince, but she would know her duty as well as he knew his.

This abrupt mention of the Norman fleet had his skin prickling. 'Norman ships, my lady?'

She is trying to distract me—there is some other matter at the heart of this, something other than her reluctance to return...

She smiled up at him, but he was learning her expressions—the smile was forced. 'Commander, as soon as we disembark, I assume you will be seeking an audience with my uncle. You will want to report to him about the fleet we saw gathering off Apulia.' Reaching for the tail of her girdle, she began playing with the fringe. 'And there were those men in Dyrrachion, too, the Franks you suspected, the spies—he will want to know about all these things.'

'Naturally I shall seek an audience with the Emperor, but not until you are settled in your new quarters.'

Ashfirth tamped down a flare of irritation. He did not need the Princess to remind him that it was his duty to make a full report as quickly as possible. In normal circumstances, once he had dismissed his men, delivering his report would have been his first priority, but in this case he was glad to have a legitimate excuse to delay it. It had been some months since he had last been in the City and there were questions he wanted answering before he saw the Emperor. He would find the answers in the barracks.

Was the City still in a state of unrest? Was it true that the army had acclaimed General Alexios emperor? Where was General Alexios, and how much support could he call upon?

*And last, but by no means least, had the current Emperor
shown any sign that he could command his body-servants,
let alone an empire? Or was he, as Ashfirth suspected,
sliding into senility?*

'I know my duty, my lady…' Unfortunately, Ash knew
it too well. In his heart he might wish that Alexios Komnenos was already wearing the Imperial purple. Alexios
Komnenos outranked this woman's uncle in almost every
respect, he was a better leader; a better general; a better dip-
lomat…the list ran on. He smothered a sigh. Such disloyal
thoughts could never be uttered, and particularly not to the
Princess. 'But I am not at liberty to discuss the details of a
confidential report with you, my lady,' he finished stiffly.

Her forehead cleared and something flickered at the back
of her eyes. Ashfirth did not think it was anger because he
had rebuffed her—how odd, for an instant, it looked like
relief.

A trumpet blared from one of the towers. The Guard
were taking up positions on the quays; their dress uniforms
immaculate, their axes polished till they shone like crescent
moons. The Empress's ladies were streaming on to the landing stage, brighter even than the Princess's entourage in
Dyrrachion; they were certainly louder, they were squawk-
ing like magpies.

The ship bumped gently against the dock, mooring lines
snaked through the air, and moments later the merchantman
was alongside and the gangplank was dragged into place.

'*Despoina—*' Ashfirth gestured at the quay '—it is time
for you to disembark.' Her throat convulsed, those brown
eyes stretched wide—she looked as though she was on the
point of making a run for it. 'My lady, you are ready?'

'Yes, Commander, I am ready. Anna?'

'Here, my lady.'

The Princess lifted her skirts and took in a deep breath.

She looks as though she is going to her execution. She looks exactly as I must have done on the eve of my first battle.

'My lady?'

He had taken her arm before he had realised it, and when she turned to him, Ashfirth understood that despite the gulf between them he had come to care about this woman. If he could spare her this ordeal, he would.

'Commander?'

'The Empress is not among those ladies. If you are… fatigued, I can see to it that the others do not delay us.'

She looked doubtfully at the noble ladies clustered around the columns on the Imperial landing stage. 'You can do that without causing offence?'

'Certainly.'

This smile was genuine, it lit her whole face. 'Thank you, Commander, I would appreciate that.'

Ashfirth Saxon was as good as his word. In no time, Katerina had stepped off the ship and had been escorted past his red-uniformed Guard with their gleaming battleaxes, past the stone lions and oxen, and the smiling, staring ladies. He led her up some steps to a pair of double doors that were at twice as large as any she had seen in her whole life.

The Boukoleon Palace seemed to have been built entirely from marble.

As Katerina entered the portico she struggled to look as though she walked through palaces like this every day of her life. It wasn't easy. So much marble! There was a wide staircase with a marble handrail and carved balusters, and a marble colonnade with a view of the sea. She nodded at several more ladies, she smiled until her face ached. She accepted a spray of spring flowers from a servant girl…

Commander Ashfirth bore her inexorably on. He swept

her up the wide stairs, higher and higher until they stopped at an airy landing. 'The women's quarters, my lady.'

Katerina managed a nod. More marble, in every colour of the rainbow—purple, cream, green, ochre… They passed into a reception chamber that was large enough to house the entire population of her home village.

'These are your apartments, I hope they meet with your approval.'

'This is lovely, thank you,' Katerina said, although the word 'lovely' scarcely did justice to the splendour in which she found herself. It was exactly as Anna had described, painted frescoes adorned the walls—birds and several unknown and exotic animals were frolicking amid the fountains of a pleasure garden. On one side of the reception chamber, the entire wall was taken up by a line of windows. The shutters were open and a dazzle of light fell into the room. Flimsy draperies hung from brass rods, billowing softly in the sea breeze. Skirts skimming silently across the smooth floor, Katerina went to the nearest window.

Directly below them, the stone lions and oxen cast stumpy shadows on the wharves of the Imperial Harbour. Beyond the harbour walls lay the Sea of Marmara; flocks of gulls were rocking on its silvery surface. There were several ships, and an exceptionally large galley with two banks of oars and a turret in its bow caught her eye. 'There is much sea traffic,' she said. The faint pulse of a drum reached her as the galley cut through the water towards a group of gulls. As the vessel bore down on them, the birds swirled into the sky like leaves in a gale. 'Surely that ship is not a trader?'

There was movement behind her. Commander Ashfirth's breath warmed her cheek as he leaned past her to see for himself.

'That is a battle ship, my lady. A dromon.'

'What do you think is happening?'

For once, that blue gaze was evasive. He looked troubled. 'Of late there has been some…unrest in the city. I need to confer with officers who have been on duty here to discover how matters stand today. In my absence there may have been…developments. As soon as I know that these apartments meet with your approval, I must go straight to the barracks.'

'They will suit me very well indeed, sir.'

The double door at the other end of the chamber opened and Anna came through. A line of men followed with the baggage, they were dressed identically in short tunics of plain bleached linen.

'The bedchamber?' Anna asked, looking at the Commander.

'Through that door, I expect.' He pointed. 'The slaves will know where to go.'

Slaves.

Katerina's heart twisted as she watched the men carry the baggage through the bedchamber door.

Slaves.

Her fingers tightened on the spray of flowers. 'Commander?'

'My lady?'

'Are there many slaves in the Palace these days?'

'Hundreds, if not thousands.'

Thousands…

'And are they…are they well treated?'

'Well treated?' He shrugged. 'I suppose they are as well treated here as anywhere. But I confess, I have never given it much thought. I do not own slaves myself, my lady.'

Katerina set the flowers on a narrow wall-table. More questions might rouse the Commander's suspicions, but she could not help herself. Ever since the days of her personal slavery had ended, she had longed to do something to alleviate the plight of others. Most of them would have been enslaved through no fault of their own, as had happened in her case. Now at last her moment had come; she had arrived at the Palace and the Princess had given her the means to help at least some of them. She must act quickly, she might not be in this position for long...

She drew in a deep breath. 'Do they beat slaves in the Great Palace when they make a mistake, do they whip them? Do they feed them well?'

The slaves emerged empty-handed from the bedchamber doorway; they bowed in Katerina's direction and left the apartment.

'Those fellows look strong and healthy enough to me,' the Commander said. 'Now, my lady, if you would excuse me...'

'One moment, sir.'

'My lady?'

Under her sleeve, Katerina fingered her bracelet. It wound several times round her wrist; its head and tail were that of a dolphin, and it had sapphires for eyes. Of all the gifts the Princess had given her, this was her favourite.

'You may recall my saying that I would like to buy some slaves, sir, and since I am no longer familiar with the city, I would be grateful for your help.'

He gave her a searching look. 'You still wish to buy slaves?'

'Yes. If I want to give them their freedom I will have to buy them—I cannot free slaves I do not own.'

Ashfirth Saxon tucked his thumbs into his belt. He was impossible to read, but she sensed her request had surprised him. She gave him a superior look such as an Imperial princess might give a barbarian born outside the Empire.

'Commander, I am asking for your help, I need to go to the slave market. What is it like? Is it safe to go there?'

'What do you mean, is it safe to go there? Surely you are not thinking of going *in person*?'

Katerina turned the golden dolphin on her wrist. 'How else might I choose slaves? I will buy them and free them.'

'You will have to do more than that, they will need to be given work. If you turn them out on the streets, they will be little better than beggars.'

'I realise that. I will give them work for as long…as long as I may. In any case, I need a new body-servant, since my old one—' she sent him a dark look '—is no longer with me.'

'Princess Theodora, I am sure there are plenty of suitable slaves the Emperor will gift to you if you ask him, there is no need for you to go anywhere near such a place as the slave market.'

'Is that your way of telling me that the slave market is dangerous?'

'It is not—' he hesitated '—the most pleasant of places.'

'Pleasant? *Pleasant?* How could a slave market possibly be pleasant?'

'*Despoina?*'

Katerina dug her nails into her palms. *Careful, careful.* In snapping at him, she had roused his curiosity. She gave a light shrug. 'As you say, it cannot be pleasant, but I need a new body-servant and if I am going to employ a freed slave, which is my intention, I should like to choose her myself.'

He stepped closer, so close that she caught a faint herbal scent. It must come from the soap he had been using. Beneath the tang of the herbs lay another, more musky masculine scent, and she realised with a start that she recognised it. That musky scent was personal to him, to Ashfirth Saxon. Surreptitiously, she inhaled.

Saints, what was she doing? To her horror, she realised she had been about to sway towards him.

Cheeks heating, she jerked back and stared out of the window, looking beyond the harbour walls and the wheeling gulls, beyond the galleys and merchantmen...

Behind them, the door slammed.

Silence dropped over them. It was a large silence, and it seemed to tell her that something large was about to happen. She swallowed.

'Princess, do you really wish to help slaves?'

'Yes.'

When his hand came towards her and hesitated, her belly quivered. When his fingers curled round her wrist next to the bracelet, she forgot to breathe.

'My lady?' He took another step and then he was directly in front of her, blocking her sight of the sea. His hands closed over her shoulders.

Katerina stared at the gold braiding round the neck of his tunic. Her mouth was dry.

How impertinent he is to stand so near. I can feel the heat of his body, which must mean he is not wearing chainmail beneath that tunic. He ought not to be touching me either. No, he isn't merely touching me, he is holding me—and he most certainly ought not to be holding me!

'I am the Princess.'

'I know it,' he murmured, and Katerina realised she must have spoken aloud.

Beneath her veil, one of his thumbs, *both* of his thumbs, moved. Once, twice, thrice. Slow, secret caresses on her neck.

Her stomach swooped. What had happened to the air? This chamber should be full of sea air, instead it was suffocating, she couldn't breathe. Most surprisingly, she felt no fear. For the second time, Katerina found herself wrestling with the embarrassing impulse to lean towards him. *Is this what happens when one is touched by a man one likes?*

The thought had no sooner formed, than she shied away from it. *No. No! I do not like men, I do not trust them.*

Not even this one?

No! It is impossible, I am here on false pretences. I have a task to perform, I cannot allow myself to like this man.

'You really do want my help to buy slaves.' His voice was husky.

She gave a slow nod, speech was beyond her.

That dark head came close, his thumbs continued to move on the side of her neck. Up and down, up and down. She ought to object. *I am the Princess.*

'Commander—' When finally she got her voice to work, it was as croaky as his. 'You must not...not...' His eyes were so dark, and that musky male scent was stronger than incense, it was drugging her senses, dizzying her thoughts.

'Princess Theodora, I cannot recommend that you visit the slave market until I...oh, to hell with this.' His grip shifted, his head came down and his mouth was on hers.

For the briefest of moments, they both froze.

He has surprised himself, he has certainly surprised me.

His arm went round her waist, bringing her full against him. He groaned and his mouth shifted against hers.

Katerina made no protest. It was astonishing, the way her mind was entirely free of fear. Hard. *His mouth is hard and his arms are like iron bands—why am I not afraid?* His lips were moving firmly over hers, pressing fiercely, insistently. He was not being gentle, but he was not forcing himself on her, far from it. It was a struggle to keep herself from reaching for him.

Remember, I am the Princess.

His hand slid round the back of her head and his fingers caught on a hair pin.

'Ouch!'

His grip eased. He muttered something that might have been an apology and his lips softened, but the kiss went on. Confidently, inexorably.

Beautifully.

Katerina had never been kissed like this. She ached—no, she burned to respond, but her legs were weakening, buckling beneath her, so she must reach up and cling to his red tunic. And then, before she knew it, she was hanging on to those wide muscled shoulders.

Must push him away, must...

Her breathing was most erratic, her fingers curled into him. And still there was no fear.

'Princess.' He eased back and looked down at her, his mouth edging up at one side. 'Little Princess.' His head came down as her mouth lifted to meet him.

His fingers were in her hair, not pulling against the pins, but smoothing, stroking, mimicking the movements of his tongue on her lips. So soothing, that stroking.

Katerina's senses were reeling, her knees had lost their strength. Far from pushing him away, she was pulling him to her. She was responding on her own behalf, not as the Princess would respond. And she did not care.

When his tongue urged her mouth to open, it opened eagerly.

Katerina had been little more than a child when she had been enslaved, she had not been much older when Vukan had propositioned her. He had not been cruel, she had agreed to go to his bed, but she had not gone from love. It had simply been a matter of survival. Her lover had been the strongest of the slaves, he had sworn to keep her for himself. Other slave girls had been treated far worse.

It was true that she had had no choice; the strongest slave had wanted her for his bed partner, and she had had to endure. But no one else had come near her. That had been the way of things until Princess Theodora bought her. She had learned to endure Vukan's touch, his kisses.

In a secret corner of her mind, in the part reserved for her most private hopes and longings, Katerina had wondered if she would ever find pleasure in a man. Today she had her answer. There was pleasure here, a world of it.

Ashfirth's tongue met hers and she was melting, she was wax in his arms. Eager. She drew back, startled at the ease with which he stole her breath. The sensations this man created inside her were exquisite to the point of pain. When his black lashes lifted, those haunting turquoise eyes seemed equally startled.

Longing shivered though her—it was almost unbearable. *If only...*

Tipping back her head, she raised her mouth.

A kiss feathered across her lips, he was easing away.

She murmured a protest and pressed closer. Shocking though it was, she ached to encourage him. In one sense, Ashfirth Saxon needed no encouragement—he was already blatantly aroused. He might be trying to retreat, but she had felt him pressed against her belly. Hard and full of desire. For her.

Or was it a princess he wanted? The question hit her like a splash of cold water.

Does he desire a princess, or me?

Yearning was a blade in her breast, but he was lifting his hands from her, and then there was space between them and the breeze from the sea was rushing through it.

She shivered and blinked up at him. Standing very straight, he shook his head. Like her, he was out of breath. His brow furrowed, a soldier struggling to control himself.

'Princess Theodora, I...I can only say that I am sorry, that should not have happened. You should have stopped me.' His frown deepened, his tone became less certain. 'You could have stopped me.'

You are the Princess, that is what he is saying.

Katerina lifted an eyebrow. 'Could I?'

'You could, and you know it.'

He held himself as he would on parade, but he was watching her mouth. Triumph flared. *He might believe he has been kissing a princess, but it is my body that attracts him, it is my person he lusts after.*

'You are the Princess Theodora, are you not?'

His question threw her, and for a moment she could only stare. Was he in earnest? Had he found her out? Had that kiss—which for her had been a revelation—merely been his way of testing her?

'I thought—' a muscle jumped in his jaw '—a princess might punish her bodyguard for such insolence.'

Katerina smiled. His gaze had flickered briefly to her mouth and up again.

He was attracted to *her*. That gave her power over him, power that was entirely unconnected with her role as princess. Ironically, if she was going to allay any suspicions as to her true identity, it was becoming clear that she must use that power. He would expect Princess Theodora to be confident...

'Men have been flogged for less, I am sure,' she said, mildly. 'But I do not think I shall inflict that on you.' Willing herself to maintain her composure, Katerina tidied her veil and straightened her gown, which seemed somehow to have been pulled all awry.

And not a moment too soon. A latch clicked behind her and the door opened, Anna was returning with a slave bearing the enamelled jewel box.

'Besides, sir, you belittle yourself,' Katerina went on coolly. 'You are much more than a mere bodyguard.'

A faint smile flickered across his lips, and he leaned closer. 'What am I, my lady?'

'You, Ashfirth—you did say I might call you Ashfirth, did you not?'

'As you wish.'

Katerina looked up at him from under her eyelashes. She had seen the real princess give Prince Peter just such a look in the days before his death, it was blatantly flirtatious. 'You, Ashfirth, are a Commander. *My* Commander.'

And then—God knows how she found the courage with Anna's footsteps fast approaching—she moistened her lips. And had to hide a triumphant smile when once again his eyes sought her mouth, and his fingers tightened on the hilt of his dagger.

He bowed. 'As you say, my lady, I am yours to command, but if you will excuse me, I must confer with the garrison officers before presenting my report to His Imperial Majesty.'

'Very well, Commander.'

Nodding curtly at Anna as he passed her, Ashfirth—after that kiss she could never think of him as the Commander—strode to the doorway. Reaching for the gilded handle, he glanced back. '*Despoina*, pray remember—until I have discovered the mood of the city, no slave markets. You are safe here.'

Katerina gave him her best smile. 'I shall remember your advice, Ashfirth.'

I shall remember it, but I shall not necessarily follow it.

Chapter Eight

Several of Ashfirth's Varangians were sitting around the wall-benches in the guardhouse a few floors below Princess Theodora's apartment. They were sharpening their axes, polishing shield bosses and helmets. As Ashfirth entered, they leaped to their feet.

'Welcome back, Commander.'

'My thanks, Halfdan. Radwald, arm back to full strength?'

'Yes, Commander.'

'Sergeant Toki?'

'Sir?'

'Everyone off the ship?'

'Yes, sir.'

'Good. Briefing in the armoury in ten minutes. Find as many of the squad as you can, I should like to speak to all who are not on duty.'

'Yes, sir.'

Ashfirth was praying that none of them could read his befuddlement.

What had come over him? To have kissed Princess Theo-

dora in such a way! He had hauled her into his arms as though she were his sweetheart! The Princess! She had said that she would not see him flogged, but in truth men had been flayed alive for less.

Although—he hid a smile—*she had not objected.*

Until that kiss, he had thought her innocent, he had made the assumption that her rank had protected her during the time of her betrothal to Prince Peter. He couldn't have been more wrong. There was nothing innocent about the way that small and beautiful body had relaxed against his, nor the way her lips had softened and her tongue had come out to meet his.

Princess Theodora was no more innocent than he. She had smiled so suggestively at him. So warmly. And what was it that she had said…*you are a commander, my commander.*

Hell. These were treacherous waters. It had been obvious from the first that Princess Theodora had not the slightest desire to marry the Duke of Larissa. She would not have made herself so hard to find.

You are a commander, my commander.

Was she asking him to take her as his lover?

Was that what princesses did when they wanted a lover? Ashfirth had never thought to look so high, but a certain tension in his loins told him that part of him, at least, was more than a little interested in the possibility. Was she asking him to have an affair with her?

Clearly she was more sophisticated than she had at first appeared. *Doe Eyes.* Perhaps she thought to while away the time until Duke Nikolaos arrived at the capital? Many of the ladies of the court took lovers. Ashfirth had always taken pains to avoid such entanglements—the complexities of such liaisons had never appealed.

But…the Princess? Temptation personified.

Sigurd, one of his captains, set his axe in the wall-rack and came over. 'It is good to see you, Commander. What do you make of the news?'

'What news is that, Captain?'

Half-listening to Sigurd, Ash allowed his thoughts to run where they would. An affair with a princess was not unheard of. It was risky though, damned risky. It would be hard—no, he must face this—it would be impossible to keep news of such an affair from Duke Nikolaos. The Duke wouldn't take kindly to discovering his betrothed had been playing him false.

Was she hinting at the possibility of an affair? He must have misread her. Her response had been…unexpected, to say the least, particularly when she was said to be carrying a torch for Prince Peter.

How she had kissed him! A grieving woman would surely not have kissed him quite so…enthusiastically. It was most odd, he hadn't judged her as the faithless type. Spoilt? Perhaps. Driven by whim? Possibly. But faithless? Ash sighed. Even if she was asking him to take her as his lover, he couldn't do it. She might have made it plain she did not want to marry the Duke, but he still couldn't do it.

Damn. He held down a reminiscent grin. What an armful she made! And that little wriggle she had given as she pressed herself against his manhood, that breathy moan… that hint of bliss to come. She knew what she was about, did the little Princess. An affair with her might just be worth the risks…

But, no. He could not in all conscience take matters further. It had taken him years to fight his way to this position in the Palace. It was a position of trust, of responsibility. An affair with Princess Theodora would destroy everything he had worked so hard to achieve.

'So, Commander, what are your views?'

Sigurd was looking expectantly at him. Recollecting himself with a wrench, Ashfirth realised that not only had he not heard half of what his captain had had to say, but Sigurd—and the rest of the guardhouse, by the look on their faces—were waiting for Ash to make some pronouncement.

'My apologies, Sigurd—you were saying?'

'Alexios Komnenos—do you think he intends to storm the city, or is he merely posturing?'

Ashfirth called his thoughts to order. *General Alexios— storm the city?*

Alexios Komnenos and his brother Isaac had until recently both been loyal to the current Emperor Nikephoros. And while general disaffection with the Emperor had grown, surely they would never take such drastic action? Unless... Ash had not been able to believe it, but...could that wild rumour of the army acclaiming General Alexios as Emperor actually be true?

'I have been away far too long if matters have indeed reached such a pass. I have only this moment returned from escorting Princess Theodora to her apartments and I have the devil of a thirst. Call for wine to be sent to the armoury, would you? And then you may bring me fully up to date with events.'

'I thought you knew,' Sigurd said. 'The Imperial army has acclaimed Alexios Komnenos Emperor.'

Ashfirth stared. 'It is true, then? The army has acclaimed Alexios?'

Sigurd nodded.

Good choice. The disloyal thought was out before he could check himself. *Good choice, but...*

'This is evil news, there will be bloodshed over this,' he said. 'What does Emperor Nikephoros have to say?'

Sigurd shrugged. 'God knows, the Emperor is holed up

in his apartments and refuses to see anyone. Word has gone out that this has driven him over the edge.'

Ashfirth swore.

'Where does that leave us, sir? The world knows that General Alexios has the makings of a fine emperor...'

He has indeed. Sweet Mary, save us.

'So where does that leave us, Commander?'

'Our position is quite clear.' Ashfirth put steel in his voice. 'We made our oaths to Emperor Nikephoros. He pays us, we owe him our loyalty—it is as simple as that. Where is General Alexios?'

'He has set up camp outside the Adrianople Gate.'

Ashfirth drew his brows together. 'The Adrianople?'

'Yes, sir.'

Frown deepening, Ashfirth shook his head. 'Not one of ours.'

'No, sir. Manned by Germanic tribesmen.'

A slave appeared in the doorway with a tray of wine. 'Do you wish to take this in the armoury, sir?'

Ash waved the slave away. 'My thanks, but later. Come, Sigurd, I've heard enough.' He glanced about the guard-house. 'The briefing will have to wait. First, I need to consult with our Emperor.'

'But, sir, he refuses to see anyone!'

'He will see me,' Ashfirth said quietly. 'He is in his apartments, you say?'

'Yes, sir.'

'Captain, you will accompany me.'

Unlocking the enamelled jewel casket, Katerina eased back the lid.

Happily unaware that the Empire was shaking on its foundations all around her, she was sitting next to Anna on a couch in the bedchamber. The jewel box lay between them. The bulk of Katerina's new wealth sat in this box, carefully wrapped in silk. Picking up one of the bundles, she took out the gold diadem and set it on her knee. The gems in the headband sparked coloured fire; the pearls in the trailing pendants gleamed, cool and smooth to the touch.

'Anna, would you say this was one of the more costly items?'

'Oh, yes, the diadem is easily the most valuable piece.'

'And this—can this be gold, too?' Katerina held out a cloak fastening shaped like a round shield, it was studded with garnets and sapphires.

Anna took the cloak fastening, weighing it in her hand. 'It is heavy.'

Katerina smiled. 'Good, the gold is more likely to be pure. It should fetch a fair amount. I shall sell the dolphin bracelet, too.' She loved that bracelet. She had been wearing it when Ashfirth kissed her into forgetting who she really was, when Ashfirth made her wish she was a woman he might come to care for rather than an impostor.

'Yes, but—' Anna looked wistfully at the diadem on Katerina's knee '—are you certain about this?'

'Quite certain.'

'You are not likely to see such riches again, Ka—Theodora.' Impulsively, Anna laid her hand on Katerina's arm. 'Do not sell everything! Keep something back for yourself.'

Katerina looked at the diadem, at the jewel box. 'What use have I for such baubles? My freedom is gift enough.'

Sighing, Anna replaced the cloak fastening in the jewel box. 'Very well. But you would be wise not to sell everything at once.'

'Why?'

'There is simply too much, and it is clearly so precious. One glance at the contents of this casket and anyone would know it must come from the Great Palace. Such treasures could only belong to someone in the Imperial household. There will be questions, questions—' Anna lowered her voice '—that at the moment neither you nor the real princess would care to have answered.'

'Yes, I see, that does make sense.' Katerina gave a jerky nod. 'Thank you, Anna.'

'We will start with a few items, then?'

'Agreed.' Katerina caught Anna's eye. 'But only if you are confident that our intermediary will be completely trustworthy. Whom do you have in mind?'

'I thought Sergeant Toki would be a good man to approach.'

Thoughtfully, Katerina wound a pearl pendant round her finger. 'As long as he is made to understand he must not breathe a word of this to Commander Ashfirth. I have received the distinct impression that he does not approve of this venture.'

Anna nodded. 'Rest easy, I will make sure Toki understands.'

Both the clouds and the Sea of Marmara were tinged with pink when the guard opened the door to re-admit Anna to the apartment.

'Here, Theodora—' Anna dropped a red leather purse into Katerina's palm '—I have brought you your money.'

'Thank you.'

The red purse was heavy and the coins made a satisfying chink. Katerina opened it and several gold coins winked up at her. 'Not half as pretty as the diadem, but far more useful.' Pulling the drawstrings tight, she smiled at Anna, the aristocratic lady she now counted as her friend. Mindful of the guard at the door, she whispered, 'How many slaves do you reckon we may buy with the contents of this purse?'

Anna spread her hands. 'That will depend on many things. On the age of the slaves, on their sex, on their strength and condition…'

Katerina grimaced. No one knew better than she what privations the slaves might have suffered. 'I want to make the best use of this money.'

'By that I take it you want to use it to save as many slaves as possible?'

'Yes.' Katerina nodded at the brilliant sunset that flamed across both sky and sea. 'I would like to act straight away, but we shall have to wait until tomorrow.'

'The slave market opens early.'

'Did you remind Sergeant Toki not to breathe a word of this to Commander Ashfirth?'

'Of course.'

'Anna, I am most grateful for your help, I would be completely at a loss without you.'

Anna gave her a strange look. 'I doubt that very much. In your own quiet way, Ka—Theodora, you are one of the most determined people I have ever met.'

At breakfast, the sunrise echoed the sunset of the previous night, as a fiery sun rose over the hills on the eastern arm of the Empire. When the shutters in the reception chamber were opened, a tide of apricot-coloured light washed over the marble floors.

Katerina and Anna ate a frugal breakfast in the apartment—some warm bread, brought by one of the slaves, a handful of dried fruits. They had dressed plainly, in brown woollen gowns the fabric of which might have been woven on any household loom, and the red purse was fastened to the plainest belt that Katerina could find. Their veils were as simple and unremarkable as their gowns.

When they had finished eating, Katerina reached for her

cloak. 'No adornments, Anna,' she said, noticing a golden bangle on Anna's arm. 'There must be nothing to mark us out as ladies from the Palace.'

'I understand.' Anna removed the bangle.

'What time did Toki say we would set out?'

Even as Katerina posed the question, someone rapped on the door and Sergeant Toki came in.

'Princess Theodora, good morning.' He bowed. 'Lady Anna.'

'Good morning, Sergeant.' Briskly, Katerina fastened her cloak. She looked past him. 'Where is our escort?'

'Waiting outside the Palace gate. In view of your instructions, I thought the less fuss, the better.'

'Quite right, Sergeant, quite right.'

Shrugging deep into their cloaks, they left the apartment and began making their way down the wide staircase. The door to the guardhouse loomed large in Katerina's mind. Would Ashfirth be in there? She pulled her cloak hood more closely about her face. Would he choose that moment to come out?

Katerina's mind was sliding all over the place, and a cold sweat was trickling down her back. She did not have to look far to find the reason. This was an echo of the dread she had felt when she had been forced on to the slave block. Her fingers clutched at her skirts as they left the women's quarters and approached the floor where the Varangian Guardsmen were billeted. The bread sat heavily in her stomach.

Think of Ashfirth, do not think about the hell that is a slave market.

Ashfirth might be angry that she had ignored his advice yet again, but nothing, *nothing* could compare with the sinking, shaming dread of being forced onto the auction block. It was far worse being stared at, being poked and prodded and made the subject of lascivious remarks. Notwithstanding that, Katerina did not want Ashfirth to see her—he would be bound to ask questions.

The thought of him filled her own mind with questions. *What is he doing? Has he seen the Emperor? Does he think of me when we are apart? How will he react when he learns the truth about me?*

Katerina could not get him out of her mind. *If only I could be open with him, if only I could tell him the truth.*

A soldier she did not recognise was on duty by the guardhouse. She scuttled past him, head down. They crossed more marble floors; they hurried past alcoves filled with statues of pagan gods and goddesses; they went through a wide door with gilded handles. Another.

And then they were outside, and the walls of the Boukoleon Palace were behind them and the lighthouse tower was rearing up on their right. The morning breeze was cool on Katerina's cheeks; she could smell baking bread and roasting meats.

Her mouth fell open at the size and grandeur of the Palace. There were lawns and gardens with sparrows chirping in the bushes. There were fountains and paved courtyards, buildings with tiled roofs and domes and columned porticoes; there were arcades that seemed to run on for ever. Sergeant Toki hustled them along while her eyes darted this way and that. She must memorise every inch of the grounds.

But there was so much!

It was shortly after dawn and already the paths and courtyards were filling with people. Slaves were rushing to and fro with trays and serving vessels. Fresh-faced eunuchs stalked along, juggling the scrolls, parchments and quills that marked them as scribes. Courtiers in long silk tunics jostled each other for space on the walkways…

There was a wall ahead. Sergeant Toki escorted them past a sentry post at a gate, and another courtyard opened out in front of them. It was surrounded by stately buildings in the style the Romans had favoured. There were more fountains, and when that courtyard was crossed, they faced yet another.

'Surely we are not still in the Palace?'

'Yes, all this is the Palace.'

'It is like a city, I remember being told as much, but I did not believe it.'

The Sergeant grunted. 'This way, if you please.'

Katerina glanced over her shoulder, half-hoping and half-fearing to see Ashfirth striding up behind them, ordering them to stop. There was no sign of him. They passed under an archway and through another gate. She kept her hood firmly up and avoided looking at the sentries.

'We're out of the Palace,' Anna whispered.

Two men pushed away from the Palace wall and came to join them. They were not wearing the uniform of the Varangian Guard, nor were they carrying the distinctive axes, but they were wearing swords. Katerina recognised them from the ship.

She nudged Anna in the ribs. 'They are Ashfirth's men?'

'Yes.'

'Will they be discreet? I don't want him to know about this.'

Anna gave an impatient sigh. 'They will be discreet. They are off duty, anyway.'

It was odd, but once they were free of the Palace and were truly on their way to the slave market, Katerina's sense of dread eased. Perhaps it was because every step was taking her closer to her goal. Her heart was set on freeing as many slaves as possible.

Sergeant Toki pressed on. Flanked by the Guards,

they hurried down a broad avenue lined with prosperous houses with gardens. They turned down another street, and another, each busier than the last. Men were pulling handcarts heavy with coffers and cooking pots; women were carrying babies on their backs; there were donkeys with laden panniers...

Why were so many people on the move? 'What's going on? Is it always like this? The whole city must be out on the streets,' Katerina said.

Anna shrugged and plucked at her sleeve. 'Let's get this over with.'

The road sloped down and the smell of the sea grew stronger. The gardens became smaller and then there were no gardens at all, just row after row of wooden tenements. Refuse littered the road. A mangy dog was nosing through a pile of rubbish, a rank stink caught in her throat. There were people here, too, lots of them. And more handcarts, more overburdened donkeys.

What is going on?

'Not far now,' Sergeant Toki announced.

The road widened, the guards stood close, the crowd thickened. A stone building lay directly ahead; the ground floor was all round arches and entirely open to the elements. The slave market. The city walls and a glimpse of sea were just visible beyond.

And there—Katerina bit the inside of her mouth—there were the slaves. Poor souls. The air was foul with the smell of fear and pain. Dread washed through her. She had to force her legs to carry her towards the auction block—it was that or run screaming from this place, and that would do nobody any good.

Anna linked arms with her. 'You are trembling, my lady.'

'I...I am remembering.'

Anna nodded and squeezed her arm, half-supporting her as Sergeant Toki shouldered through and secured them a place at the foot of the platform.

Katerina cleared her throat. 'You can tell much about a slave master by the condition of his slaves. See, over there, under the third arch on the left...' She gestured towards a particularly bedraggled group in filthy homespun.

'That little girl,' Anna pointed, 'she cannot be more than two!'

The child's hair hung in rat's tails about her face, a face that was pitifully young to be so drawn and dirty. Her eyes were red-rimmed and she was gripping the hand of an even smaller child whose wretched clothes made it impossible to determine whether the child was a girl or a boy. Heart twisting in sympathy, Katerina forced herself to release Anna. Her nails dug into her palms.

'Look, Katerina, that other one is little more than a baby!'

Katerina fought off a wave of nausea. She had known this would be difficult, but the echoes were stronger than she had anticipated. 'Anna, your family own slaves, you knew about this place.'

Anna grimaced. 'Naturally I knew about it, but I have never actually been here myself and...and my parents have always treated their slaves well. I confess, I never gave it much thought. But this...' Tears welling, she stared at the children. 'You must buy those two, you must!'

A heavily chained young man stood behind the children. He was swaying on his feet, his fair hair was matted and dull and his cheekbones were bruised.

Anna caught Katerina's arm. 'That male slave is hurt, look at that stain on his tunic—it...it's blood!'

'You are right.' The young man's tunic was splotched with rust-coloured marks. He was very tall and he might be well built, if he were not so thin. A giant. 'He looks like a brawler to me.'

The little group was herded and, in the case of the male slave, goaded on to the auction block.

'They are half-starved,' Anna muttered. Her eyes never left the male slave. 'Buy him, you must buy him!'

Deeply troubled, Katerina frowned. 'I don't think he is a good choice, he looks like a troublemaker.'

'Why should that matter? You don't intend to keep him.'

'No, I told you, I shall feed them and clothe them, give them work for a time and then give them their freedom.'

'Buy him as well as the children.' Anna's fingers dug painfully deep. 'Please, Ka—my lady, I…I don't have money of my own, but I will pay you back somehow. You can have my gold bangle, and the rest of my jewellery. You can sell the lot and buy *more* slaves.'

'You have no money?' How odd, Lady Anna's father had an estate outside the City.

'My father's revenues are small, he spent much buying me my place at Court. My lady, I will give you Zephyr, you can sell her too.'

Katerina's mouth fell open. Zephyr was Anna's horse, Anna adored her; she had brought Zephyr with her when she had first arrived at the Rascian court.

'You would sell your Zephyr for a slave?' She looked doubtfully at the fair young man on the auction block. 'Anna, he looks…dangerous.'

'I would sell her for that one. Please.' Anna clasped her hands together. 'I will make sure you don't regret it.'

Back in the women's quarters of the Boukoleon Palace, Ashfirth rapped on the main door of Princess Theodora's apartments. A young boy let him in.

'I need to speak to the Princess,' Ash said. The reception chamber appeared empty, no one else was about. Hell, where was she?

Ash had a thousand things on his mind, but his conscience would not let him rest until he had made sure that Princess Theodora understood that for her own safety, she must remain in her chambers. He had enough to do without worrying about her, too. Outside the massive city walls, the Imperial generals were banging the battle drums, and the Emperor had abandoned any pretence of being in control. Matters were worsening by the hour.

Would Alexios Komnenos actually break into the city?

The boy—his short tunic marked him out as a slave—looked apologetic. 'The Princess is not here, sir.'

'Where is she?'

'I…I do not know, sir. I am sorry.'

Ash swore and the blood drained from the slave's face. The boy had the dark eyes and curly black hair that Ashfirth had learned to associate with several of the Armenian tribes.

'Where are you from, lad?'

'Armenia, sir.'

'I have travelled there, I know your people. Are you sick?'

'No, sir.'

The boy was very pale. And if he wasn't sick, perhaps he was lying, he was certainly being evasive. 'Do you know who I am?'

The boy's Adam's apple jerked up and down. 'Yes, sir. You are C-Commander Ashfirth of the Varangian Guard.'

'Indeed. Now I shall ask you this question again, and I would recommend that you think carefully before you answer. *Where is Princess Theodora?*'

The boy dropped into a crouch at Ash's feet and pressed his forehead to the marble tiles. 'Please, sir, don't ask me.

Please, sir…she ordered me, she *ordered* me not to tell anyone. Please, sir…'

Ash regarded the dark curls for a moment before lifting the boy to his feet. 'Go on. Where is the Princess? No harm will come to you, if you tell the truth. Understand this, I need to know because I am pledged to protect her.' He made his voice stern. 'On the other hand, if you persist in withholding information concerning her whereabouts, I may have to take strong measures.'

'S-slave market.'

'The Princess has gone out to *buy slaves*?' Ash swore. Did that woman never listen? He had told her that a visit to the slave market was inadvisable. Despite what had passed between them, she didn't think enough of him to heed his advice. With General Alexios camped outside the walls, apparently on the point of forcing his way in; with the Imperial throne tottering and Constantinople in turmoil, this was the last thing he needed.

Am I to go chasing all over the city looking for a spoilt princess? Is she so impatient that her whims must be instantly satisfied? Blessed Mary, give me strength!

'Please sir, don't tell her I told you, she will have me whipped!'

The boy's dark eyes filled with tears.

With his mind already halfway to the slave market, Ash shook his head. 'I doubt that, I doubt it very much. What's your name, lad?'

'Orchan, sir.'

'Thank you, Orchan.' Ash hurried to the door. *To save time, I will have to ride.* 'I will see you do not suffer for the help you have given me.'

Chapter Nine

Ash rode to the slave market with a handful of the Guard, all of whom were wearing ordinary clothes rather than their uniforms. Discretion would be needed.

Somewhat to his surprise, the auction hall was a hive of activity, people were spilling out on to the street. Leaving the horses with one of the men, he forced his way through the group round the slave block. Sigmund and Tidulf were hard on his heels.

Where the devil is she?

There!

She was standing with her lady-in-waiting at the foot of the platform, enveloped in a voluminous brown cloak. Toki stood at her side... *Toki was with them?*

At least she had had the wit to dress modestly, neither her cloak nor her gown was designed to attract attention. And she had brought an escort, but Ash would have to have words with Toki later. That must wait though, the bidding was starting.

Ashfirth squeezed through. A child in ragged sackcloth was up on the block. Huge eyes, a shivering, unhappy bony body. Ash felt his heart clench. An even smaller child was clinging to the girl's legs. Behind them, wavering slightly, was a fully grown male. His face was black and blue.

'That man is barely conscious,' Ash murmured to Sigurd.

A heavily veiled woman on his right slanted him a knowing glance. 'Handsome brute, though. I can see why she wants him.'

'She?'

'That woman at the front. She seems quite determined to buy him, she has put in three bids already.' The woman's smile was suggestive. 'I expect she hopes he might be tamed. I can see that it might be…interesting, taming a man like that.'

The Princess was bidding! She had mentioned choosing a slave who might become her maidservant—what on earth was she doing bidding for these wretches? She must have taken leave of her senses! Ash forged on until he stood directly behind her.

'My lady.' Ash spoke softly, he had no wish to publicise her identity and draw unnecessary attention to her. Or worse, cause a scandal. If it became known that an imperial princess had left the Palace with so insignificant an escort…the best she could hope for was to be named eccentric—imperial princesses simply did not wander the city at will.

Her hand—she had been lifting it to signal a higher bid—froze. 'Ashfirth!'

She looked different this morning, and it was more than just her everyday clothing. Her face was clear of court paint and she looked much younger. More approachable. She had that vulnerable air that Ash had glimpsed the first time he had seen her through the convent grille.

'I see you ignored my advice.' He attempted to take her

arm, but she wrenched free and completed her gesture to the auctioneer.

Her bid was bettered. The auctioneer looked her way. She nodded and the bidding continued.

'I told you, Ashfirth, I wish to buy slaves.'

'A maidservant! You said you needed a maidservant.'

'Did I?'

'You know you did. In any case—' Ash threw a scathing glance at the pitiful souls on the block '—your choice is poor. Those children are far too young to be freed, you will have to look after them for years. And if you have a mind to train them as servants, it will be years before they are of use to anyone. Indeed, it may not be possible to train them at all, they have clearly been badly used. And as for that male slave…he looks to be in a very bad way. I doubt that he will take instruction.'

'Ka—Theodora!' Lady Anna nudged the Princess. 'Bid again, or you will lose them!'

Princess Theodora nodded in the direction of the auctioneer while, up on the auction block, the male slave had noticed that she was bidding for him and was looking intently at her. Willing her to buy him?

Ashfirth's stomach tightened. He really did not want the Princess to buy the man, though he could not have said why. It was almost as though he felt….jealous, but that was impossible. It was simply that the Princess Theodora had been placed in his charge and, although she was a wilful woman who had clearly been very spoilt, he had a developed a liking for her. He did not want her to waste her wealth on such a poor bargain.

More to the point, though, was the fact that General Alexios might break into the city at any moment. The sooner she was safely back in the citadel, the better, but they could scarcely argue the point in public.

'Sir, I will make my purchase.' She raised her hand and nodded yet again to the auctioneer.

Had anyone thought to explain to her how much matters had deteriorated during her long sojourn in Rascia? Did she know her uncle seemed to have lost all reason and that he had practically surrendered the day-to-day running of his affairs to the Empress? He doubted it. If she knew that Constantinople was like so much kindling, ready to burst into flame, she would surely have heeded his advice and remained at the Palace.

Whoever was bidding against her was faltering, Ashfirth craned his neck to see them, but a pillar blocked his view.

The gong rang. 'Sold!'

The slaves were hustled away and put in a pen under one of the arches. More wretches were dragged on to the block.

The Princess exchanged glances with her lady-in-waiting and gestured at Toki. 'Here, Toki, take these to seal the deal.' Taking coins from the red purse at her belt, she handed them to him.

A scribe was sitting at a table near the slave pen, behind a pile of scrolls. Toki cast a sheepish grin at Ashfirth and took the money to the table.

Ash sighed. 'My lady, you will have to sign the transfer of ownership personally,' he said.

'I realise that.'

Her voice was brittle, Ash searched her face. Something was amiss, he was sure of it. When he saw her mouth tremble, the thought came to him that she was concealing some profound hurt. And yet…those brown eyes were alight with triumph and she was smiling. 'Excuse me, Commander,' she said. Arm in arm with her lady, she started towards the slave pen.

Ashfirth had no option but to follow her.

Stupid, stubborn woman. What the hell is she intending to do with those infants? And as for that male slave...?

'That man will cause more trouble than he's worth,' Ash muttered, as they reached the slave pen.

She sent him a dismissive glance and then—the idiocy of the woman—gestured at the guard to admit her. Slowly, she approached the male slave.

Fearing for her safety, Ash stuck close, close as her shadow. Not that the poor wretch could do anyone much harm in his current state. He was leaning against a pillar, head drooping, eyes half-closed. He must be in considerable pain, he was white about the mouth and was cradling his right arm in his left. He straightened as she reached him, his chains rattled. He attempted a smile, though Ash could see that it cost him. It came to him that the slave was younger than he appeared, pain did age a man.

Princess Theodora gave her new slave the sweetest of smiles, and a knife twisted in Ash's insides. When she leaned forwards and murmured in the slave's ear, the knife turned to fire.

What the hell is she saying to him?

And why the hell had his wayward mind chosen this moment to remind him how the Princess had felt in his arms and of the pleasure that was to be found in her kisses?

Ash flexed his fingers to stop them curling into fists. The heavily veiled noblewoman's words were echoing in his head, that lascivious murmur was going round and round— *Handsome brute...I expect she hopes he might be tamed.*

He glared at the Princess's back. *If only I could see into your mind—but what man has ever seen into a woman's mind?* All Ash could see was the knowing smile of the veiled noblewoman. Many of the ladies of the Court entertained themselves by taking unsuitable lovers, but the Princess would not. *Would she? She wouldn't take a slave...*

In her apartment, after they had kissed—and that had been a mistake, a pleasant mistake, but a mistake none the less—she had said, 'You, Ashfirth, are a commander. *My* commander.'

Had that been her subtle way of propositioning him? At the time, Ashfirth had understood her to be merely flirting with him. His head began to whirl.

Had he got it wrong? Had she in fact been propositioning him? If so, she might believe he had rejected her. Was this her solution? On the other hand, he definitely recalled her mentioning wanting to buy slaves and free them. Had her purchase been motivated by altruism? This man would make a pretty strange maidservant…

He sent the blond slave a black look. Damn it, that woman in the crowd had a point, under the bruises and filth he *was* handsome. Even Ashfirth could see how such a man might appeal; many women loved nothing better than to nurture a wounded man… Hell. He shook his head. No, no, it was scarcely credible unless…

'My lady, are you set on angering Duke Nikolaos?' He had taken her arm, and only realised it when startled brown eyes met his. 'Is that what you are doing?'

'Ashfirth?'

'I know you wanted to delay meeting Duke Nikolaos. Are you set on angering him to such as extent that he will set you aside? Is that it?' Noticing Lady Anna drifting towards the male slave, Ash gestured at his captain. 'Sigurd, stand by Lady Anna, lest she should need assistance.'

'Yes, sir.'

The Princess was staring haughtily at his hand. White fingers—he was holding her too tightly. Ash released her. Their eyes met and his stomach muscles tightened. Leaning towards her, he whispered in her ear in the same way he had seen her whisper into the slave's ear. 'You would not take such a slave as your lover…would you, my lady?'

A surprised laugh emerged and her eyes began to dance. Ash caught the faint fragrance of roses and musk and the warm scent of woman. The Princess might have left her purple cloak and her diadem back at the Palace, but she could not change her basic self.

Woman, she smells of woman and I want her. Desperately.

The thought caught him off guard. Ash had never felt desperate for any particular woman before and he did not want to start now. More specifically he did not want to feel desperate for the Princess. Shocked at where his thoughts had taken him, he stepped smartly back.

Her eyes sparkled. 'Why, Ashfirth—' her voice softened '—don't tell me you are reconsidering our conversation of yesterday?'

He looked from her to the blond slave and back again. She was laughing openly now, damn her, while his guts were twisting into knots and some wholly unwanted images of her and that wretched slave began to take shape…

Holy Virgin.

'Reconsidering what?'

Her lips formed a tempting pout. Brown eyes gleamed up at him from under long lashes, he could see the tiny green flecks. 'You don't remember yesterday? Ashfirth, I am devastated, simply devastated.'

Ash gritted his teeth. 'Naturally I remember.' And then, oh, Lord, he had done it again—unconsciously reached out and regained possession of her arm. 'We cannot discuss this here, I have to take you back to the Palace.'

Her lips twitched. 'That sounds *very* promising…'

'Stop that. There are matters, serious matters, that I need to discuss with you.'

She was watching his face most intently, he prayed she was not going to argue. Ash knew he ought not to be addressing her in so familiar a manner, but she drove a man wild. And he could not, he simply could not stand here in the middle of the slave market discussing whether or not she wanted to have an affair with him.

If, indeed, that is what we are discussing.

He dragged his hand through his hair, as a dozen conflicting thoughts warred within him.

A plucked eyebrow arched as she looked at the male slave. 'You are not jealous, are you, Ashfirth?'

Jealous? Ash opened his mouth to deny it, but thank heaven he had retained some control and the words remained unspoken. He gave her an ironic bow. 'You are goading me, my lady. I am glad I amuse you.'

'Mmm.' The slave slumped against the pillar, and her attention shifted while Lady Anna and Sigurd lowered him to the ground. Nearby, the small girl hugged the infant to her, her eyes huge in the thin, dirt-streaked face.

The Princess sighed, all trace of amusement gone from her face. 'It is time, I think, to sign those documents.' With a twist of her wrist, she freed herself and joined Toki at the scribe's table.

Wits scattered to the four winds, Ash stood like a man turned to stone. *That woman, that woman...*

She picked up a quill and turned, seeming to look through him. 'Lady Anna, would you spare me a moment? I need you to witness my signature.'

Her lady-in-waiting straightened and hurried over. The Princess signed with a flourish and handed Lady Anna the quill.

The hairs on the back of Ash's neck prickled and he narrowed his gaze. Something about the way the Princess had looked straight past him and had summoned her lady struck a jarring note.

I was closer, why not summon me?

And as to the way the women were positioned, standing so as to shield the document from him…that was surely no accident?

Was she simply taking pains to conceal her identity from everyone here? Did she not trust him? Did she fear he might inadvertently reveal who she was?

No, she must know he would not betray her to the crowd, there was something else here, something he had yet to fathom…

Ash was puzzling over what that might be when Lady Anna's voice reached him.

'He is a Frank, you know.' Lady Anna waved towards the pillar where the blond giant was slumped.

Norman! Every muscle in Ash's body went tight as a bowstring. *Norman!* Normans had destroyed everything he had ever held dear—was he never to escape them? Bad enough that they were nibbling away at the edges of the Empire, but to have Princess Theodora actually buy one…!

She was looking at the wretch, eyes full of compassion.

She had bought a Norman! Why? For purely altruistic reasons? God, he hoped so.

Ash's thoughts had become so entangled that he scarcely knew himself. And she was to blame. The kiss they had shared was large in his mind; her scent was lingering in his nostrils, but what did he really know about her? Until a few weeks ago he hadn't even met her. When she had spoken to him through the gate of St Mary's Convent, she had not struck him as being particularly sophisticated—rather the reverse. And though it should be nothing to him how the Princess chose to behave, he had liked her rather better when he had believed her unworldly.

She wanted a lover, their kiss should have told him as much. If he hadn't been dwelling on his duty to her uncle, he would have realised. He might have responded differently.

The question was, why did she want a lover? For herself? Or to taunt her unwanted fiancé, to goad the Duke of Larissa into breaking their contract?

He let his breath out in a rush. *She has bought this handsome, ill-used brute—yes, the man might be Norman, but he is unquestionably handsome—what the hell is she planning to do with him?*

'Anna—' she was smiling at her lady, handing out more coins from the red purse '—I shall entrust my purchases to you. Find the young man a litter. Take Toki as your escort, I—' a small hand was placed on Ashfirth's sleeve '—shall be walking back with Ashfirth.'

And then those doe's eyes were looking up at him and she was smiling again. This smile was sensuous, intimate even. A smile a woman might give to her lover. His breath caught. His thoughts became even more entangled.

'Ashfirth, will you be so good as to walk with me back to the Palace?'

Say something, don't stand there gaping.

Ash was beginning to feel a certain sympathy for the Duke of Larissa. He cleared his throat. 'You did not ride?'

Her lips curved. 'Me—ride? Ashfirth, you cannot have forgotten my dislike of horses.' She favoured him with another look that could only be described as smouldering.

What was she up to? She was taking his breath away, that was what she was up to. The witch. She was putting foolish ideas in his head about him taking a princess as his lover, she was making him dwell on that illicit kiss…

Thank God they had come to the slave market incognito, because if word got back to the Duke of Larissa that the

Princess had been seen in public, flirting shamelessly with the man assigned to protect her...

Keeping his face a blank, he covered her hand with his. As an attempt to control her it was a fruitless gesture—this woman was beyond his control. Hell, who was he fooling, it was a caress. 'Sigurd?'

'Sir?'

'Return to the barracks, and take Caesar back to the stables. I shall accompany my lady back to her apartment.'

'You are going on foot, sir?'

Irritable for no reason that he could point to, Ashfirth waved the captain away. 'We go on foot.'

She was looking wistfully at her Norman.

'Come on, my lady, the stench of Frank in this place is rather too strong for my liking.'

Setting his jaw, Ash marched her through the bustle and shove around the auction block. He felt her watching him, but she didn't speak until they had left the slave market and were out in the street by the market stalls.

'You dislike Franks because of what happened to your country?'

'It cannot surprise you, my lady. They crossed the Narrow Sea, invaded our land and killed our king. An entire generation of Anglo-Saxon warriors was lost in the Great Battle.'

'Your father Thane Aiken included.'

'Yes.' He towed her on up the street, past a man selling nuts and dried fruits. The man had a monkey on a chain, it was offering dates to passersby.

'Remind me how old you were when this took place.'

'Ten.' Ashfirth checked and came to an abrupt halt. Their conversation must be confusing her, the Princess had been about to take a wrong turning. Ahead, over the top of the sea wall, he could see a glimmer of sun on the waters of the Golden Horn. 'Not that way, my lady, this way.'

'Oh!' Her cheeks coloured, her eyes fell. It was a moment before she picked up the thread of their conversation. 'So... you were ten when the Franks invaded England, I remember. Well, I would judge that slave to be younger than you by at least a couple of years. Which would make him about eight years old at the time of the conquest. Were you present at this Great Battle, Ashfirth?'

Ashfirth. Why did she have to pronounce his name in that breathy way? And had he imagined it or had those little fingers that were resting on his arm just given him a gentle squeeze?

They progressed up a slight incline. The wind teased a glossy brown strand of hair free of her veil. Startled by an impulse to smooth it back, Ash swallowed and dug his nails into his palm.

'So, Ashfirth, did you take part in the Great Battle?'

'No. I was at Ringmer with my mother and my brother.'

'You will see then that it is very unlikely that my Frank was even in England at the time. It is far more likely that he was at home with his mother, too.'

'You are probably right.' Ash conceded the point with a smile he knew was crooked. 'I have not heard that Norman children took part in the Great Battle. Boys, yes, children, no. And so I must agree that it is indeed most unlikely that your slave was anywhere near Hastings.' He shrugged. 'It is not easy abandoning one's prejudices.'

She nodded. 'But you have found your place here, I think. This has become your home.' A wave of her hand took in the city, encompassing not just the wide colonnaded avenues, nor the narrow streets and cramped tenements, but the Palace, the Great Church, the Forum...

She came to a dead halt and frowned about her. 'Where

are we? I seem to have missed my way.' Brow wrinkled, she pointed up a side street. 'Does that lead to the Palace?'

'I thought you knew where you were going, my lady.'

She was looking extremely uneasy, guilty even. *How interesting.* When she bit her lip, goosebumps rose on Ashfirth's skin. *Very interesting.*

'Yes, so did I. Particularly since it can't be much more than an hour ago that we left my apartment.' Her high colour was back and she was having great difficulty meeting his eyes. 'My memory of the city is faulty, it seems.'

Ashfirth said nothing—it was suddenly most important to see what she would say if he did not prompt her. A couple of the domes in the Palace were peeping over the rooftops of the neighbouring buildings like rising suns; and a few yards farther on, the top of the lighthouse tower would easily be visible. The Princess ought to know this, yet she was giving every appearance of being a stranger to the city, a *complete* stranger.

The scales fell from his eyes. *The landmarks mean nothing to her, she is blind to them, because they are new to her!*

'Ashfirth, is the Palace this way?'

'No, my lady, but you are not far out.' He observed her as though from a great distance. *Constantinople is unknown to her, but how can this be?* 'That street leads directly to the Hippodrome.'

'The Hippodrome!' Her eyes lit up, her fingers squeezed his arm. 'Ashfirth, I should like to see the Hippodrome.'

'You remember it?'

'I…I have faint memories of watching a chariot race from the Emperor's Box.'

She is lying. There are lies here, entangled with the truth. Ash needed to tease out the lies. Ten years ago, it was far more likely that the Princess—if that was indeed who she

was and Ash was beginning to suspect otherwise—would
have watched chariot races with the Empress. The Empress
and her ladies had their own viewing platform, well away
from the Emperor's box…

She is lying.

Not about everything—she did genuinely appear to want
to see the Hippodrome, but she was lying about having sat
in the Emperor's box. A shiver ran down Ashfirth's back,
but it was no light thing. It was like the touch of steel, it
had that same cold certainty.

She is not the Princess, this girl cannot be the Princess!

The thought had lodged in his brain, and it was the truth.

This girl is not Princess Theodora.

Who the hell is she, then? And where the devil is the real
Princess?

He forced a smile and heard himself say, 'Would you
care to see the Hippodrome before we return to the Palace?'

'Please!'

It was an artless reply, artlessly delivered. It was uttered
from a smiling mouth, a mouth that Ash had kissed. A
mouth he would like to kiss again, even though it seemed
likely that it had been lying to him from the moment he
had first seen it.

They walked on.

Knots of people were gathering by the well-heads and
outside the taverns. Ash ignored them. He was too busy
reviewing what he knew about her, searching for evidence
that might lend weight to his suspicions.

His heart sank. Once you started to dwell on it, there
was plenty to be suspicious about…

Item: she did not ride. An Imperial Princess who didn't
ride? She had claimed to dislike horses—that much he was
inclined to believe, she had undoubtedly found the ride
from St Mary's to the port of Dyrrachion an ordeal. But

the Princess had not been born who had not been taught to ride; if this girl were a Princess, she would have been educated to overcome her fear...

Item: there had been a number of times when Ash had sensed she was concealing something from him, most recently a few moments ago in the slave market. She had deliberately blocked his view of her signing that document; she had looked past him and called Lady Anna over to act as her witness...

Item: for an Imperial Princess she was appallingly ignorant of the geography and extent of the Empire. On board ship, she had not known the location of Apulia...

Item: there was that letter she had sent to the other ship... to her body-servant...to—Ash racked his brains to recall the name—to...Katerina.

Was *she* Katerina?

Katerina. A pair of beautiful brown eyes peering at him through a convent grille. Unworldly eyes. Doe Eyes.

Who was she?

Item: there was her lack of familiarity with the Palace, her dazed expression as she had looked at the stone lions and oxen in the Palace Harbour. *She had never seen them before.*

And as for those claims of a faulty memory... Ash had been ten when he had left England—the exact age that Princess Theodora had been when she had left Constantinople. Yet Ash could recall every plank and nail in his father's hall; every cottage in the village, every tree and shrub in his father's holding. He treasured his memories, they were polished with much use. In an instant, he could conjure the three old willow trees trailing their fingers in the river; he could hear the splash of an English trout, and behind him the drone of a bee blown in from the south downs...

If his memories were clear—why weren't hers?

He glanced up. 'Here is the Hippodrome, my lady.' He nodded casually at the great wall that was the outside of the Hippodrome, and held himself aloof, the better to study her reaction.

'The main gates are closed.'

Ash led her to a side gate where they would be able to see through the bars to the arena inside. 'It is Holy Week, my lady, Lenten games are frowned upon by the Patriarch. The main gate are likely to remain closed until after Easter.'

'Of course.'

'If you look through here though, you can see inside.'

The Princess looked through the bars and went very still. Ash watched her eyes widen as her gaze ran over the tiered seats and the row of statues in the centre. She swallowed as she looked at the bronze horses set high above the main gate. For the space of a heartbeat it was plain that the sheer scale of the Hippodrome had knocked her off balance, and this was certainly the first time she had seen those bronze horses.

A moment later, she had herself in hand. She smiled and looked earnestly at him. 'Oh, yes, Commander, the horses. I had forgotten the horses.'

Who is she?

Her smile wavered. 'I have never liked horses.'

'How odd that you should forget these.'

Her chin went up. 'I do remember the chariot races—I did not care for them.'

Ashfirth nodded and smiled and murmured something non-committal. *That last sounds convincing, but it does not alter the fact that you are a liar. Who are you?*

'We had best return to the Palace,' he said. 'I am sure you will want to ensure that your recent purchases are being cared for.'

She gave him a look that was, as far as Ash could tell,

completely guileless. 'Indeed I do, and what is so wrong with that?'

Shaking his head, because once again she had set off in the wrong direction, Ash turned her gently to face the Palace wall. It was only a few feet away.

You, my lady, are no more the Princess than I am.

What the hell am I going to do with you?

Chapter Ten

She is not the Princess, should I denounce her? If so, to whom should I denounce her? The Emperor is closeted in his apartments, refusing to see anyone.

In the weeks that Ash had been away, the Emperor's deterioration had been fast. Emperor Nikephoros had become little more than a puppet dancing to the Empress's tune.

Since I don't answer to the Empress, I must decide what to do with this girl.

The hand resting on his sleeve was small, the fingers slender. She was wearing one thin gold ring today, no gold bangles clinked on her wrist.

What will happen to her if I denounce her?

The answer made him hollow inside. She would be put on trial and it would not be pretty. Execution was the likely outcome. But what sort of execution would it be? Beheading? Or something more…painful? The courts in Constantinople were not known for their leniency towards those proved guilty of breaking their laws. Ash did not know what the penalty for impersonating a member of the Imperial family might be, but it was bound to be severe.

And as for himself, denouncing her at this stage might well put an end to his own career.

Commander Ashfirth, taken in by a slip of a girl.

He would become a laughing stock. A commander could not afford to lose the respect of his men.

He studied the curve of her cheek and the line of her nose. She had a pretty nose, but it was her lips, those lying lips, that held his gaze. A flash of anger almost took him, but he resisted its pull.

Think this through, Ash, think this through. It would not have been possible for her to practise this deception without the Princess's support, she has to be acting under instruction from the Princess.

So, given the weak mental state of the Emperor, who was not coping well with the crisis in his army, and who certainly could not cope with additional complexities concerning the identity of a princess he had never met, Ashfirth felt he could justify continuing to observe her for a while.

He could hardly turn back time and return her to Dyrrachion. In any case, the real Princess had boarded the second ship. Ash could do worse than wait for that ship to arrive, it should only be a few days behind them. Lord, if his suspicions were correct, the real Princess was at this moment sailing towards chaos and insurrection!

'Ashfirth, can you smell burning?'

Ash jerked himself out of his thoughts. She was right, an acrid smell hung in the air. A grey cloud of smoke was drifting towards them from the merchants' quarter.

'One of the bakeries must be using damp wood,' he said curtly. This girl confused him and she angered him, but this was no time to inform the Emperor of his suspicions. General Alexios was camped outside the city walls,

Constantinople was in a ferment, and the Emperor was ill. Should the Emperor recover and emerge from his apartments, well, that would be another matter.

The wind strengthened. The smell of wood smoke intensified; it was coming from the north of the city, somewhere near the quays that lay alongside the Golden Horn.

'A bakery is using damp wood?' She—whoever she was—was peering down an alley that was choked with smoke. 'Don't you think the smoke is rather too thick for that?'

A chill settled in Ashfirth's insides as he came to another realisation. If she was not the Princess, did that mean she was not attracted to him? That kiss...the way her eyes danced when she flirted with him...these things had seemed true, and he had enjoyed them—but were they true? Or had she manufactured a liking for him because it suited her? Perhaps she had simply been attempting to distract him, perhaps she was still trying to distract him. He ought not to mind, but damn it, he did.

They passed through the Palace gates and began weaving their way through the courtiers gathered in groups to discuss the crisis. Ash put his attraction for her out of his mind and kept his ears open. Years ago he had trained himself to listen to what the people around him were saying, a habit that had served him well on a number of occasions. Just because this girl had him tied in knots did not mean that he must set good habits aside.

By an antique statue of a Greek god, an official in a long ceremonial gown was speaking earnestly to a eunuch. 'Where is the Emperor? I heard he was dead.'

The eunuch shrugged. 'Who can say, sir? No one has seen him for days. I heard he had lost his mind.'

In the archway leading to the Imperial stables, a lute-player was telling the tale to one of the grooms. 'I was told the Emperor has been poisoned.'

'No, no, the way I heard it, it was suicide,' the groom's response was instant. 'In the taverns they are laying odds that Alexios Komnenos will be enthroned within the week.'

Small fingers clenched on Ashfirth's arm. Her face was pale and though she had a charming smile ready when he glanced her way, several fine lines had appeared around the corners of her eyes.

'There is much concern about my uncle, Ashfirth,' she said quietly, as they entered the Boukoleon Palace and began to climb the wide marble stairway. 'Tell me…do you fear there will be fighting in the city?'

'One moment, my lady.'

A guard was stationed at the double doorway that led to her apartments, a young man Ash recognised as a recent recruit. 'Kari, isn't it?'

The boy smiled and saluted. 'Yes, sir.'

'Here…' Ashfirth pressed a coin into the boy's hand. 'Follow me.'

'Yes, sir.'

Ignoring her puzzlement, Ashfirth took the arm of the girl who was not the Princess Theodora and ushered her into the apartment.

Lord, the party from the slave market had arrived before them, the outer chamber was teeming. The Norman slave was unconscious on a litter by one of the tall windows and Lady Anna was kneeling at his side. She had cut his ragged tunic and was peeling it carefully off him, handling him as though he were made of Venetian glass. Servants were rushing this way and that with linens and trays of food, and the two small children were standing together in a great copper basin, being bathed by women with sponges. The little girl had her fist firmly around a lump of bread, and was stuffing it single-mindedly into her mouth. Water splashed on to the floor.

Lady Anna looked across, her face clearing when she saw the girl on Ash's arm. Her mouth opened. 'Theod—'

'Later.' Gripping the girl who was no more princess than he, Ashfirth strode with her to the bedchamber.

'Commander Ashfirth!' Her large brown eyes were startled. 'What on earth are you do—?'

'Be silent.' He pulled her into the bedchamber. 'Kari?'

'Sir?'

'The Princess and I do not wish to be disturbed.'

The boy's eyes widened. 'I see.'

'I hope that you do. No one—' he leaned towards the boy, and jerked his head at Lady Anna '—and I mean *no one* is to enter this bedchamber.'

'No exceptions, sir?'

'None except Captain Sigurd. Do you understand?'

Kari stared at him for a heartbeat, and then at the girl. 'Yes, sir.' His skin darkened. 'I understand perfectly.'

Closing the door in the boy's face, Ashfirth slammed the bolts home.

'What is the meaning of this, Commander?' Her chin was up, her voice was strong.

Ashfirth gave her a cold look. 'It is time for this pretence to come to an end. I know the truth, and I will have you admit it.'

A plucked eyebrow lifted and her long-lashed eyes, a thousand times more alluring without their court paint, looked haughtily up at him. *She has been hiding behind those cosmetics.*

'You know the truth? Commander, what are you talking about?'

'That's good. Very convincing.' Ashfirth folded his arms across his chest. 'How long did it take you to perfect that look?' Having seen through her, it was obvious she was playing a role—why hadn't he realised sooner? 'It wasn't easy seeing past that stuff you have been plastering on your face,' he continued thoughtfully. 'You have been using it as a mask, haven't you? You are a performer and the gowns and jewels fitted you for your role. And they worked, they dazzled. *You* dazzled and I did not see you clearly. Did Princess Theodora find you in a circus?'

'You are insolent, Commander.'

Whoever she was, she was a natural performer. It was no coincidence that his moment of realisation had come when she had left off her cosmetics and her jewels. 'Did Princess Theodora give you the jewellery? Is it payment for a perfect performance?'

'Commander, I think you must be…unwell.'

Katerina's finger-ring caught the light as she moved away, turning her back on him. *He knows! What shall I do? I cannot admit anything, not yet, it is too soon. I promised to try to buy the Princess a few weeks' grace once we reached the capital, but it has only been days…*

She put iron in her voice. 'Commander, if you would be so good as to unlock the bedchamber door and release me, I will say nothing of this, I—'

'You are no more the Princess than I am.'

Katerina stared blindly through a window. *Saints, he sounds so certain! Admit nothing, he may believe you. And if he does not…well, you have used your body once before and it did not kill you, you may have to use it again. You must distract him. This man is not Vukan, at least you enjoy Ashfirth's kisses…*

Head high, she turned to meet his eyes, praying her expression was well under control. If she was going to convince him he was mistaken, it was imperative she appeared calm and composed.

'Not the Princess? Commander, you really have taken leave of your senses—of course I am the Princess!'

Ashfirth propped a shoulder against the door. This won't take long, he thought, she can't keep this up for ever. Deliberately, he allowed the silence to stretch out between them. If she were unnerved, she might confess to the truth. While he waited for her to break, he ran his gaze around the room. Like the rest of her apartments, the bedchamber was spacious and airy. The shutters opening onto the sea had been flung wide to admit the spring sun; three flares of light were creeping across the creamy marble.

And the bed! It was vast, piled with cushions and bed coverings the colour of ripe mulberries, an island of lavishly embroidered silk. There was some sort of canopy above the bed, draped with yet more of the mulberry-coloured silk. Nimble fingers had artfully looped the bed hangings into swags and tied them back with gold braid; chunky gold tassels hung at the corners.

Ash had never seen such opulence, it was oddly arousing.

It was also, he told himself firmly, pure theatre. It was a lie.

An image burst in on him. Of her—*what is her name?*—lying naked among the mulberry-coloured silks, of slender limbs peeping out from under the rich covers. It seemed to him that those doe's eyes were beckoning him, a silent invitation.

'A princess who is not a princess,' he murmured, finally pushing himself away from the door and starting towards her. 'Doe Eyes.'

'Commander?'

'I prefer it when you call me Ashfirth,' he continued softly, half-smiling as she edged away. When her calves hit the bed she halted, eyes wide. She was biting her lip, worrying it with small white teeth. Not quite so lofty now…

'Your mouth has always told lies, but your eyes—' reaching out, he stroked her cheek with the tips of his fingers, before drawing her firmly into his arms '—your eyes tell another story altogether.'

She stood unresisting in his arms, not pliant exactly, but neither was she drawing back.

The kiss was hard. It was harder than Ash had intended because there was some anger in him, and when he pulled that small body against him, he found he was not entirely under control. He was squashing her lips into her teeth. His groin ached. He lifted his head, and was momentarily transfixed by a slash of colour across her cheekbones.

'You are not the Princess, admit it.'

'I am the Princess.'

She was a liar. A determined liar whose hands were pressed up against his chest, a liar who brought them to rest on his shoulders. He wondered whether she had decided to hold him to her or to push him away. He forced himself to become gentle, nibbling at her lower lip while he allowed the smell of her, of the pretty girl who had caught his attention at St Mary's, to swirl through his brain.

It was difficult to keep in mind that she was a liar while he was kissing her. She made the hot blood rush to his braies, she made him throb and pulse. He adjusted his hold, sliding an arm round her waist and raising his head long enough to unclasp her cloak. *I will have the truth out of her. Lord, who would have thought she would be so resistant?*

Katerina stood firm. Ashfirth's kiss had weakened her limbs, exactly as it had done before, but she stood firm. His blue eyes had darkened, but they remained keen, watching for the slightest hint of uncertainty on her part. This man desired her, but he was holding to his intention of wringing a confession out of her. That must not happen!

Distract him a little more. Use your body. Look at his eyes, he desires you...let him think he may have you.

She allowed herself to go lax in his arms; in truth, with this man, that was easy. She gave a breathy sigh; that, too, was easy. The coy smile was harder, but she managed it.

Ash was beginning to feel confused. He couldn't read her, he couldn't read her at all. What was real here? 'An Imperial Princess...' As her cloak slipped on to the bed his voice cracked, it was unrecognisable. 'An Imperial Princess should not permit a Varangian Guard such liberties.'

'This one would.' She gave an unsteady laugh and moistened her lips with her tongue. Lips that his kisses rendered far more alluring than any cosmetics.

Briefly, Ash closed his eyes and when he opened them again she was watching him. Despite the sunlight pouring into the bedchamber, her eyes were dark as midnight, drawing him in. *Those eyes cannot lie.*

'My lady, I thought at first you were set on angering Duke Nikolaos, that you wanted him to set you aside, but in that I was mistaken.'

'You are mistaken in everything!'

'I do not believe I am. It is your eyes, you see.'

'My eyes?'

'Yes.' Ash lowered his head for another kiss, he couldn't resist. This one was soft as a whisper. It was a puzzle the way his anger against her was draining away. 'Your eyes tease me, but they are beautiful, they tell the truth.'

'Commander—'

'Ashfirth, remember?'

'Ashfirth, you are mistaken, I *am* the Princess.'

'You admit nothing?'

'There is nothing to admit!'

He lowered his lips to her ear, and whispered. 'I will seduce the truth out of you.'

She gave one of those startled laughs and her bright eyes turned to his. The little green flecks were dancing, definitely dancing. 'I hope that is a promise, sir.'

Ash found himself grinning down at her. He might be all kinds of a fool, but she was utterly delightful when she put her mind to it. 'It is.'

She wound her arms about his waist. *You may want to seduce the truth out of me, but I shall seduce you into forgetfulness. You shall not learn my secret, not yet.*

Ash was planting a row of kisses along her neck, working his way slowly, inexorably to her mouth. As he deepened the kiss, her heart thudded.

She moaned and twisted her body closer, pressing her breasts against his chest. His manhood nudged her belly. She flickered her tongue over his lips, hesitating long enough to hear his groan and then she was pushing her tongue into his mouth, sliding it provocatively against his. Her hands were firm on the back of his ribs, holding him to her. She did not have to pretend to be aroused. Her nipples were twin points that moved against his chest, reaching for him, eager for him to explore them fully. *Touch me, touch my breasts.* Neither the fabric of her gown nor the stuff of her tunic could hide the fact that she wanted him as much as he seemed to want her.

She is aroused. Ash lifted his head to see if this truth, the truth of her body, was mirrored in her eyes.

'Ash?'

Her hands were growing bold, they were far too bold for a princess who had not yet wed. One outlined the shape of his buttock while the other tugged at his belt buckle.

He couldn't breathe. 'Your eyes—' Ash was pleased with what he saw '—they do not lie.' Further explanation was impossible, need was clawing in his guts, his loins were on fire for her, the girl had addled his brain.

Clumsily, he wrestled with pins and ties. Her veil drifted down, becoming a puddle of silk on the sun-warmed marble.

She made not a protest.

Princess Theodora would have protested.

Instead, those quick fingers were working at his belt; a dull clink marked the moment it joined her veil on the floor.

'Who *are* you? Is your name Katerina?'

'I am the Princess Theodora.'

He was watching her lips as she spoke. 'Liar.'

His hand closed over a breast. She moaned and her eyes glazed over. Her eyes did not lie; they desired him. Her breast tightened under his hand. Ash did not think that her breast lied either; that, too, desired him.

He planted another row of kisses down one soft cheek. Her eyelids lowered. Her hair had been dressed in a loose knot at the nape of her neck, as simple as the clothes she had worn to the slave market. Ash found the hair fastening and her hair fell free. It was soft as a whisper, a shining fall of hair running over the back of his hands. The perfume it released into the air was spicy and exotic. That scent—musk and roses. Her. His 'princess'.

'What is your name?' He nibbled her ear, inhaling her. He pressed himself against her and groaned. 'Is it Katerina? Tell me the truth.'

'I am Theodora.'

'Liar.' Her belt fell, snaking over his in a patch of sunlight.

'The-o-do-ra.'

Slender fingers burrowed into his hair, insisting his lips remain on hers when he would have pulled away to ask once more: *'What is your name?'*

And then it no longer mattered whether she was the

princess or not. It no longer mattered that Ash did not know her name, because her hands were sliding down his neck and shoulders; they were stroking his sides, leaving a trail of heat where she had touched him. His pulse pounded in his temples. He throbbed. She made his head swim; if he wasn't careful, she would unman him…

She was lifting his tunic, unfastening him, freeing him from the restriction of hose and braies…

While he— Lord, she had better not be the Princess, because he had snatched at her gown and dragged it over her head, heedless of where it fell. He sighed. She stood before him in a plain linen undergown, a small dark girl whose slim arms reached for him. That finger-ring flashed, her lips curved in blatant invitation and she pulled him down with her on to the mulberry silks.

And then her undergown was gone and they were naked together on the great mulberry-coloured bed.

Holy Virgin, let her not be the Princess.

Ashfirth gazed at her, stroking her flank from breast to hip, drawing her close. She was moaning in much the same way as he had been doing a few moments ago, twisting her head from side to side, loosening that glossy dark hair so it trailed over the silken pillows.

She was kissing his chest. Running delicate fingertips over him, touching his scars lightly, one after the other, kissing them.

Leaning up on an elbow, he drank in the sight of her. So small to be so determined. So beautiful. 'Beautiful Doe Eyes.'

One kiss led inevitably to another, he couldn't stop himself. There were reasons he ought not to be doing this… she ought not…but the reasons were lost at the back of his mind. Lost behind one kiss, then another, then another. Their bodies writhed, two bodies with but one thought between them, skin must touch skin. The mulberry bed-clothes tangled beneath them. He found a rosy nipple and toyed with it, his mouth followed.

That slight body strained against him. 'Ashfirth.'

Princess or not, Ash loved the sound of his name on her lips. Since he had come to Constantinople, only a handful of people used it. Brand was one, and now this girl…

'Damn it, what is your name?'

'Theodora,' she breathed. 'The-o-do-ra.'

She was bold, this mysterious girl who lied to him. Her fingers were on him, they had closed round him, they were moving up and down with a confidence that the real Prin-cess would not possess. Instinctively, he pushed into her hand.

No matter. No matter that she is not the Princess. 'Thank God, in fact.'

'Hmm?'

He shifted over her; she was guiding him into her, show-ing him how ready she was. *She wants me. Her body does not lie.*

At the last moment, he paused to find her eyes. She smiled and gripped him by the hips. Ash gave a hard, strong thrust and then he was inside, buried to the hilt.

She is not a virgin, she is not the Princess.

Saints, but it was a relief to be in her. Ash moved again, and she came to meet him, placing a kiss on his shoulder when he was at his deepest. At his third thrust, a kiss landed on his cheek; at the fourth, on his neck. At the fifth…he was not going to last, not this time.

Lord, it had been too long and this girl lying on the Princess's bed, her doe eyes dark with a lust that matched his—he was not going to last. Oblivion was but a heartbeat away.

Withdrawing slightly, he reached between them. When

his fingers found her, her breasts rose and fell. Her breathing was ragged, her cheeks pink. She arched into his hand.

He bent his head, licked her breast, caught the tip, and licked again.

A moan. He sucked.

'Ashfirth.'

When her hips bucked and her breath sighed out between her teeth, he took her by the buttocks and plunged deep.

'Again,' he murmured.

She arched towards him, mouth seeking his.

As their lips joined, she shuddered beneath him, tightening around him. He drove home. Once more. Twice.

'Ashfirth.' She was kissing him like a Fury. 'Ashfirth.'

Every muscle trembling, Ash was on the brink. He pushed on to his elbows and levered himself out of her; it would not do to lose all control. She was kissing his shoulder when his seed spilled on to the silken sheets.

He lay there, catching his breath.

A fine sheen of sweat gleamed on both their bodies. His tongue came out, he tasted salt on her neck. He stroked the back of her head, fingers winding into her hair.

She smiled at him, her expression adorably bemused. 'That was—' her voice was scarcely a whisper '—that was perfect.'

Winded, Ash muttered agreement, he would never move again. Perfect? Perhaps, but it had been so swift and withdrawing at the last moment had almost been impossible. Whoever she was, she would not want him to father a child on her.

'You, my lady,' he said, catching his breath, 'are definitely not the Princess.'

Her eyes opened wide, her smile never faltered. 'Commander Ashfirth, you are wrong. Quite, quite wrong.'

'I am not wrong.' He stroked her breast, cupping it in

his palm, watching as the small bud tightened. 'You, my lady, were no virgin.'

Katerina allowed her smile to widen, her gold ring caught the light as she reached up to run an exploratory fingertip across his cheekbone. The slight roughness of his cheek fascinated her.

The urge to tell Ashfirth part of the truth, of *her* truth, was dangerously alluring. 'Princesses are not always innocent when they go to their marriage beds,' she said. 'Sometimes—for political reasons—they are forced to surrender their virtue early.'

His brows snapped together, he was immediately on the alert. 'You were forced? You are saying that Prince Peter forced you?'

Wishing she could snatch back the words, Katerina shook her head. *No, no, what are you doing? You cannot imply that Prince Peter forced Princess Theodora, particularly when they adored each other.* 'No…no, my apologies…I did not mean…I…I should not have said that. Prince Peter did not force me.'

Ashfirth watched her. 'You were no innocent a moment ago.'

'No.'

'Nor are you the Princess, I am certain of that.'

He cannot be sure, he has no proof. The Commander had not seen her signature at the slave market; neither had he seen her document of manumission—the paper that had set her free. Before they had left the slave pen, Katerina had asked Anna to put the slaves' documents safely under lock and key.

A smile came and went on his face, those blue eyes never left her, he was waiting for her to make the smallest slip.

Not yet. I cannot confide in him yet…I may never be able to confide in him.

He was playing with her hair, weaving a strand in and out of his fingers. Her belly fluttered, her heart constricted. She liked his touch and there he lay, watching. Waiting.

I must brazen this out. Katerina longed to unburden herself, she wanted to tell him *everything.* Instead she had to content herself with giving him a smile that came from her heart. She rested her head against a broad shoulder.

'Thank you, Ashfirth. That was most…enjoyable.' In truth, Katerina was stunned—she had never experienced such pleasure in her life. When he had pushed her into this bedchamber, intent only on revealing her identity, she had set out to tempt him, to distract him from his purpose. Except that she had been the one to lose her purpose. Ashfirth, with a few gentle touches, had transported her—she would need time to recover herself.

'You are welcome.' His lips twisted. 'I am happy that as a lover I meet with your approval.'

He can never know all of my truth, that I am a maidservant who was once a slave.

It was bad enough that Ashfirth Saxon, a man she had come to admire, should discover that she had been deceiving him, but for him to learn that she had herself been a slave…that she could not bear.

Katerina had lost her innocence to Vukan in the days before the Princess had bought her. No love had been involved and, on her part, little attraction. Katerina had never enjoyed relations with him. She had simply been thankful there had never been a child.

The window hangings swayed and a shaft of sunlight fell across the bed. Ashfirth had become her lover and the world was a different place. Sliding an arm about his waist, Katerina allowed herself a smile. Most enjoyable was perhaps not the best description of how she felt now. The sensations had astonished her.

From head to toe, all was bliss. It was a complete revelation. For the first time in years, she felt truly at ease with a man. With Ashfirth's heartbeat in her ear, she felt safe. It was utter folly, their liaison was impossible, but it felt as though Ashfirth Saxon had stripped her of her past when he had stripped off her clothes. At this moment, it even seemed possible that she might learn to trust a man again.

Trust a man? What a terrifying idea! Katerina had not had such a thought since her father had sold her into slavery. Yes, Ashfirth was a skilled lover, yes, he made her body glow from head to toe, but that was no reason for her to lose her head over him.

She shifted her cheek against his chest. It was astonishing how pleasurable it could be to listen to a man's heartbeat. *Small pleasures, I can allow myself small pleasures.* She had been attracted to Ashfirth from that first look through the convent grille. Initially the attraction had been superficial, but every moment spent in his company had revealed more that was likeable about him. Gradually liking had turned to admiration.

None the less, she had been unprepared for how overwhelming it was to make love with a man one admired. *One touch and I was lost—what a horrifying thought. Except that with Ashfirth it is far from horrifying.*

His large, gentle fingers were caressing her cheek, sliding back into her hair, tipping her head back so their lips could meet…

Gentle. He can be so gentle.

Ashfirth's lips were warm and soft as they moved over hers. Loving. She felt herself warming inside.

Loving? She drew back with a frown. They had come together and while Ashfirth Saxon clearly had the power to transport her, she must not delude herself. This was not love. He was a man and she was a woman; the attraction between them was carnal, nothing more.

The Commander of the Varangian Guard had taken her because he no longer believed her to be the Princess. The act of love was for him yet another weapon in his armoury, a weapon he had not hesitated to use because he hoped to lure the truth out of her. At her tiniest slip, he would pounce. His hands might treat her kindly at the moment, but would they continue to do so when he discovered her low status? Commander Ashfirth, taken in by a freed slave!

Anger had prompted her father to sell her into slavery—what form would this man's anger take?

He was smiling, leaning over her so that those finely curved lips could chase hers.

This cannot go on for ever. This may be the only time we have together...

She kept smiling as she allowed his mouth to settle over hers. He had her firmly pinned to the bed with his hands on her shoulders and she *was* enjoying it. *Bliss, this man makes me melt...*

The kiss drew out until longing was a fierce pain in Katerina's belly. He lifted his head and gave her a smile so sweet she blinked.

'Ashfirth?'

A strong thigh inserted itself between hers and he pressed against her, hot and hard. Ashfirth Saxon wanted her again.

'Already?'

'If it pleases, my lady.'

It did please. It pleased very much, because while they were...making love, Katerina could stop worrying about deceiving him and what form his anger might take when she did at last admit the truth...

Chapter Eleven

Sated, content in ways he did not care to examine, Ash pillowed his head on his hands and looked past the gently wafting curtain. Gulls were calling in the harbour below, dusk would soon be darkening the sky. He could hear the clipped commands of a sergeant changing the guard and the tramp of booted feet.

They had not left the great bed for hours, making love time after time while the sun inched its way across the mulberry sheets. He could not stay closeted in the Princess's bedchamber for ever. Soon, he must leave.

Whoever you are, we have managed to cause a scandal between us. To have remained in this bedchamber together for so long...!

It was a wrench to drag himself back to his duties, and as Ash forced himself to do so, his sense of contentment faded.

Had General Alexios made a move? Probably not. If Alexios Komnenos had entered the city, Sigurd would have summoned him, this was the lull before the storm.

And what about Emperor Nikephoros? With luck, the

Emperor might have returned to his senses, he might be an inadequate ruler, but an inadequate ruler was better than none. When Ash left these chambers, he had best be prepared for anything.

Ash glanced at the 'princess'.

I should not have seduced her, I have learned nothing.

She had fallen asleep with his name on her lips. Half-hidden beneath one of the mulberry-coloured sheets, she was tucked against his side, a slender ankle hooked over his calf.

Ash hadn't been able to stop himself. Not that he had tried very hard. Initially, he would swear that the passion that had flared up between them had startled her—but once it had been ignited, she had been as hungry for him as he had been for her. In the end, he had resorted to drawing a sheet over them both. As an attempt to kill the desire he felt for her, it had been utterly futile—that slight, sweet body drew him as none had ever done. He wanted her still.

Perhaps I should have resisted, but I hoped she might betray herself.

Unfortunately, she had not.

Thanks to her, Ash found himself in an untenable position. Without doubt, she was not the woman he had been ordered to bring back to the capital, but he wanted proof. At the least, he wanted her to admit what she had done. Ash gave a self-deprecating smile. The only thing that this woman had revealed was an intensely passionate nature.

Who is she?

Each time, and Ash had lost count of how many times their bodies had joined, he had been careful to ensure that he had not left his seed inside her. He had not lost control.

Who is she? It was likely she would have been chosen from the most faithful of Princess Theodora's ladies-in-waiting. As such, she would certainly not welcome quickening with his child.

Who is she? As the light faded to violet and the shadows began to thicken, he felt his face soften as he studied her. Why did she draw him so? She was surely out of bounds for him, he should never have touched her.

What if—his skin iced over—*what if she is married?*

No! She was not married, she could not be married, her responses were so warm, so unfeigned. Unfeigned? Holy Virgin, what was he doing trying to justify her? The woman had deceived him, she was continuing to deceive him!

His fingers crushed the silk sheet. A trace of anger remained, confusingly mixed with what Ash recognised was concern. God's blood, he should not feel concern for the woman, that had not been part of his plan.

Who is she?

The most loyal of Princess Theodora's ladies? She looked heart-wrenchingly young. So small and defenceless tucked up against him. That air of unworldliness had taken him in from the start. Could it be that she was unaware of the enormity of what she had done? Of the penalties that might be imposed upon her? Banishment…torture…*death*.

She had mentioned the Prince of Rascia—had hinted at being forced. Frowning, Ash reached for a shining strand of hair and wound it round his finger. That simply did not fit with what Ash knew. Princess Theodora was said to have been enamoured of her prince. Was it likely that the Princess would entrust the extraordinarily challenging task of impersonating her to a woman she did not trust? To a woman who had had relations with her prince? If Prince Peter had forced this girl—no, the Princess would have to be a saint to have kept this girl in her entourage after that.

Ash stared at the sleeping face so close to his on the pillows, and sighed. She was so beautiful. Why had she mentioned being forced in that way? Again the thought came to him that the truth was there, interwoven with lies. It would be good to think that she wanted to give him the truth, and that it was loyalty to the Princess that prevented her from giving him more. Could her evasiveness be caused by more than loyalty, could fear also be part of the weave? Lord.

She had been no innocent when they had taken their joy of each other. She had been startled, pleased even, but she was definitely no innocent. It was possible that somewhere in her past someone *had* forced her. His chest tightened. Shaking his head, he ran his hand down a length of soft, perfumed hair. *Someone had forced this girl.* His jaw clenched as the thought became cold certainty. How could they? She was so delicate and fragile, so caring of those around her—the Princess, the slaves...

Who cares for her? This girl may not be the Princess, but surely she is just as deserving of protection?

Silk rustled as he shifted. Was he being taken in by a pretty face? It was possible. No one knew better than he what it was like in Imperial service, having to jump the moment word was given. Ash had seen a servant beaten to within an inch of her life, simply for dropping a glass goblet.

The Princess might have some hold over her...

A glossy strand of hair fell over her face, Ash stroked it away. For this girl to keep up the pretence once she had left the Princess's sight, her motive must be powerful indeed.

What kind of a hold might the Princess have over her?

The jewel chest—was that her motive? The Princess must have given her those jewels, and there was more wealth in that enamelled casket than most people saw in their entire lives.

Motive enough, but not for this girl.

Pensively, Ash rubbed his face. The girl slept on. She had bought slaves today. The large Norman and the two babes. Had she sold some of the Princess's jewels to buy them?

Why buy slaves? Some ladies bought slaves to puff up their consequence.

Not this one. In the slave market her expression had been compassionate, and she had asked Lady Anna to find a litter for the Norman.

She wants to help slaves, why? There was some connection here that he had yet to fathom. Ash grimaced. There was so much about this woman that did not fit. Hell, the only thing that fitted was the way she had come into his arms, the way they had taken pleasure in each other. In that way, they were a perfect match.

The door rattled. Someone—Lady Anna, if he guessed aright—was outside and she sounded agitated.

'Theodora, let me in!'

Another voice, this one low and male, murmured back. Kari?

And then it was Lady Anna again. 'They have been in there the whole afternoon—I must see her!'

Ash eased the girl's head from his shoulder and slipped out of bed. From the rising pitch of Anna's voice, Kari would not be able to keep her at bay much longer.

Ash scooped up his clothes and dressed quickly. As he moved towards the door, he couldn't resist a last look at the girl curled beneath the disordered bedclothes.

If only I knew her name...

Katerina woke with a start. Someone had opened the bedchamber door, she heard a curt muttered exchange.

Then, *'Princess!'*

She jerked upright, clutching the sheet to her breasts. As

the door swung shut, she saw Ashfirth striding through the reception room beyond. His leg must be getting better, his limp was barely noticeable.

'Are you mad?' Anna rushed over, her eyes practically starting from her head. 'What in Heaven is going on?'

Embarrassment was a hot flare in Katerina's cheeks. Truth to tell, the sudden flowering of intimacy been her and Ash had shocked her. *It is so easy to respond to him! It is all pleasurable with Ash...and not only that—Ash makes it a pleasure to give him pleasure.* However, Katerina was far from ready to admit as much, even to Anna. She lifted her shoulders as though she did not care. 'I would have thought that was obvious.'

Anna's jaw dropped. 'The C-Commander and you...?'

'Yes, Anna, the Commander and I...'

Anna bent to pick up Katerina's gown and veil. 'It must be the strain,' she muttered. 'I told the Princess that you were not suitable to take her place. She should have sent someone with real knowledge of the Palace, someone who understood the protocols.'

'Someone with more breeding, you mean,' Katerina said, drily.

'Since you care to put it like that, yes! Someone with a little more breeding would have had some idea of what is, and what is not, acceptable behaviour.' Anna met Katerina's gaze squarely. 'Princess Theodora would *never* have invited Commander Ashfirth into her bedchamber. Or into her bed.'

'Pass me that robe, please, Anna.'

Frowning, Anna flung the robe at her, and Katerina got out of bed. 'Really, Katerina, you should not have done it. And so blatantly! You are quite without shame.' There was more muttering. 'The Princess should have sent a lady in her stead, not a peasant! I told her, I told her!'

Katerina set her teeth. The first mention of her humble background had wounded her, she had ignored it out of deference to Anna's nobility. But that did not mean she was going to permit her to rub salt in the wound. 'I may only be a peasant, Anna, but I am doing my best to help Princess Theodora.'

'I hardly see that sleeping with Commander Ashfirth was called for!'

'If you would calm down and hear me out, I would be happy to explain.' Katerina knew that there was no explanation for the way that intimacy with Ashfirth had turned out to be so wondrous an experience, but she could at least make Anna understand what she had set out to do.

Anna put her hands on her hips. 'I am listening, but consider this: Princess Theodora would *never* have slept with one of the Emperor's Guard.'

'The Court is renowned for many things, but you must know that a strong sense of morality is not one of them. Why, back in Rascia, I heard one of the Princess's ladies commenting on the prowess of a lover in the Varangian Guard.'

'The Princess would not have done it,' Anna insisted.

'Would she not?'

Anna made an impatient sound and looked sharply away. Her jaw was set in stubborn lines. 'You should not have done it.'

'That is as may be, but I consider I had to. He was becoming suspicious.'

'Sweet Mother, you slept with him to distract him?'

'In a nutshell, yes.'

'Save us, the girl has taken leave of her senses! How can becoming *more* intimate with Commander Ashfirth possibly help? Surely it would have been better if you had cultivated an air of distance?' She leaned closer. 'Well? Tell me, did it work?'

Katerina gave a rueful smile. 'Not exactly. It did distract him, but he remains suspicious. Anna, I am sorry, I know my behaviour falls short of what might be expected from the Princess, but—'

'You panicked.'

'It was all I could think of.' *And then delight caught me unawares, and I was caught up in the moment, a moment which may never return...*

Anna sighed, her mouth relaxed into a smile. 'That is because you like him. I observed this on the voyage home. There is a definite *frisson* between you.'

'*Frisson?*' The word was new to Katerina.

'It is a Frankish word. It signifies the...charged atmosphere that can develop between a man and a woman when they are attracted to each other.'

'*Frisson.* I like it. Anna, you are perceptive, I am attracted to him. Even more so now.'

'But?'

'He has divined the truth.' Anna made a convulsive negative gesture and Katerina shook her head. 'Rest assured, I never admitted it, but Ash knows—'

'*Ash?* Never tell me you refer to him as Ash!' Anna tutted. 'Such intimacy.'

Cheeks warming, Katerina looked down at her toes and flexed them. The floor tiles were cool and faintly patterned by striations in the marble. 'Anna, have you noticed the swirls in this floor?'

'Don't change the subject, Ka—Theodora. Ash, indeed!' Anna shook her head. 'In truth, I am beginning to think you are already half in love with the man.'

'I am not in love with him! It is true that I admire him, but...'

'But?'

Regret was heavy in Katerina's chest. 'He came to this bed, hoping to catch me out.'

Anna gave a disparaging sniff.

'Anna, you are in the right, I am a peasant. Only a peasant would have used such a method to try to distract him.' *And I failed, utterly.*

Slowly, Anna shook her head and reached for Katerina's hand. 'I was wrong to be so rude, I didn't mean it. I spoke out of turn because I was worried. You are a natural lady.' She jerked her head towards the reception chamber. 'And in view of what you are doing for the slaves out there, it was particularly ungrateful.'

Katerina squeezed Anna's hand. 'How are they?'

'The children are playing with one of the eunuchs, it has been difficult to get them to stop eating.' Anna's expression clouded. 'As for the Frank, he has yet to speak. He has been badly beaten and it may take some time for him to recover.'

'And his arm?'

'Thankfully it does not seem to be broken. It is bruised to the bone, but not broken.'

'He has recovered consciousness?'

'Yes. He has eaten, but so far he has said scarcely a word. I know his name is William, but I can get nothing else out of him.'

'That is odd, the auctioneer said he could speak Greek. I do hope his mind has not been damaged by the beatings. I understand that sometimes—'

Anna went pale. 'No, Theodora, do not say so!'

'I shall pray he recovers well.' Katerina lifted an eyebrow. 'It has not taken long for this man to become important to you.'

Anna gave an awkward nod. 'So it would seem.'

'You need to get out of the apartment for a time,'

Katerina said, moving away. Their pretence had put Anna under strain too. 'We both do. And since Commander Ashfirth is no longer breathing down our necks, we should make the most of it.'

'Oh?'

'This is the perfect moment for you to give me a tour of the Palace. This morning when I was on my own with Ash…with the Commander, I lost my way, it was most disconcerting. I should like to explore the City too, but—' flushing, Katerina eyed the thickening dusk outside '—given they will be lighting the lanterns any moment, I expect we should stay within the Palace grounds.'

'That would be wise. Tomorrow I can show you the City.'

'Anna, is there any way we might leave the Palace without an escort? It would be good to talk freely.'

'We can say we want to attend church. Hagia Sophia is only across the square, there will surely be no need for guards. As for this evening, a tour of the Palace should certainly be possible.'

'Thank you, Anna. Do you think we might start with the bathhouse? I overheard one of the servants mentioning a ladies' pool—I should like to try it.' Katerina grinned. 'And before we do that, I must eat, I am ravenous!'

The following morning, after breaking their fast and having seen to it that the children—who were named Daphne and Paula—and William had eaten their fill, Katerina and Anna tiptoed softly out of the apartment and down the long, marble corridors. No one challenged them; they were free of an escort.

'Take me to Hagia Sophia first,' Katerina murmured. 'I need somewhere peaceful to think.' Ashfirth would be too busy with military matters to be worrying about her, but the fact remained that he was suspicious of her. *What if he decides to discuss his misgivings with someone else? Will he betray me? After all, his duty is to the real Theodora.*

Yesterday afternoon, when Katerina had woken to see him hurrying from the apartment, she had been lost in a haze of bliss that had hidden all doubts. This morning the haze had evaporated. *Will he betray me?* That one thought dominated her mind.

Outside the Boukoleon Palace the sky was leaden, a soft rain was falling. Katerina drew up her hood and glanced at the lighthouse. The warning beacon had only just been extinguished; wisps of grey smoke lingered round the top of the tower. It seemed they had beaten the crowds of courtiers; only servants and slaves were moving through the fountained courtyards.

'Thank Heavens for the rain.' Anna exchanged a look of relief with Katerina as she, too, shrugged into her hood. 'With luck Commander Ashfirth—if he is about—won't see us. But to be safe, I think we had better choose one of the less popular paths.'

Holding their skirts clear of damp paving, they scurried past domed buildings and ancient palaces. Some areas were surprisingly rundown, with overgrown gardens and silted-up ponds.

'That is the Hall of the Nineteen Couches,' Anna murmured, pointing to a boarded-up building with a caved-in roof. A row of statues guarded the portico; several had lost arms, one its head.

Katerina shivered. 'It looks derelict to me.'

'Yes, it's been empty for years.'

'Creeping about like this makes me feel like a criminal,' Katerina said. 'I suppose in the eyes of the Commander I am a criminal.'

'You told me you had admitted nothing!'

'Nor did I. But I do feel guilty for misleading him. Perhaps it was short-sighted of me, but I had not expected to feel quite so...bad.' They were approaching a small gate and Katerina fell silent until the sentries and the Palace walls were behind them. 'Anna, yesterday I overheard something very strange...'

'Oh?'

'One of the grooms said that a soldier called Alexios Komnenos was making a bid for the throne.'

'I was hoping you wouldn't hear about that.'

'So it's true? Why on earth didn't you mention it?'

'I thought you had enough to worry about, and after we got back from the slave market I was somewhat distracted.' Anna laughed. 'We both were. By the time the Commander had left your bedchamber, it had quite slipped my mind.'

'You don't think there will be fighting in the city, do you?' *Ashfirth!* Katerina's heart missed its beat. Ashfirth would have to defend the Emperor, he could be hurt, he could be killed...

'It is possible, but I do not think it likely.'

The colonnaded avenues and wide streets were eerily clear of people. The only noise came from some geese flying overhead and a flock of starlings in a nearby plane tree.

There is nothing to be gained by worrying about something that may never happen. And why should I be concerned for a man who thinks I am...what? An impostor? A liar, a deceiver, a traitor?

Ashfirth Saxon could look after himself.

'Mercifully, the city seems peaceful this morning,' she said. 'Thank the Lord we got away without any guards seeing us.'

Two beggars were sitting by the gutter, holding their hands out for alms. Seeing them, Anna flung a worried glance over her shoulder. 'I am not so sure. Don't you think we should have brought at least one servant with us? Is it really safe to wander around the city unattended?'

'Anna, you may be used to the pomp and ceremony of the Court, but I—as you were so quick to point out yesterday—am a simple villager. For one morning, just one morning, I need to escape an escort and all that entails. I really need to think.'

Anna's gaze was curious. 'About the Commander?'

Katerina concentrated on rearranging her hood. 'In part. He is an honourable man and I do not like deceiving him.'

'You agreed to it.'

'I know. It is just that I did not realise how it would be, once I had got to know him.'

'You like Commander Ashfirth, you trust him. Yes, I can see how that might make difficulties. It must be strange trusting a man again, I imagine.'

Katerina's throat closed up, it was hard to get words out. 'Trust him? Trust a man? Anna, I am not so sure I can ever trust a man again, not after my father...'

Anna pressed her arm sympathetically. 'I think that you do already trust the Commander. He is, as you say, a man of honour. And now you and he have become...intimate.'

'It does complicate matters.' *Where is he? What is he doing this morning? When shall I see him again?* Katerina had wondered if he might return to check up on her; she had been both looking forward to it and dreading it, in equal measure. *What shall I say to him? How should I behave towards him?*

Anna tugged her sleeve. 'Was it pleasurable?'

'I...*what* did you say?'

'We have all heard about the staying power of Varangians, about their reputation as lovers. Is it true?' A sly smile hovered on Anna's lips. 'And your Ashfirth is their Commander, he must have more stamina than most.

Besides, you cannot deny that you were locked in that bedchamber together for *several* hours.'

Katerina's cheeks stung. 'Anna, you never cease to amaze me. One moment I think you were made to be a nun and the next…goodness, what's that noise?'

They turned a corner into a square and came to an abrupt halt. There was a colossal bronze column in the centre and hundreds of people were milling around it. Her eyes widened. 'No wonder the Palace is deserted, everyone is here!'

Richly dressed courtiers were heading towards a gate in a wall. Katerina could see domes behind it, presumably the domes of Hagia Sophia.

Rain-sodden banners were being borne aloft; pennons hung limp and dripped on to flagstones that were shiny with wet. There was a distinct atmosphere of unease.

Several grand ladies forced their way through, retinues trailing after them. The ladies were dressed sombrely, but there was no Lenten sackcloth that Katerina could see. Brocades, damasks and silks were being paraded in front of each other, while armies of attendants, servants and guards jostled for position. Mouths were pursed tight, expressions were dour.

Katerina and Anna—swallowed up by one of the retinues, squashed on all sides—found it impossible to break free. They passed through the gate in the wall and were borne towards the great church doors.

Katerina was resigned to being swept inside, until Anna leaned towards her.

'I wonder if Empress Maria is here?' she whispered.

Katerina snatched at Anna's hand. 'You haven't seen her?'

'No, but…'

Shrinking further into her hood, Katerina tried to hang

back, but a woman behind her muttered an objection and prodded her in the shoulder blades.

'Anna, I cannot meet the Empress,' she hissed, steadying herself. 'Empress Maria knew the Princess before she was sent to Rascia!' Yes, the Princess had been a child at the time and it was unlikely that the Empress would realise Katerina was an impostor, but she had no wish to put her likeness to the Princess to the test. Not with someone who had known Princess Theodora.

Mouth dry, Katerina fixed her eyes on a lady in grey brocade with an elaborate headdress and was carried into the church, pressed between courtiers' bodies.

The air was heavy with incense, with perfume and the smell of human sweat. About them there was a dull gleam of gold mosaics. Ornately decorated walls flickered in the light from a thousand hanging lamps. Shadows shifted. Voices were hushed, footfalls soft; and behind these sounds came the plaintive backdrop of chanting monks.

'It is Holy Week,' she managed, frantically searching for an escape route. There were too many people! 'The whole Court is attending.'

'Most likely.'

Gripping Anna's hand, Katerina forced her way to the side. Holy Week! How could she have forgotten? She must get away!

'Anna, half the Court is here, I can't let my guard down for a moment.' She grimaced as people poured through the door. There were rosy-cheeked eunuchs; soldiers in dress uniforms that were spotted with rain; ladies pulling faces as they shook water from rain-darkened hems; black robed monks; bearded priests… With every moment that passed more and more pushed in. 'The whole Palace is here! Is it always like this?'

'I must say have never seen it quite so full.'

'Is there anywhere else we might go? Somewhere more peaceful?' *Somewhere where there is no chance I might bump into the Empress.*

'There is another church nearby. Katerina, I don't think you need worry about meeting the Empress. If she is present, she will be up in the gallery.' Anna waved at the cavernous space above them, so large a space, it made ants of the entire Court. Katerina saw rows of round arches, more gleaming mosaics, the glow of a lamp.

'I can't take the risk—oh, Lord, those ladies are gesturing us to that stairway. Anna, get us out of here!'

It is a good thing one of us knows her way about, Katerina thought, as at last they had fought their way out and had dived into the quiet of a side street.

The rain fell steadily, the sky was darkening. Smoke caught in the back of her throat, they must be near one of the city bakeries.

With the main thoroughfare behind them, Anna turned towards a church that stood slightly apart, among some cypresses. 'There it is, Hagia Irene.'

Several men on horseback were galloping through the trees, churning up the turf. Anna pushed back her hood and frowned. 'Listen, did you hear that?'

'I can't hear anything except hoofbeats—' Katerina broke off. There *was* something else...the faintest of sounds. It was like a winter wind whistling through pine trees. No, no, it wasn't, it was... Her skin chilled.

Someone is crying out, screaming...

A bell began to toll and then, from all quarters, other bells joined in.

'Th-the prayer bell?' she asked, gripped by a sick dread. That was no prayer bell.

White about the mouth, Anna shook her head, pulling at her. 'Alarm, that's an alarm—we must get back to the Palace!'

Katerina pointed at the church among the cypresses. 'The church is nearer, we will be safe there.'

'No!' Anna's face was tight with fear. 'Look, I don't know why the alarm is sounding, but I do know that General Alexios had troops outside the city. It's possible they have got in—we will be safer in the Palace.'

Raindrops blurred Katerina's vision, she blinked them away. 'The General is making his bid for the throne?'

'He must be.' Anna yanked frantically at her hand. 'Come on, we may only have minutes. There may be... violence... Please, Katerina, come on!'

'But General Alexios is Greek.' An ominous grey cloud was drifting towards them from the west. Except that it was not a cloud, it was the smoke Katerina had smelled earlier and it was not from any bakery. 'Surely he would not attack the citizens?'

'He has mercenary troops and they are not choosy about how they get their coin. Oh, Lord, I expect that is why there were so many people in Hagia Sophia...'

'They knew this was about to happen, they were seeking sanctuary?'

'Yes, *yes*! Come on, *please*!'

A shout drew their gaze to a contingent of foot soldiers hurtling out of a side street. Under their helmets the soldiers' faces were streaked with dirt. They saw the girls and clattered to a halt.

Time seemed to freeze. The world fell silent.

A smile split the face of the lead soldier before his harsh voice shattered the silence. 'Look here, lads...*ladies*! Real ladies.'

His beard quivered. He was close enough for Katerina

to see the redness of his mouth, and several broken teeth.
He licked his lips.

'Sweet Mary, help us.' Katerina's guts turned to water.
'I don't recognise that uniform.'

'Neither do I. Run, *run*!'

Chapter Twelve

Ash took the stairs to the Princess's apartments two at a time; in a matter of moments, he would learn her true identity.

With General Alexios on the verge of entering the City, Ash had much on his mind, but he hadn't been able to shift the image of a slender girl lying amid disordered mulberry-coloured sheets. As soon as he learned who she was, he could concentrate on his military duties.

I should have thought of this earlier, undoubtedly I would have done, had I not been seduced by a pair of mysterious brown eyes...

'Befuddled by lust,' he muttered as he reached the half-landing overlooking the Palace garden.

It was odd, because lust was something Ash had learned to control since joining the Guard. Until now it hadn't been hard—there was no shortage of women in Constantinople willing to offer comfort to soldiers in the Emperor's Guard. Come to think of it, there had never been a shortage of such women in the Great Palace either; in the last few years he had turned down several. He had never lost his head over a woman, certainly not to the extent of losing his wits as he seemed to have done over his 'princess'.

He found her irresistible. There was something about her that had made him set aside his decision never to become involved with a lady of the Court. It was too late for regrets, this intriguing slip of a girl had him well and truly befuddled; he couldn't stop thinking about her, couldn't stop worrying about her.

Arriving at the doors to her apartment, Ash exchanged a greeting with the guard.

I should have thought of this earlier.

Telling himself that self-flagellation served no purpose, Ash marched into the reception chamber. With General Alexios poised for battle, he could no longer prevaricate, but for his own peace of mind he needed to discover her true identity.

His footsteps slowed.

The apartment was ominously quiet, empty but for the two children and a smiling maidservant. The baby was waving a coral teether and the little girl was rolling a wooden ball to the maidservant. The Norman's pallet was empty.

The Norman's pallet was empty?

Ash frowned. He had left two men to watch over her, the man at the door and...

'Kari! *Kari!*'

Kari emerged from a side chamber. 'I am sorry, Commander.'

'Where is everyone?'

'I...I am not sure. I think the Princess and her lady have gone to church.'

Ash's skin chilled. 'They've left the Palace grounds?'

'I...I think so, sir.'

'Did they take an escort?'

Kari shook his head. 'The Princess didn't want one.'

'Devil take you, you were supposed to keep an eye on her, not let her run loose in the City!'

Kari scratched the back of his neck 'Who am I to refuse the Princess?' He spread his hands. 'She is a member of the Imperial family, we are sworn to obey.'

Ash felt like tearing his hair out. 'Your orders were clear, your duty is to *me*! You were to watch over her, to make certain she was safe. How the hell can you watch over her when you are not with her?' He waved at the empty pallet. 'And where the devil is that Norman slave?'

'I…I don't know, sir. He was there when the Princess and Lady Anna broke their fast. He got up shortly after they left. I thought he had gone to relieve himself, but…'

Ash made an exasperated noise. 'Don't tell me—he never returned?'

'That's it, sir, that's it exactly.'

Ash fought to remain calm. 'Not only have you let the ladies leave the Palace without an escort, but we also have a runaway slave to contend with.'

Kari shuffled his boots. 'I am sorry, sir, but the Princess…'

Ash sighed. 'Kari, I am most displeased.'

'Yes, sir. My apology—'

'Yes, yes, I heard the first time. How long since the ladies left?'

'It's not been long.' Kari brightened. 'I could go after them, I might be able to catch them.'

'No, I want you here.'

The little girl smiled warily at Ash. Scrubbed clean and wearing decent clothes, he wouldn't have known her for the pitiful scrap the 'princess' had brought from the slave market. 'Do you think you are up to watching children?'

Kari went crimson. 'Yes, sir.'

'Good. If the Princess returns, your orders are to stick to her like a burr. You are not to let her out of your sight. Understood?'

'Yes, Commander. And if she decides to leave the Palace again…?'

'Stop her. Bind her hand and foot if you must. Until this business with General Alexios is settled, I don't want her setting a toe outside the Palace.'

'Yes, sir.'

Ash strode into the bedchamber, confident that this was where he would find what he was looking for. The slaves' document of ownership. He had watched her sign it at the slave market, and for it to be valid she would have to have used her real name.

Where the hell would she have put it?

Several travelling chests were lined up against a wall, Ash recognised them from the ship. There was no sign of the jewellery box. His gaze settled on an archway leading off from the main bedchamber. Ducking under the arch, he found himself in what appeared to be a dressing room. An icon lay on a table, an ivory comb, a silver-backed mirror…

There! The enamelled box was on the floor under the table. Ash picked it up.

It was locked, as he had expected. The lock was sturdy, but not sturdy enough to withstand a man with a little determination. He would soon have it open. Not wanting to blunt the blade of his dagger, Ash tucked it under his arm and went back under the arch.

Kari was in the reception room, staring moodily at the children. He eyed the casket with interest.

'If the Princess returns before I do,' Ash said, 'tell her I have taken her valuables. I am putting them into safe-keeping and will return them to her when the City has been restored to order.'

Kari saluted. 'Yes, sir.'

In his private quarters a couple of floors below the Princess's apartments, Ash worked at the lock with the pin
of a cloak fastening. The lock was more delicate than he
had thought, and more intricate, as was the detailing on
the casket itself. What a beautiful object! The surface was
studded with enamel plaques, with gemstones and coloured
glass—in itself the box probably represented several years'
pay. Ash grimaced, he was loathe to destroy it to get at the
contents, but get at them he would.

This had to be where she had secreted the documents of
ownership, the documents he had seen her sign at the slave
market.

Her name has to be on them, her real name...

He bent over the lock. The cloak pin bent. Swearing
softly, Ash found a belt buckle with a pin that had more
substance to it and tried again. The lock was resistant and
he was on the point of resorting to brute force when it gave
a soft click and the lid popped open.

The scrolls were on top. Holding his breath, Ash picked
one out, unrolled it and peered at the signatures. In his early
days in service with the Emperor, Ash had found it hard to
grasp Greek lettering, but he had been ambitious, he had
learned to read.

And there it was, clear as day. Large and curiously ill
formed. *Katerina.*

'Katerina,' he murmured, staring bemusedly at some
extremely misshapen handwriting.

Her name is Katerina! Katerina...

Next to Katerina's signature, written with a practised
flourish, was another name: 'Anna.'

Puzzled, his eyes went from one signature to the other,
the contrast between the two couldn't be more marked.
Katerina's was crabbed and awkward, almost childish in

its execution; Lady Anna's on the other hand, was polished and sophisticated.

Katerina, her name is Katerina...

Ash was frowning bemusedly at the ill-formed signature when someone rapped on the door.

'Commander?' Captain Sigurd stood there, bristling with news.

Ash shoved the scroll back into the box and closed the lid. 'Captain?'

'The General's troops have got into the City.'

'Already?' The last Ash had heard they were camped outside the walls, he had hoped it had been a bargaining position, to put pressure on the Emperor. He had prayed they would not actually break in...

'Yes, sir. A contingent has reached the aqueduct. And it as you feared, they are out of control.'

Ash secured the casket in one of his coffers. 'Come, we had best get to the guardhouse. Captain, full report! How did they get in?'

Sigurd answered as they sprinted down the stairs. 'Word has it that the Germans let down ladders and they climbed over the bastion.'

'Holy Mother. Alexios Komnenos is honourable, but his soldiers are largely mercenary, they may run amok.'

'Sadly, sir, it appears you are right.'

Ash squared his shoulders as they entered the guardhouse. 'The next few days are likely to test us, Sigurd.'

'I know it, sir.' Sigurd swallowed hard. 'It does not look good for our Emperor.'

Indeed it does not. And that was a thought Ash would not speak out loud.

'Many of the men would as lief take orders from General Alexios as from our Emperor,' Sigurd added, with a swift sideways look.

Ash glared at him.

'I am sorry, sir, I spoke out of turn.'

You and half my men, I'll be bound.

'Captain, has anyone seen our Emperor this morning? Has he left the Palace?'

'It is possible, there is no sign of him in his apartments, and a guard at the Chalke Gate reported seeing a courtier resembling the Emperor heading towards Hagia Sophia.'

'Wasn't he sure?'

'No, sir. The man was heavily cloaked and the guard forbore to ask his name.'

'Hell.' Thoughts racing, Ash ran his hand round his neck. The Emperor's weak state of mind had meant that Ash had been unable to deliver his report on the build-up of Norman forces off Apulia. The matter was urgent, yet he had been forced to sit on it. And with General Alexios choosing today to make a bid for the throne…

Ash had long admired the General and until this moment he had thought it impossible that he would end up facing him in battle.

A battle in the city. Lord, save us. Not only will I be limited in where I might deploy the troops, but it is inevitable that civilians will get hurt.

His life had become a nightmare.

Emperor Nikephoros might be old, his wits might have gone begging, but he deserved protection.

As for Katerina, the girl he had bedded in the Princess's bedchamber, she was one worry Ash could well do without. Nevertheless, she had been put in his charge, he was responsible for her safety—particularly after what had passed between them.

She is wandering about Constantinople without an escort— what if she runs into trouble?

'God save us.' Ash moved to a window overlooking the city. The sky was lightening and the rain easing. Dense black smoke was hanging like low-lying cloud over some of the roofs. 'The merchants' quarter along the Golden Horn has been fired.'

Sigurd leaned past him to see for himself. 'Yes, sir, I think you are right.'

'Fighting inside the streets is the last thing we want. Innocents always get hurt.' Ash shook his head. 'There is little else for it though, we are sworn to support the Emperor. Are the men braced for fierce action?'

'They are.'

'Good man. Listen, General Alexios will be heading this way. Deploy the men in the main square in front of the Milion Arch. In close order.'

'Yes, sir.'

Ash gave one last look out of the window, but no one resembling Katerina was in sight. If it was within his power he would help her, but his duty to the Emperor must come first.

Let her be safe. Dear God, let Katerina be safe.

'Run, *run*!'

The mercenaries lurched towards the girls, howling like wolves. 'Ladies, real ladies!'

Heart pounding, Katerina dived for the church door. The soldiers' gait was unsteady, they must have broached more than one wine barrel, but it had not slowed them down.

Her hands shook; she fumbled the latch.

Behind her, harsh voices were arguing over whose turn it was to go first, and which girl they wanted.

'The one in the red dress.'

'I'll take the other. Then we can swap.'

The good-natured tone to the quarrelling chilled her to the marrow. *They have done this before, it is nothing to them.*

Katerina leaned her weight against heavy oak and tripped over the threshold.

'Anna? *Anna?*'

Anna was not there. Chest heaving, Katerina stared in disbelief at the empty footpath. No Anna. But Anna had been right behind her—where had she gone?

The mercenaries had split up. Three of them were weaving, with drunken doggedness, towards the church, the others were no longer in sight.

The others are chasing Anna.

Instinctively, Katerina backed into Hagia Irene. She was vaguely aware of rows of arches that were busy with mosaics of saints, of purple marble, a lofty space. Something rustled behind one of the pillars. Her heart banged against her breastbone as a man in black robes stepped into the light. Katerina let her breath out in a rush as another man followed. Monks!

'Thank God! Please, brothers, help me!' She clutched wildly at a black habit. 'My friend is out here and those men...' Trembling from head to foot, she pointed shakily at the approaching mercenaries.

The monk made a swift negative gesture and reached for the door.

'Brother, *no!*' She hung on to his habit. 'What about Anna?'

'My apologies, sister, but you are at risk—there is no sense in two ladies being hurt.'

She struggled, but the other monk took her arm and pulled her deeper into the church. His face was kindly and creased with concern, but he was implacable, his grip unshakeable.

The door shut with a clang. A large key was turned and a bolt scraped home. Outside, something thudded against the wood.

'Just in time, Dimitri.' The monk relaxed his grip on her arm.

Katerina glared at him. 'You don't understand, my friend is out there!'

'I shall pray for her, sister, and I suggest you do the same. Compose yourself. Come, we were about to pray for a peaceful outcome.'

Peaceful outcome? Does everyone in Constantinople know more about what is happening than me? Why has no one discussed this properly with me?

The answer came swiftly. *Because it concerns a rebellion against the Emperor and you are masquerading as the Emperor's niece...*

Another thud had her shrinking deeper into the church. 'What is happening? Has the world gone mad that two women are not safe within yards of the Palace?'

'Where have you been, sister, that you have not heard? General Alexios and his mercenaries have entered the city.'

So, Anna was right, that was why the alarms had rung out. Her skin iced over. Ash must be defending the Emperor...God save him. His face swam into focus in her mind's eye—the gleaming black hair, the vivid blue eyes, that beautiful mouth. Ash was a mercenary—not all mercenaries were as unscrupulous as the men out there. *If only Ash was with me now, then I would know he is safe.*

As Katerina was ushered into the church, she put a hand to her mouth to stifle a moan. *Anna, where are you? Are you all right?*

At the east end, the apse was dominated by a huge black cross. Below it were tiers of stone benches, many monks were already at prayer.

'Come, sister—' the kindly, implacable monk tucked his hands into his sleeves and moved towards his brethren on the tiered benches '—join us in our prayers for peace.'

The Guard was well drilled. Within minutes, Ash had five hundred men in place, and was himself standing with them in the square in front of the Milion Arch. The red dress uniforms had been replaced with battle armour, and their helmets and battle-axes, row after row, were like silver sharks' teeth pointed at Heaven.

It was ironic that they had taken up position by the Milion Arch. A glorified milestone at the centre of the Empire, the Milion was the start point for measuring distances to towns and cities in every province. The Varangians were thus awaiting their first sighting of General Alexios at the very heart of the Empire that he was hoping to rule. The wall of the Great Palace lay on their left hand, hiding the sprawl of elegant buildings within; the domes of Hagia Sophia mushroomed out behind them.

A rook cawed overhead, a man coughed.

This coup has come dangerously close to ripping the Empire apart.

A grey-bearded warrior was lining his men up alongside the Varangians. The warrior's name was Nikephoros Palaiologos and he and his family exemplified the rift. Palaiologos was the head of his dynasty, a dynasty that was just as aristocratic as the Komnenos dynasty. Loyal to his marrow, Palaiologos was determined to stand shoulder to shoulder with Ash and the Guard.

Sadly, not everyone in the Palaiologos family was as loyal: his son, George, was siding with General Alexios. Foreign mercenaries were not the only ones putting their lives at risk today. In this battle—in the city!—it was going to be Greek against Greek.

The men stood firm behind the shield-wall. Chainmail chinked, battle-axes gleamed like crescent moons.

'Commander!' Captain Sigurd pointed down the street leading to the Hippodrome. 'Do you hear them?'

Men on the march. Not in view yet...

There!

A troop of foreign soldiers charged round a corner at the opposite side of the square. They were in disarray and when they saw the Varangians, they came to a ragged halt.

In one of the side streets a woman was screaming. Ash clenched his teeth. *Katerina! Where is she?*

'Hold the line, Captain. Hold the men steady.'

'Yes, sir.'

In the corner of his eye, Ash caught a flash of movement. His heart sank. *Lady Anna!* She was pelting along behind the Milion, eyes large with fear. If Ash had looked but a moment later, he would have missed her. Her skirts were bunched up about her knees and she had lost her veil. Her hair had broken free of its pins and was streaming out behind her.

Katerina! Where is Katerina?

Mind full of that one question, Ash's heart began to pound. He glanced towards the Hippodrome. The rebel troops were milling about in front of it, no one seemed to be giving them orders. There was likely to be a stand-off while they waited for their general to appear.

Good, that gives me some time. Where is Katerina?

He snatched up his shield. Inside, he was fighting his own internal battle. Yes, he was in command here, but the Emperor had also charged him with protecting Lady Anna and her 'princess'.

'Captain?'

'Commander?'

'You know the orders?'

'Yes, sir. We shall not give up an inch of ground; Komnenos will enter neither the Palace nor Hagia Sophia.'

'Hold to those orders come what may. If in doubt, look to Palaiologos for command.'

'Yes, sir.'

Ash turned and broke into a run, but Lady Anna had vanished.

Where is she? She cannot have gone far...

He circled the Milion. She was racing past the myrtle bushes that grew alongside the avenue. His gaze sharpened as he saw who was after her—three of General Alexios's mercenaries.

He raised his arm. 'Lady Anna! This way!'

She swerved in his direction. 'Commander!'

Keeping a close eye on the mercenaries, Ash unhooked his battle-axe and ran like the wind. He reached her by the buildings over the Palace Cistern. Wild eyed, she lurched towards him.

'Thank God!' Lady Anna's chest heaved as she sucked in air. 'Those men…'

Ash gripped his axe and looked past her. *What the devil?* The street was dominated by a large, half-naked man— mere sight of him seemed to have put the mercenaries to rout.

'Holy Virgin, it's Katerina's Norman!' The man was brandishing a sword and the mercenaries were backing off.

Shoving back her hair, Anna turned and went very still. 'So it is.'

Yes, it was unquestionably the slave who had vanished from Katerina's apartment. He stood in the middle of the avenue, legs braced slightly apart in the stance of a practised warrior. His upper body was covered in bruises and his sword arm was bandaged, but the grip on that sword told Ash that he was looking at a seasoned fighter.

What is he doing here? And how the hell did he get hold of that sword?

Whatever the man was doing, his appearance was timely. The German mercenaries must have decided that whilst an unprotected woman was fair game, one who could call on a Varangian Guard and a half-naked warrior with a sword was another proposition altogether.

'My lady, where is Katerina?'

Lady Anna's mouth opened and shut.

He gave her a gentle shake. 'My lady?'

'You…you know?'

Keeping the Norman in sight, Ash nodded and shook her again. 'The time for pretence is over. *Where is Katerina?*'

Lady Anna was staring at the slave. 'Safe. In Hagia Irene.'

Relief went through Ash like a wave. *Safe!* Briefly, he closed his eyes. 'Thank God.' He raised his voice. 'You there! Slave!'

The Norman met his gaze, Ash noted that he did not lower his sword.

'Yes?'

'You will look after Lady Anna?'

'Yes.'

Ash wondered whether he could believe him. Runaway slaves were not known to be reliable, and this one had managed to steal a sword. But he had put himself in harm's way for Lady Anna…

Ash looked at Lady Anna, and jerked his head towards the soldiers mustered behind the Milion Arch. 'Time is short.'

'I understand,' she said. 'You had to know she was safe.'

He gave a curt nod. 'Do you trust this Frank?'

Anna looked at the slave. The slave looked at Anna. She

nodded and gave Ash a little push. 'I will be safe with him. Go back to your men, Commander.'

Ash fixed the slave with his eyes. 'You are to protect Lady Anna with your life. Take her back to the women's quarters in the Palace. Understand?'

The Norman lowered his sword and held out his hand. Anna moved towards him. 'I understand.'

At that moment a roar went up from behind the Milion Arch.

Chapter Thirteen

Katerina was kneeling in Hagia Irene, staring up at the black cross in the apse when she became conscious of the rustle of dark robes beside her.

'Excuse me, my lady.' Brother Dimitri was gesturing towards the west end. 'Someone is enquiring after you.'

Katerina craned her neck, but she could only see monks. In the vicinity of the church entrance, a hanging lamp had blown out, grey ribbons of smoke were trailing through the air. 'You opened the door, Brother? Was that wise?'

'Under the circumstances, I thought it safe. He is waiting for you in the cloisters.'

'He? Who…?'

But Brother Dimitri had bowed his head and drifted away to tend to the smoking lamp. These monks, as Katerina had already discovered, hoarded most of their words for their worship.

Picking up her skirts, wondering that she could have been so lost in her thoughts that she had not noticed the door being opened, she hurried down the nave. It could

only be Ash, the monks would not have opened that door
to anyone they did not trust—not today.

Please let it be Ash.

She swept by the mosaic saints gazing calmly from their
lofty perches on walls and arches and entered the cloisters.

Sweet Mary, they have admitted him in his armour!

Ash was standing near a stone bench at the far end of the
southern cloister, fingers drumming the hilt of his sword.
He looked every inch the warrior. His battle-axe and helmet
lay on the bench and when he saw her his forehead cleared.

'My lady!' Striding over, he took her hands. His face was
strained, his hair was much disordered, but as those blue
eyes searched hers, he gave her a lop-sided smile. 'You are
unharmed?'

Katerina gripped him. 'Yes, but Lady Anna, she—'

'Lady Anna is safe.' Releasing a hand, he reached up and
ran a finger gently down her cheek before sliding it round
her neck in a hold that was suddenly, achingly, familiar.
He stared soberly at her for a moment, tugged her towards
him and hugged her fiercely.

His chainmail nipped her breasts through the stuff of
her gown. It felt cold and hard. Alien. *He is a barbarian,*
she reminded herself, staring at the shoulder-strap from
which he hung his sword. She did not need to examine
his battle-axe to know the edge would be razor sharp. *An
Anglo-Saxon warrior. This is what he is.* For a moment she
could not breathe and something shifted in her mind.

Bemused, she reached up and ran her fingertip along
his shoulder-strap. *This man ought to feel foreign to me,
yet here I am in his arms and all I feel is...complete.*

'Ash?'

Warm fingers were massaging the nape of her neck.
'Mmm?'

'What happened to Anna? Tell me! I have been praying and praying. We were walking in the City when—'

His eyes became cool, his hand fell from her neck. 'You left the Palace without an escort.'

Although he was no longer standing so close, he had retained one of her hands and was running his thumb back and forth, lacing his fingers in and out of hers, squeezing them. She had the impression that he was unaware of what he was doing and would be irritated when he realised.

'I know it was foolish, but I needed to escape the Palace for a time. I needed to think.'

He said nothing, merely watched her through slightly narrowed blue eyes. Unreadable. Ash was a chilling sight in full battle gear, yet paradoxically there was something endearing about the way that dark hair was sticking up in untidy spikes; her fingers itched to tidy it. What a mystery he was, and what a rarity. She had made love with this man and he had ensured that her pleasure had been as great as his.

'Ash, I had to get away! And then some soldiers appeared, I think they are in the pay of General Alexios.'

'They were certainly not the Emperor's men. I saw them, but you need have no fears for Lady Anna, she has found herself a champion.'

'She has?'

'Your Frankish slave.'

'William?'

A dark eyebrow shot up. 'I was unaware of his name, but suffice it to say that he found himself arms and seems to have appointed himself her protector. I have asked him to escort her back to the women's quarters as soon as he may.'

Katerina felt some her tension ebb away. 'Thank God.'

A couple of the brothers entered the cloisters and stood a few feet away, muttering to each other.

Releasing her, Ash pulled up his mail coif and shoved on his helmet. She bit her lip. With the noseguard hiding half his face, he was transformed in an instant to a terrible stranger. Scooping up his axe, he crooked his arm at her. So fierce looking…so polite. 'Shall we?'

Hesitantly, she laid her fingers on his arm and he led her along the cloister, away from the monks. They turned a corner.

'My lady—' he cleared his throat '—or perhaps I should say Lady Katerina—if I may call you that?'

She came to a dead halt next to a carved column. *Lady Katerina?* 'Commander…?' She swallowed. His tone made it clear that this time he had proof of her name. *Except that he does not know the half of it. He thinks I am a noble-woman, but I am only a potter's daughter from Crete—a potter's daughter who was once a slave…*

I am a peasant and Ash believes me to be of noble blood!

When Katerina opened her mouth, he stopped it with his fingers. 'It is useless continuing to deny it.' He bent towards her. 'I have seen your signature on the documents you signed at the slave market.'

She stiffened. 'You have been through my belongings? I had hoped that you were above such tactics, Commander.' She made to remove her hand from his arm, but he held it in place.

'Gently, my lady, gently.' He indicated a knot of monks standing in the central courtyard. One of them was staring at them, brow wrinkled with worry. 'You are upsetting the good brothers.'

He propped his axe against a slim column. 'Lady Katerina, I must soon return to my men. Unless you can discuss this sensibly here, we shall have to continue later at the Palace. For myself, I would rather have the truth now.

'My lady, we are standing on hallowed ground. Do you think that here you might admit to the truth? I know you are not the Princess, but what is your full title? Katerina of…?'

At a loss as to how to respond, she shook her head. 'I…I cannot say.'

His lips thinned. Behind the noseguard, his eyes were bleak. 'I am trying to help you—is that so hard to believe?'

Katerina stared at him; the ache under her breastbone spoke of a desperate longing, one that—because of the gulf between them—could never be satisfied. 'I want to trust you, but it is hard.'

'Why, what on earth has happened to you? Someone has clearly hurt you, but surely you know by now you may trust me?'

Her cheeks burned. 'Sir, you are right, I have been… hurt. In my experience men use women. They abuse them because they have stronger bodies and may force them to their will. Ash, there has not been one man in my life who has proved himself to be worthy of trust.' There! She had revealed a little to him, not a great deal certainly, but it was more, much more than she had revealed to any man.

'There is me,' he said, quietly. 'I have no wish to hurt you. Katerina, you may trust me.'

In an agony of indecision, she reached towards him, curling her fingers into his shoulder-strap. 'My father,' she began, 'he…he…betrayed me.' The blue eyes were fixed on hers. Intent and no longer quite so bleak. 'And later there was a man who…' But then Katerina's throat closed up and she was unable to continue. Hanging her head, she managed to whisper. 'I…I want to tell you everything, Ash, but it is too painful, too shaming.'

'I am sorry if your experiences have given you a mistrust of men, but I am trying to help you. Listen…' He lowered his voice. 'As I mentioned, I do not have long, so I will come straight to it. You are of good family and there is your reputation to consider. We have had…intimate knowledge of each other and I should like to make provision.'

She wrinkled her brow. 'Provision?'

'In case there is a child.' He sighed. 'Lady Katerina, I am asking you to marry me.'

Marriage! Katerina's breath left her in a rush. *He is asking me to marry him?*

'M-marriage? You and me?'

'Yes. *Yes.*' Voice edged with impatience, he glanced at the monks in the centre of the courtyard. 'In England I was considered to be of a good family—a thane's son—but I realise that I shall never be noble in your eyes; your family will likely be disappointed in the match. I am an Anglo-Saxon, a barbarian.' His cheeks darkened. 'But this I swear, Lady Katerina, if you were to accept me, I—'

She stepped back, stunned by his offer. *He thinks he is offering for a lady-in-waiting. He cannot possibly want me!* 'You were so careful. When you…when we…you made certain to…' All too aware of the good brothers' listening ears, it was Katerina's turn to flush. She finished in a whisper. 'You made certain…you were careful.'

He caught her wrist and drew her to him, so they were once more standing chest to chest and his body armour was hard against her. 'Such methods are not entirely reliable, my lady.'

Katerina's thoughts were spinning. Ashfirth Saxon, the Commander of the Varangian Guard, had asked her to marry him!

He had learned her name, but he was making a very large assumption—he thought her family aristocratic! He would never offer marriage if he knew the truth. In all likelihood, he believed her to be a cousin of the Princess, a member of the Doukas family. It would never have occurred to him to offer marriage if he knew she was a simple village girl.

'I…you do not know me, Commander. In any case, as you realise, long before I met you, I had…relations with another man for a time and…well, to put it bluntly, it is quite possible I shall never conceive, so your offer, while honourable, is unnecessary.' She tried to twist free and his grip tightened. She could scarcely believe it—he had offered for her and he was looking so sincerely at her. His expression was thoughtful, if a little guarded. *If only I could tell him the whole truth. But I cannot. Ash must think marriage to a relative of the Princess would serve his ambitions. I must tell him the truth.* But she couldn't tell all of the truth. She couldn't bear to see his eyes darken with disappointment; she didn't want to watch that beautiful mouth curl with scorn. And that would be bound to happen, when Ash learned that she was just a potter's daughter from Crete, a girl whom the real Princess had rescued from slavery.

She could, however, give him another fragment of the truth—he deserved that much. She held her head high. 'Commander, I have to tell you, I am not a member of the Doukas family.'

'Not cousin to the Princess?'

'No.'

'No matter.' Easing his grip, he raised her hand to his lips, gently kissing the back as though he were truly courting her. Her heart twisted in an agony of longing. 'My offer stands. I would be honoured if you would be my wife.'

Her chest felt as though it would burst with pain—why must wanting hurt so? Truly this man was exceptional, she ached to turn him down, but turn him down she must. This was the Commander of the Varangian Guard while

Katerina, as Anna had so rightly reminded her, was only
a peasant. She was the last woman a proud and ambitious
man like Ash should be choosing. 'No, Commander, I am
sorry, but I cannot marry you.' Finally, she tugged her hand
free. Her skin was burning where he had kissed it.

He stood very straight, a muscle flickered in his jaw.
'No?'

'No, sir, I am sorry.'

He gave a brusque nod and turned away to frown at the
axe leaning against the column.

Katerina's eyes smarted, hastily she averted her head.
Through a mist she saw that the sun had broken through
the cloud and was shining on the centre of the courtyard
where the monks were standing. A sparrow flew to the
edge of a puddle and started pecking about. Surreptitiously
she wiped away a tear. When she had first walked into the
cloisters, his arms had felt like home to her, but now...now
she was in exile. She had never felt so alone.

'So be it.' Ashfirth swung back to her and offered her
his arm. 'I have time to escort you to the Palace gate.'

'Commander, I—'

'My lady, I must ensure your safe return.'

'Thank you, Commander.'

They left the cloisters and passed the lines of saints
watching from the walls. As they approached the studded
oak door, he paused. 'Lady Anna knows your identity?'

'Yes.'

'But you will not tell me?'

'No, Commander, I will not.'

His expression hardened and the eyes behind that noseguard became so cold that it seemed impossible that Katerina had ever kissed this man, let alone shared a bed with
him.

'Before we leave, my lady, you may rest assured that

while I know you to be an impostor, I shall not reveal it to anyone. For the time being, as far as everyone in the Palace is concerned, you shall remain the Princess Theodora.'

She sighed in relief. 'Thank you, sir.'

A monk came out of the shadows to open the door and they left the church.

Ashfirth's blue eyes were sombre. 'I cannot promise to protect you indefinitely, but as long as this uncertainty continues, I see little point in revealing you as an impostor.' He gave a bitter laugh. 'It would seem that the General's bid for the throne is working in your favour.'

'How so?'

'In normal circumstances, the Empress would have summoned you to meet her in her chambers. You have been spared that trial.' He continued down the path, battle-axe resting on his shoulder, expression distant. 'You would also have been summoned to the Doukas apartments. Did you know that General Alexios is married to Irene Doukaina?'

Katerina stared at him, trying to follow the thread of his thoughts. What a tangle! Clearly, relationships in the Palace were a web of complexity. 'Princess Theodora is related to General Komnenos's wife? As well as to the wife of the current Emperor?'

'Just so.'

'Then if General Alexios succeeds in becoming Emperor, Princess Theodora's place at Court will be assured?'

'Exactly. As will the places of other members of her family…her cousin, for example.'

'For Princess Theodora's sake, I am glad that is the case. But, Commander, I have already told you…the Princess and I are *not* related.'

He stopped mid-stride to look frowningly at her. And then he set off again, escorting her swiftly through the milling crowd in the square outside Hagia Sophia. One thought occupied Katerina's mind. *Ash thinks this rebellion will end badly for him.* By the time the bronze column stood behind them and the Palace walls loomed up in front of them, her throat was tight with dread.

'Comm—Ash?'

'My lady?'

Her fingers clenched on his arm, but she doubted he would feel it through his mail shirt. 'Tell me, do you expect to be defeated?'

Startled blue eyes met hers. 'I do not consider defeat, my lady, but I had better warn you, I may not always be in a position to protect you. My Emperor has lost much support.'

'The Varangians remains loyal, though.'

'Naturally, it is a point of honour with us. If necessary, we shall fight to the death. We do not consider defeat.' Catching the eye of a guard at the gate, he waved him over.

'Sir?'

'Please escort the Princess back to her apartments in the Boukoleon.'

'Yes, sir.'

'And whatever might happen in the City, make sure one of my men remains posted outside her chambers at all times. For the Princess's protection.'

'Yes, sir.'

Giving her an ironic salute, Ashfirth swung on his heel and turned, the curve of his battle-axe winking as he went. She stared after him, dread lifting the hairs on her neck. Apart from Ash, the square appeared deserted.

'Guard?'

'My lady?'

'What lies across that square?'

'Why, the Milion Arch, my lady.'

She almost took an involuntary step after him. Would

she see him again? Commander Ashfirth was a brave man, noble and honourable. Was he walking to his death?

His parting words rang round her brain. *'I do not consider defeat.'*

He is expecting to be killed!

Her heart was like lead. Ashfirth Saxon was a man like no other, he did not deserve to die. Although angry that she had deceived him, he remained mindful of her well-being. Of course, his Emperor had put her into his care; doubtless Ashfirth's sense of honour forced him to care for her even though he knew she had deceived him.

She sent the man at her elbow a wry glance. *If setting a guard over me could be construed as looking after me...*

Am I your prisoner, Ash?

It was a question she was unable to answer.

The square behind her was entirely empty, Ash had passed out of sight. She forced her lips to smile and looked expectantly at the guard. 'Very well, you may escort me to my apartments.'

The Varangians were in exactly the same position as when Ash had left them, drawn up in close battle array in front of the Milion. Palaiologos and his men stood alongside. Little had changed.

On the other side of the square, by the Hippodrome, a few more German mercenaries had arrived, but their ranks remained thin. Ash felt his lip curl; he would wager that at least half their number were on the rampage elsewhere on the City. Clearly discipline was poor in the enemy camp. The usurper's mercenaries. Lord, he had never thought Alexios Komnenos would push matters this far!

'Still at a stand-off, Captain?'

'Yes, sir. There's nothing to report.'

Ash took his place by the standard and settled in for what

looked like a long wait. He had caught himself unawares when he had proposed marriage to her.

Marriage!

The strain of these past days must be taking their toll, Ash had bedded women before and marriage had never occurred to him. Had thoughts of death goaded him to pose that particular question today? Katerina. He had told her that he had not considered defeat, and that much was true. Death, on the other hand, was a real possibility.

Ash turned to face his men and lifted his axe high. Five hundred pairs of eyes locked on to him. His lifted his voice. 'Varangians, are your blades hungry?'

As one, five hundred axes crashed against the shields; five hundred voices cried, 'Aye!'

'Varangians, will your axes taste blood?'

This time the axes crashed three times, steel against lime wood, as they yelled, 'Aye! Aye! Aye!'

Helms and chainmail glittered as Ash strode to and fro before them and the cheering went on.

'For the Emperor!'

'The Emperor!'

Finally, Ash raised a hand for silence. 'For now, men, we wait. And we watch.' He turned to face the enemy.

Until today he had thought it no great matter if he should die in the service of his Emperor. It would be a glorious death, one for the bards, but now...now...

In his mind's eye Katerina was smiling up at him and her mouth—that lying mouth that would not tell him everything—was as tempting as ever.

I do not want to die!

He eased his shoulders. For the tenth time that day, he tested the blade of his axe for sharpness and checked his sword. All was in order. Except for his thoughts. They seemed to be taking more twists and turns than the labyrinth of corridors under the Palace.

Why propose marriage? It is not as though I cared for the girl. How could he care for a woman who refused to admit who she really was?

To serve the Princess in such a way, she must be one of her ladies-in-waiting. Not a relation, though, if she was to be believed. She would be safe now, back in the apartments, thank God. Oddly, the mystery of Katerina's full identity seemed less important than it should. The crucial thing— the only thing—was that she must not come to harm.

Lord, he did care for her! It would seem that the pretty girl who had assumed the identity of the Princess had somehow found her way into his heart. He was oddly unsurprised.

She has refused you. And in any case, you are not likely to see tomorrow's dawning. He shook his head. This must stop! Too much introspection could weaken a man.

Ash scowled across the square at the random group of mercenaries by the Hippodrome and stamped his feet to keep his blood moving. What the devil was causing the delay?

'Has General Alexios shown himself, Captain?'

'No, sir.'

Katerina. What did he know about her? He knew her name. He knew she served the Princess, but there had to be more to it that that. To be willing to put herself into such danger, Katerina had demonstrated rare loyalty.

Why? Simply so the Princess might avoid marriage with Duke Nikolaos? Was that a good enough reason to risk angering an Emperor?

Ash might not think so, but clearly Katerina did.

He ran his gaze over his men, it was important to maintain morale. As if he had not a care in the world he shouted, 'Sergeant Toki!'

'Yes, sir?'

'Give us one of your songs.'

One of the troop's most popular men, Toki launched into a bawdy drinking song. Moments later, the entire Guard was belting out the familiar words.

Was Katerina driven by family loyalty? She had said she was not a member of the Doukas family, but she had lied to him before. Or might there be another reason? He eyed his troop, singing their hearts out. They were loyal to the last man. The Guard were paid to be loyal, and while they served they received the companionship of their comrades. A companionship that might—for those who had lost homes and family—come to mean the world. As it had for him, until today.

Katerina.

What other reasons might she have for serving the Princess with such devotion? Ash could think of none, not one. What else did he know about her?

She roused protective instincts in him, instincts he had not known he possessed.

She made him lose control—he would never forget the way she had looked lying across those mulberry sheets, holding out those slender arms for him. Even the memory had heat pooling in his groin.

But she has refused you.

Why? She liked him. Ash was not vain, but a man knew when a woman liked him. True, she mistrusted him, but she had confessed to mistrusting most men. She liked him, and when they had tumbled into those silken sheets, the joy had not been entirely his. Katerina might remain a woman of mystery, but she had taken her joy of him under those silken bed hangings.

Might she be promised elsewhere?

No, that did not fit either.

So…her name was Katerina. Faithful to a fault, she served her princess with unswerving loyalty. She mistrusted men, but she must feel more than a little liking for him to have responded so warmly when they had lain together in that bed.

If he got out of this in one piece, he would build on that liking. *One day, Lady Katerina, you shall trust me.*

And love? Ash pushed the thought away—he had no time for love. Katerina had found a place in his heart, he was fond of her, but that was as far as it went. He would have to do his best to see that she did not suffer for playing the role the Princess had set her.

Ears ringing with Sergeant Toki's lewd song, Ash stared blindly across the square. Whatever happened here, if he was alive at the end of it, he would help her.

It did not seem likely that Emperor Nikephoros would be sitting on the throne for much longer. Ash clenched his jaw. He would fight, he would ensure that his men conducted themselves with honour. And after that he prayed he would be given the chance to teach Katerina to put her trust in at least one man. Him.

Her father had—what had she said?—her father had betrayed her. She had told him that men had used their superior strength to impose their will on her, to abuse her.

Dear God, had she been raped? It would seem a possibility. Whatever had happened, she felt shame and obviously the hurt cut deep.

But it is not her shame! When this is over I will convince her she need not feel shamed by the sins others have visited on her.

When she understood that, she would realise there were

no barriers between them. *I will win her round to my way of thinking, she will marry me.* Ash gave a grim smile. In this, as in other matters, he refused to consider defeat.

Chapter Fourteen

Ash marched up and down before his men. What he needed was more information about what the rebel troops were up to elsewhere in the City. 'Captain Sigurd?'

'Sir?'

'Send three scouting parties, two men in each. Different directions. To report back in half an hour.'

'Yes, sir.'

On his left, towering over a wall, the column in the main square gleamed like gold in the evening rays. Almost as tall as Hagia Sophia, it was crowned with a bronze statue of the Emperor Justinian astride his horse—he was said to be wearing the armour of Achilles. It must be true about the armour, Ash thought wryly, for Justinian had ridden up there like a god for centuries. And most likely he would continue to do so, long after the dust had settled from today's crisis.

Twilight was thickening about them. The beacon had been lit in the Palace lighthouse; the Varangians had been battle ready for hours. At this rate, his troops would be exhausted before battle was joined. Ash was on the brink of redeploying more of the men simply to keep their minds occupied, when a red-faced messenger sprinted up to the standard.

'Sir!' The messenger saluted, panting for air.

'About time,' Sigurd muttered. 'It has been far too quiet.'

The older warrior, Palaiologos, was nearby, tugging at his beard. Ash gestured him over. 'Please, sir, come and share this news.' He nodded at the messenger. 'Go on.'

'Commander, the Patriarch has called for the Emperor to abdicate!'

Ash felt his captain's rising excitement and deliberately avoided his gaze. The Patriarch, as Head of the Orthodox Church, was almost as powerful as the Emperor. He was bound to be concerned about bloodshed in the City, not to mention the looting and rapes.

'Has the Emperor responded?'

'He is resisting, but he has been made aware that most of his support has melted away.'

'Apart from the Guard,' Sigurd said grimly, fingering the grip of his battle-axe.

'Yes, sir, apart from the Varangians.'

Sigurd made a convulsive movement, his eyes gleamed. 'Commander, I hope Nikephoros does abdicate, he is a pitiful excuse of an Emp—'

'Enough, Captain!'

Sigurd's gaze fell. 'My apologies, sir, but you know my views.'

'And you know your duty.'

'Yes, sir.'

Ash gestured at the empty streets. 'That explains the lull—everyone is hoping diplomacy might win the day, everyone is waiting.'

'Yes, sir.'

Abdication! How long will it take for the Emperor to

*come to his decision? How long did they have before hell
broke loose?*

The messenger shifted. 'Commander, there is more.'

'Continue.'

'The fleet is on the move. Sentries on the sea wall have
reported seeing warships moving towards the straights.'

'Is the Bosphoros clear?'

'No, sir, they say there are ships everywhere.'

Ash glanced at Palaiologos. 'Your son's handiwork?
George is Admiral of the fleet, is he not?'

'Yes, Commander.' Palaiologos ground his teeth
together. 'And from this day forward, he is no son of mine.'

Ash had no reply to that. The poor man was deeply
embarrassed by his son's disloyalty, and deeply wounded
by Alexios Komnenos's bid for power, which had liter-
ally torn his family in two. The father had remained loyal
to the ruling Emperor, while the son, George, supported
Komnenos.

'Sir, you are not responsible for the actions of your son,'
Ash said.

Palaiologos mumbled into his beard.

'You are not responsible for George's disloyalty,' Ash
repeated. 'That was his choice and his alone.'

The glow of the lighthouse beacon caught his gaze. As
Ash looked at it, an idea began to take shape…the lighthouse…something to do with the lighthouse…

'Hell, this will mean more waiting, while the Emperor
makes his decision,' Palaiologos growled. 'Nothing is likely
to happen until dawn.'

'I am not so sure, there may be something we can do,'
Ash said. He was transfixed by that lighthouse. 'Advise
me, sir. I have a question and it concerns seamanship.'

'Seamanship?' Palaiologos gave him a black look. 'It is
my son who is Admiral, Commander, not I.'

Ash pointed at the glow around the lighthouse. 'It is a simple question. At night, how much reliance would you say the fleet places on the lighthouse?'

Palaiologos stared blankly at him for a moment, before giving a reluctant smile. 'You are thinking of dousing the light, Commander?'

'Wouldn't you?' Ash spread his hands. 'The lighthouse is sited in the Palace. It is under *our* control and, unless I am mistaken, the fleet relies on it to navigate around the point.'

'That they do, Commander. Douse that light and at the least you will cause confusion.'

Ash grinned.

'Shall I send someone back to the Palace, sir?' Sigurd asked.

'No, since we find ourselves in something of a lull, I shall see to the dousing of the light myself,' Ash said. 'Send a runner if you need me. There are other matters in the Palace that need my attention—in view of this news, I need to amend the orders of the Treasury guards.'

And there is a certain brown-eyed lady-in-waiting called Katerina...but she will have to wait, of course, until after I have completed my military duties.

He became aware of Sigurd exchanging remarks with Palaiologos. 'What was that, Captain?'

'Whatever the Emperor decides, we shall come out of this with honour.'

'That is my hope,' Ash said. 'I am also determined that we shall come out of this *alive*.'

Servants had lit the braziers and lamps in the reception chamber, they were closing the shutters and drawing the heavy brocade curtains against the oncoming night. As they did so, Katerina noticed that the Sea of Marmara was filled with sails. Hundreds of them were bellied out with the wind, like ghosts on the evening sea. The faint pulse of a drum reached her, and then the shutters were closed and the curtains were pulled across. The drumbeat faded.

On the north side, the windows overlooked the Palace terraces and courtyards, the City lay beyond. Moving across, Katerina hooked back a curtain and peered out.

What is happening out there?

It was very quiet. One or two torches lit up the pathways and fountains, shadows shifted in the courtyards, but she saw no one, not even a patrolling guard. Katerina had not been a resident of the Palace long enough to know it in all its moods…but something had changed. Was it her imagination, or did the grounds seem much darker than usual?

The lighthouse has gone out!

Now that her eyes were adjusting to the intense gloom, Katerina could make out the tall black point that was the lighthouse tower. On previous nights, it had lit up the Palace grounds like a giant's torch, blazing a warning to ships: *Land ahead! Beware the approaching landmass!* Not tonight.

She chewed her lip. Had the lighthouse guards abandoned their posts? Or had the fire not been lit in hopes of putting the Emperor's enemies into disarray?

Behind her, Paula, the older of the two children, murmured a sleepy protest, but before she could go to see what was wrong, Sylvia was kneeling in a pool of lamplight at the child's side, stroking her brow. Sylvia was the maidservant Katerina had put in charge of the children and she was proving to be a good choice. Katerina smiled at Sylvia as she soothed the girl, her smile fading as her gaze came to rest on the empty pallet of the Frankish slave. Ash had seemed confident that the slave would not harm Lady Anna, but why had there been no sign of them? Katerina

had not seen Anna since they had become separated outside Hagia Irene.

*Something terrible must have happened. Has the Frank
kept Anna safe? Or is he making a bid for freedom? Why
haven't they returned?*

Katerina stared blindly at the empty pallet. She had
had her misgivings about buying that slave, but Anna had
insisted.

I will never forgive myself if he hurts her.

Resting a hand on the looped-back curtain, she peered
into the darkness.

*If only I could see beyond the reach of those torches; if
only I could see over those walls to the Milion Arch. Has
there been fighting? Is he safe?*

There was no sound from the city, no braying donkey, no
guffawing from the guardhouse, just an ominous silence. It
was as though someone had muffled the city by dropping a
cloak over it. *Everyone is waiting, but what are they waiting
for?*

Katerina didn't want to wait a moment longer, she
couldn't bear it. She had never felt so edgy!

Where is Ashfirth?

'Sylvia?'

The maid looked up from Paula's side. *'Despoina?'*

'Is there any news from outside the Palace?'

'News?'

Katerina let the curtain fall back into place. 'It is like a
grave out there. Do you think the Guard have been routed?'

Sylvia lost colour. 'Heaven forbid. But, no, Princess, I
do not think so, we would surely have heard if battle had
been joined. I was told the Varangians were to be deployed
a stone's throw from here.'

Sylvia had to be right, she had to be. It was surely far

too quiet for there to have been fighting nearby; they would have heard shouts, the clash of arms, screams…

'The lighthouse is out,' she murmured.

'My lady?'

'Never mind.' Striding to the doors, Katerina flung them open. She was in luck, Ashfirth's manservant was in conversation with the guard. 'Hrodric, the very person!'

'My lady.' Hrodric bowed.

Does he know I am not the Princess? Has Ashfirth told him? Ashfirth had said he would not reveal that she was an impostor to anyone, but she had seen how close he was to his manservant—Ash might confide in him.

'Hrodric, have you had any news?'

'No, my lady, we have heard nothing.' Taking her arm, Hrodric led her, politely but firmly, back into the apartment. 'Please wait in here. Commander Ashfirth said he would return as soon as he is able.'

'Yes. Thank you. I…I do not like this waiting,' she admitted, as Hrodric followed her in and closed the doors. If Hrodric had been told that she was an impostor, it was not affecting the way he treated her; he was as gentle and courteous as ever.

Conscious that Hrodric had not left the apartment, she returned to where Sylvia sat with the children. Paula's fretting had disturbed Daphne, the smaller child was lying wide-eyed in her basket. She was not complaining, but she was sucking very hard on her thumb.

'Come to me, sweet,' Katerina said, bending to pluck Daphne from her basket.

Sylvia watched her adjusting the little girl's blankets. 'There's no need to do that, my lady. Daphne can't be hungry after all she has eaten today, she will go back to sleep if you leave her alone.'

Katerina hugged the child to her. 'Likely she has been

left alone too much in her short life, she can go back to sleep in my arms tonight. In any case, I have need of the comfort she can give me.'

Cuddling the child, Katerina turned and walked past the Frank's empty pallet towards the light burning on a wall-sconce at the far end of the room. The curtains shifted in the breeze, the light flickered and blew out, and a nearby brazier glowed like a dragon's eye. And, despite the warmth of Daphne's small body, her skin had come out in goose-bumps.

'It isn't easy, the waiting, is it, my lady?'

Hrodric spoke in her ear; her heart jumped to find him so close.

'No, I hate it. I am all nerves tonight.'

Hrodric's eyes were sympathetic. Reaching for a taper, he relit the light on the wall-sconce. Cupping Daphne's head as she rocked her, Katerina studied him. There were deep lines about Hrodric's eyes, and his hair was grey at the temples. She judged him to be a good ten years older than Ashfirth. It was possible he had served Ashfirth's father before Ashfirth. 'Have you known the Commander long, Hrodric? Did you come with him from Ringmer?'

'Aye. Originally I was Thane Aiken's manservant.'

'I thought as much.'

'After the Great Battle, I returned to serve Ashfirth's mother, Lady Mildryth. She sent me after Ashfirth when he had to leave Ringmer. Almost lost him altogether, but managed to catch up with him in Honfleur.'

'Honfleur?' Katerina pressed a kiss on to Daphne's cheek; the child's eyes were drooping, she was already half-asleep.

'A Norman port across the Narrow Sea.' Hrodric's gaze was unfocused as he remembered. 'Captain Brand was with him, except he wasn't a captain then, of course, any more than Ashfirth was Commander. They were both boys.'

'I imagine he grew up quickly.' It was hard to imagine Ashfirth Saxon as a young boy, cast adrift from everything and everyone he knew. Ashfirth's early life had been no easier than hers.

'That he did. I did my best to watch over him, not that he needed much watching over.'

'No.' She glanced at the child. Asleep. 'But it is good to know he was not alone. Do you miss Ringmer, Hrodric?'

'Not any more, the Commander is the best of masters. He made it easier at the beginning and then one day I realised—' Hrodric cleared his throat and looked quickly away '—my home is with him and—'

The apartment doors flew open and Ashfirth himself strode in. His helmet was under his arm, and some black smears on his cheeks had made his face a devil's mask.

He looked unharmed. Relief weakened Katerina's knees; the same emotion was reflected on Hrodric's face.

'It is good to see you, sir,' Hrodric said, quietly. He went to take Ashfirth's helmet and battle-axe, setting them on a nearby table.

How does Hrodric stand it, how does he remain so calm? He loves Ash, it must tear him apart every time Ash prepares for battle. When you love someone...when you love...

No! Katerina's blood chilled. Was this love? The agonised waiting in case he had been harmed; the savage despair at the thought of him marrying someone more suitable...

I cannot love him, I cannot! For how can he love me when he finds out who I am?

Even as she cradled Daphne to her breast, her eyes were running over every inch of Ashfirth that was not hidden by his chainmail, she could not stop herself. She must check him for injuries; she had to know he was whole.

No! This cannot be happening...

I do not love this man!

So why do I want to fling my arms round him? Why does my bloodstream heat when he touches me, when he smiles at me?

'I need to speak to the Princess,' Ash said.

'Here, Hrodric, please put Daphne back in her basket. Gently now, she is asleep.'

Lifting the infant from her, Hrodric backed softly away.

Ashfirth took her arm and another weakening rush of relief ran through her. Katerina swallowed. She found herself reaching out to touch the dark streaks on his cheek. 'You are quite unhurt? What is this? Why, it's soot!'

Ash smiled. 'Probably.' His teeth were very white in contrast with the soot and the dirt, and his smile reached deep inside, warming her to the core. 'One of the furnaces in the copper-maker's street was left unattended.'

'It caught alight?'

He nodded. 'It took a number of us to put it out.'

And then she saw it, a reddish mark on the back of his hand and felt his pain as her own. *This is love.* 'You have burnt yourself!'

'It's nothing.'

Shaking her head, she towed him back to the other end of the chamber.

'Sylvia?'

'Despoina?'

'Where is that salve that Anna used on William?'

Sylvia reached for a willow basket and drew out a small clay pot. 'Here.'

'My thanks. Is there fresh water?'

'I shall fetch some at once, my lady.'

Amused by such fuss over what was a very minor wound, Ash allowed her to lead him into the light of a table lamp.

'Here, Commander.' She pushed him on to a stool and frowned over the back of his hand.

Ash nudged her with his thigh. Her face was so serious. 'It is a very small burn, my lady. I am sure there is no need—'

She shook her head, her veil rippling out about her. 'I won't risk it getting infected.'

The water was soon brought and Ash submitted to his hand being washed and dried and rubbed gently with salve. A bandage was produced. If he were honest, he was enjoying her attention—the clean, fresh smell of her and that subtle hint of roses and musk was a balm for his soul. And a far more effective balm than that mess she was rubbing on his hand.

Although I would far rather she addressed me as 'Ash' than 'Commander'. She is trying to distance herself from me, but she cannot do it. Her nature is too generous, she is giving to a fault and she cannot help but become involved in everything that goes on around her. For all that she has been wounded in the past, her essential nature remains unspoiled. Her warm heart is revealed in everything she does, from the way she was cradling that infant when I walked in, to the way she insists on binding my hand...

Ash watched the concentration with which she began winding the bandage round his palm and allowed himself a slight smile.

'That Frankish slave you found at the market had far more serious hurts,' he said, watching her face for her reaction.

'Oh, hmm, yes, I suppose he had.'

'Did you tend his wounds too, my lady?'

Startled brown eyes looked into his. 'William? Heavens, no. It was unnecessary, Anna saw to his hurts.'

Ash's smile widened. *She cannot hold herself aloof from me.* She glared at him and his smile faded. Tying the last knot with rather more force than was necessary, she straightened. 'You command the Emperor's Guard, your sword arm cannot be put at risk.'

'Such loyalty.' He flexed his hand. 'And I thank you, my lady, it does feel much better.'

Those large eyes were on him again, they were full of shadows. 'Have you seen Lady Anna again?'

'I take it that she has not returned?'

'No.'

'I haven't seen her since I saw her fleeing those mercenaries in the company of the Frank.'

Katerina had not moved away; indeed, she was standing so near, her leg was touching his thigh. Experimentally, Ash shifted, pressing closer. She held her ground. He was tempted to pull her on to his lap, but the watchful maid and the children at the other end of the chamber constrained him.

She may have refused my offer of marriage, but she does not seem to object to my person. She would not stand so close if she did; she would not bandage my hand with such care...

An image of Katerina cradling another baby—their baby—flashed into his head. Ash felt his heart begin to soften, before he caught himself up.

This is neither the time nor the place for such daydreams!

He tried to shove the image aside, but he must be more exhausted than he had realised, for he could not shift it.

Katerina, holding our child...

She was gesturing at the windows overlooking the City. 'What's happening out there?'

'I wish I knew.' Ash rubbed his face and suppressed a yawn. He was weary to the bone and now that he was at last sitting down, it was catching up with him. He could not remember when he had last slept properly. Or eaten, for that matter. He had been walking a tightrope for days.

'It has gone very quiet.'

'Yes. I've stood down half the Guard, they are grabbing some food.' He found himself wrestling an impulse to rest his head against her belly. He glanced at the maid. Oh, to hell with it. He took Katerina's hand and at once her fingers curled into his. He smothered another yawn. 'Negotiations are apparently underway.'

Her head tipped to one side. 'Between the Emperor and General Alexios?'

'No, between the Emperor and the Patriarch. Or so we were informed, but—' the yawn finally escaped '—no one seems to know what is really going on. Lord, I must keep moving or I shall be snoring.' He hauled himself to his feet. 'Events still hang in the balance, that being so, I should like to take you to a place of safety.'

Slowly she shook her head, she was staring down at her hand as if startled to see it clasping his. Releasing him, she picked up a length of spare bandage, coiled it into a neat roll, and set it carefully on the side table.

'You think General Alexios will win the day.'

'It is possible. As I said, events hang in the balance. Whatever happens, I must see you safe.'

'Surely this apartment is as safe as anywhere? Why, we are above your barracks, are we not?'

He caught her wrist. 'There is somewhere safer. Come, my lady, you may bring only what is essential.'

Her chin lifted, her eyes shone in the lamplight. 'I have

nothing of value since you took the jewel box. Were you thinking of returning it?'

He frowned. 'Of course I shall return it—did you not get my message?'

'Kari gave me a message, but—'

'You did not believe it!' The flare of anger caught Ash by surprise. So much for him thinking that she felt warmly towards him—he was deluding himself! She mistrusted him, as she mistrusted all men! He had been out of his head with worry—for her, for the Emperor, for his soldiers—yet he had taken the trouble to let her know that her valuables were safe.

And she did not believe him.

I have not given her any reason to mistrust me...whatever has scarred this woman has left her loving nature whole, yet she is walking around with a festering wound in her soul. She has lost the ability to trust.

Which raises some important questions—has she been scarred to such an extent that she will never trust anyone— ever? Will her wounds twist her loving nature out of true?

Lord, I pray not.

'You need to talk about your past,' he said, tightening his grip when she would have pulled back. 'You need to talk to someone who will hear you sympathetically, otherwise whatever happened to you will fester in your soul and destroy you.'

Her chin lifted. 'I have talked about it.'

'To Lady Anna?'

'Yes, she knows what happened.'

Ash tightened his grip on her wrist. 'Then it is time for you to try trusting someone, you are going to have to take that risk some time.'

The chin inched higher. 'I trust Lady Anna.' With a

sidelong glance at Sylvia, she lowered her voice. 'I trust the Princess as well.'

There was hope to be found in those words, but Ash felt his stomach cramp. *I want you to trust me!*

'Commander, I shall trust you to return my jewels.'

Cursing under his breath, for that was *not* what he meant and she knew it, Ash grabbed his battle-axe and started for the door. 'Very well, my lady. Since your jewels are essential to your happiness, your jewels are what you shall have.'

He stalked past the maid, Katerina's wrist firmly in hand. The maid had picked up on his anger; her eyes were round as pennies.

She started to her feet. '*Despoina*, are you all right?'

Katerina nodded. 'Thank you, Sylvia, everything is quite all right.'

Sylvia subsided and they left the apartment. Ash forced his grip to ease and hustled her past the startled guard and down the wide stairs.

Flinging back the door of his chamber, he dropped his axe on his bed and snatched her jewel box out of his coffer. He thrust it into her arms.

'There,' he spoke through gritted teeth. She was cradling the enamelled box in exactly the way she had been cradling the infant. 'Happy?'

She nodded, but she was lying, she looked anything but happy, her mouth had turned down at the corners. It was still—Holy Virgin—it was still the prettiest mouth in Christendom, it still looked ripe for kissing, even when it was unhappy.

He folded his arms, there was a bitter taste in his mouth. 'What in Hades happened to you?'

'C-Commander?'

'You can tell me. What did your father do? Or was it

that other fellow, your lover? What makes you value the contents of a trinket box more than life itself?'

Vehemently, she shook her head. 'That's a ridiculous thing to say, of course I value life! It is just…it is just…' Her brown eyes were huge, they seemed to draw Ash to her, even with fierce disappointment clouding his judgement. He felt his anger begin to subside. 'It is just…I have found a use for these trinkets, as you call them. A *good* use.'

Ash ran his hand through his hair. His stomach growled, he could only hope that she had not heard it. 'A use for them?' He frowned at the box. *The slave market!* 'You mean to sell the contents and buy *more* slaves?'

'Yes, I shall sell everything. I want to buy as many slaves as possible.'

'Will you free them, too?'

'Yes.'

'There are thousands of slaves in Constantinople—you can't free them all.'

'I know.'

Why? Why this obsession with slaves? Ash opened his mouth to ask her, but there was a rap on the door-frame and Hrodric appeared in the opening, holding Ash's helmet. 'Commander, you might need this.' He lobbed the helmet at Ash.

With a sigh, Ash set his jaw. 'Thank you, Hrodric.' *I forgot my helmet?* Merciful heavens, Katerina scattered his wits. The question remained though. *Why? Why would one of Princess Theodora's ladies-in-waiting be so determined to free slaves?*

Later, if God wills it, there will be time to discuss this later.

Reaching his spare cloak down from a peg, Ash tossed it round her shoulders. 'Come.' He extended his hand to her and managed to smile. 'While we wait for the wheels of diplomacy to turn, I shall take you to safety.'

Clutching the box in one hand, she placed her other hand in his and he led her, more sedately now that his anger was fading, out of the Palace and into the night.

As they picked their way across the shadowy courtyard, she glanced up at the lighthouse. 'No light tonight?'

Ash grunted. 'Ordered them to douse it.'

'Because the fleet has sided with General Alexios?'

'Yes. Had to do something while we waited for the Emperor and the Patriarch to finish their discussions.'

In silence Ash escorted her past the lighthouse and across a dimly lit expanse of grass. She had the jewel box firmly under one arm. He pulled her past the fountain that was shaped like a giant shell; it was grey in the gloom. Her eyes took in the statues of the dolphins frolicking in the centre, she was biting her lip.

Why does she have this need to buy slaves? When Ash was at leisure, he would find out.

'Where are you taking me?'

'Somewhere safe.'

She dug in her heels. 'What about Paula and Daphne? I want them to be safe, too.'

He released her hand. 'Why should anyone harm a couple of slave children?'

She stepped closed, placing her fingers on his chest. His heart warmed, even though he could barely feel her touch through his armour. 'Yet you seem to believe I am in danger?'

He spread his hands. 'Your case is different. You have taken Princess Theodora's place for several weeks—there are bound to be repercussions. I want you to be safe.' He touched her cheek. It was warm. Soft. He wanted to kiss it. 'Under normal circumstances you must realise your position is tenuous, and at the moment…Katerina, I cannot say whether General Alexios will succeed in his bid for the throne or not. If he fails, Emperor Nikephoros is bound to have questions for you.'

'And if General Alexios takes the throne…' Katerina heard her voice crack, she was unable to continue. *Ash, you might be killed!*

'Whatever the outcome,' Ash continued, 'I will have you safe.'

Katerina looked up at his face, but the torch on a nearby wall had cast it in shadow and she could not read his expression. *He wants me to be safe. And I want him to be safe.*

'Katerina, we must hurry.'

Ash sounded so curt. Asking for the jewel box had clearly infuriated him, but he really did appear to care about her safety. Katerina's heart twisted. Why, she wondered, did the longing to believe him hurt so much? *This is love.*

'You are certain the children will not be harmed if they stay with Sylvia?'

'I am quite certain. In any case, they would hate it where we are going.'

'Very well, Commander. Where are you taking me?'

'To the safest place in the Empire.'

'And the children wouldn't like it?'

'It is no place for children.'

Saints, where on earth was he taking her?

Chapter Fifteen

They crossed several darkened courtyards and stopped at a plain windowless building with a line of burly men-at-arms in front of it. A flickering torch silvered the curve of their battle-axes. Varangians. They sprang to attention.

'We're going in, Sergeant.'

The Varangians stood aside to reveal a squat door, heavily banded with iron. Ash produced a key that was the size of a small dagger, and two of the men dragged the door open. Behind the door, more torches flared, lighting up soot-stained walls and a narrow stone corridor. A curl of stairs ran down into darkness.

'Shut the door behind us,' Ash said. 'I will lock it from the inside, but I won't be long.'

'Yes, Commander.'

Katerina's hand was taken in a firm grasp; Ash had to duck his head to avoid the low lintel. No sooner had they stepped across the threshold than the door thudded behind them. Ash locked it and tucked the key into his belt. *We are closed in!* Her temples throbbed.

No place for children, indeed!

'Is…is there nowhere else?'

'It is the safest place in Constantinople.'

He pulled at her hand, but she balked at the head of the stairs. Gripping the enamelled casket, she shook her head. The idea of going down into the earth made her flesh creep.

'It is the safest place,' he repeated softly. 'I do not want the Princess's lady to be harmed.'

Tell him. You must tell him that you are no lady, and you must do it this instant! He will not thank you for continuing to mislead him in the middle of this crisis. You are wasting his time and it is precious.

'Ash…' Her lips felt stiff, it was as though she had not spoken in years. 'Ash…'

Tell him!

She made her hand lie lax in his, ready for the moment when he would drop it. 'Ash, it is not necessary for me to go down there. I am no lady of the Court in need of protection. I come from Crete. I…I am only a peasant.'

His eyes were black in the poor light, he frowned down at the casket for a moment before looking back up. 'From a village in Crete?'

'Yes.' His face was a mask, it was impossible to tell his reaction to her words.

'You have no family in the city?'

'No.' Her chest felt like lead. Unable to meet his eyes, she looked at the wall behind him. 'So you see, there is no need for your concern, I am not important. I am not the Princess, nor am I a great lady.'

His fingers squeezed hers, his thumb was rubbing the skin on the back of her hand. 'Katerina?'

His voice was warm, almost amused. She risked a look. *He is smiling, Ash is smiling at me!*

Utterly bemused, for amusement was the last thing she

had expected, she opened her mouth, but, with no clear idea of how to respond, she quickly closed it.

He raised her hand to his lips. 'Katerina, you are important to *me*.' His eyes gleamed. 'And if you think a hasty confession will get you out of going down there, you can think again. I want you out of harm's way.'

He sounds as though he means it! She stared. His reaction, so different from what her experience had led her to expect, completely baffled her.

Somewhere outside, a bell began to toll. The sound was too muffled for Katerina to identify clearly, but she did not think it was the alarm bell.

'Strange,' Ash murmured; he, too, had heard the bell. 'That sounds like Hagia Sophia.' He tugged at her. 'Hurry, I must get back. It is possible the Emperor has come to his decision. One way or another I must stand with my men.'

He started down the steps, leaving Katerina no choice but to follow. His words rang in her brain. *You are important to me.* He cannot mean it…

The stairs were steep and winding. There was a hand-rope, but because of the necessity of holding the jewel box, she tripped over the hem of her skirts and almost fell head-first.

'Give me that thing.' Taking the box from her, Ash continued down the stairs.

As they went down she saw faint light ahead. *Praise be, there are torches down there!*

It was very cold. At the bottom of the stairs, they came face to face with another door; this, too, was heavily banded with iron. More Varangians were on guard, helmets shiny in the yellow torchlight.

'Open it.'

And then they were hurrying along winding corridors, some lined with stone, others with brick. *Are we in the dungeons? Some sort of crypt? Whatever this place is, it is incredibly old.*

They passed yet more locked doors, more Varangian Guards, more doors. As they moved on and through, each door was locked behind them. The walls glistened with damp, salt crystals bloomed in broken plaster. The air became still, the torches fewer; the flames no longer flared and spat, they streamed steadily upwards.

Goosebumps rose on Katerina's arms; the hairs lifted on the back of her neck. Down here, it was as chill and as quiet as a tomb. Passages ran off to left and right. There were shadowy tunnels that appeared to go nowhere, some were bricked up a short way in.

It occurred to her that if Ash were angered by her confession, he could leave her down here as a punishment. But he did not seem angry any more, certainly not as angry as he had been when she had asked him to return the jewel chest. Rather the reverse, in fact.

'Where are we? What is this place?'

'You sound afraid—don't be. We are underneath the Palace.'

'Yes, but wh—?'

'This is the Imperial Treasury.'

'The Treasury!' Her jaw dropped; she felt the blood drain from her face. Surely he could not have brought her to the Emperor's Treasury?

He took her into one of the smaller tunnels running off the main corridor. It had a barrel-vaulted roof and was empty save for a worm-ridden storage chest. He set the jewel box on the chest and stared pensively at it. 'You are not a lady-in-waiting?'

'No.'

'So you have no lands, no great estates? In short, this—' long fingers touched the box '—is all you have.'

'Apart from a small gift of land, yes.'

'And you would use your jewels to free slaves.' Turquoise eyes held hers; never had they watched her so intently. 'You are a remarkable woman, Katerina. Quite remarkable.'

She had no answer for that. Were her lack of estates and family connections a disappointment? Ash did not look disappointed, in truth, his eyes were warm, but again this man was leading her into uncharted territory, and she did not know how to respond to him.

Her palms felt clammy, she wiped them on her skirts. 'Am I your prisoner, Ash?'

The warmth left his expression. 'Is that what you think? I thought you understood, this is the safest place in the Palace.' His lips twisted. 'In the entire Empire.'

Her throat worked. 'But, Ash...the Imperial Treasury? You are going to lock me in the Treasury?'

'You are afraid.'

'*Yes!* I...I don't like the thought of being trapped.'

He gestured back at the corridor. 'This cellar is open. See? No door.' He gave a strange laugh. 'You have been given the run of the vaults.'

'I don't like it. I am still locked in down here, and it is dark.'

He frowned at her for a moment and went out into the corridor.

'Ash? *Ash!*' Pulling his cloak more closely about her, Katerina shivered. *I must not scream, I must not scream...*

He was back with one of the corridor torches before panic had time to take hold. Jamming it in a rusting wall bracket, he pulled her to him. 'That should keep the demons at bay.'

She looked at the torch and back into his face. A warm hand slid round her neck and he pulled her to him, bending his head so their foreheads touched. 'Katerina, try to remember, I seek to protect you. My men will guard you with their lives.'

'Even though I have confessed my true worth? I am nothing, nobody!'

He grimaced. 'Do not underestimate yourself, Katerina.'

'Please, Ash, let me out of here.' She put a hand on his chest. 'I would far rather be back in the apartment. I hate to be confined.'

'You will be released.' Easing back, he shook his head. 'For pity's sake, try to trust me. Always you expect the worst of me. I am a man and so I am condemned. If you do not take care, Katerina, you will turn into an embittered woman. Can you not try trusting at least one man? Hmm?'

'But, Ash…' Her fingers would have curled into his mail coat, but she could get no purchase on it; the metal links were rough on her fingertips. Hard. Cold.

He stepped back, glancing at the corridor. 'I must go. Have no fear, you are not chained, after all. This is a storage vault, not a prison cell. Have faith, Katerina.'

Have faith. If I could have faith in anyone, it would be this man.

She managed to nod. She even tried to smile.

'That's better.' His face lightened. 'You will not be alone. I will send Hrodric to bear you company. Unless you would prefer Sylvia?'

She shook her head. 'Sylvia would loathe it here. Besides, the children need her. I…I should like to see Hrodric, though.'

'Very well. Stay calm. I hope to return soon…but I can make no promises.'

Hooking his hand round her neck in the familiar way, he brought his mouth to hers and kissed her. At once she began to melt against him, but the contact was fleeting, he had lifted his lips from hers and was gone before she had a chance to respond properly.

Take care, Ash, take care.

She strained to hear his footsteps, but soon they were lost behind the clang of a distant door and the scrape of a lock.

Like a moth to a flame, Katerina returned to the circle of light beneath the torch. Ash's cloak was heavy round her shoulders and she was grateful for it. Without it, the chill in these vaults would soon seep into her bones. The cloak smelt faintly of him; she could almost imagine his arms were about her. Enfolded in his cloak, she prayed the torch would last until Hrodric reached her.

This place was like a tomb. If something happened to Ash, would anyone remember where she was? She might die and lie undiscovered for eternity...

Hurry, Hrodric, hurry—before I forget Ash promised to send you.

It seemed like an age, but in truth it could not have been long before she heard the rasp of a key and the groaning of a rusty hinge.

'Hrodric, thank God you are here!'

Hrodric gave her a quiet smile. 'Couldn't have you down here alone, could we?'

Hrodric had brought the welcome glow of an oil lamp with him. There were more footsteps and a Varangian guard appeared, carrying a roll of blankets, a sack and a couple of wine-skins. Setting them in front of the wooden chest, the guard bowed to Katerina and withdrew.

Hrodric untied the sack and pulled out a loaf of wheat bread and a round of goat's cheese. He also produced several slices of meat wrapped in a cloth, and a small pot of olives. Katerina watched with widening eyes as he set them on a platter on the wooden chest and offered her one of the wineskins.

'A drink, my lady?'

She shook her head. *As if she could!* 'No, thank you, later, perhaps. Hrodric?'

'My lady?'

'There is no need to address me in that way, Hrodric. I...I don't know if Ash told you, but I have no title. I am... Katerina, simply Katerina.'

Hrodric nodded. 'Very well, Katerina.'

Thoughtfully, she watched for any reaction, but Hrodric seemed no more shocked by her admission than his master had been. His eyes were just as kind as ever, just as calm; indeed, his demeanour was sympathetic enough to encourage a confidence.

'Hrodric?'

'Katerina?'

'I should have told him to take care of himself.'

'He has been doing that for a long time, my l— Katerina, never fear.'

'He is a fool!'

Hrodric's brows rose. 'Katerina?'

'It strikes me he is fighting for a lost cause. Emperor Nikephoros has lost control of both his army *and* his navy. The Patriarch is suggesting he abdicates, yet Ash must return to his men.'

'Such is the nature of the vow he has made. Men of the Varangian Guard remain loyal till death.'

'I know, I know.' Suddenly close to tears, she wrapped her arms around her middle. Why was it that worry made one weak? 'It is that wretched honour of his. But Ashfirth is a fool, Hrodric, a fool! If that damned honour of his gets him killed, I shall never forgive him!'

Hrodric simply smiled. 'May I ask a question?'

'Please…'

'The Commander told me you have a fear of confinement, but when I entered it struck me that you were not letting your worries rule you.'

'Your point being?'

'You are concerned for the Commander, of course, but you never doubted that I would come, did you?'

'He said he would send you.'

'And you believed him.'

'Yes.'

'I hope he knows this, it would gladden his heart to hear you admit it.' Hrodric glanced at the wine-skin in his hand, shrugged and took a long pull from it. He wiped his mouth with the back of his hand. 'That's better, I needed that. Katerina, forgive my impertinence, but what do you plan to do when he returns?'

Ask him to forgive me for the trouble I must have caused him.

'I am…undecided. If, no…*when* he returns, I expect I shall have to face his anger. I deceived him and if the Emperor survives this attempt to topple him, Ash will have to answer for my actions.' She looked him square in the eyes. 'How long have you known?'

'That you are not Princess Theodora? Almost as long as Ashfirth.'

She grimaced and felt a light touch on her arm, a reassuring touch.

'Katerina, you must not fear that I shall betray you. Doubtless you were acting on Princess Theodora's orders?'

'Yes.'

'And you think Ashfirth holds this against you?'

'He must do. He was ordered to bring the Princess back to the Palace and instead he brought…me.' She stared blindly at the opposite wall. 'I am a very poor substitute for the Princess—he must feel betrayed. Hrodric, please understand, I never wanted to take Princess Theodora's place, but I owe her a great deal. And later, once I came to know the Commander and to...to like him, it became doubly difficult.' She gave a brittle laugh. 'In his place, I would be furious!'

'Did Ashfirth strike you as furious when he left the Treasury? Did he berate you? Did he threaten you in any way?'

She twisted her fingers together. 'Ash has never threatened me. Not when he discovered how he had been misled, nor when I confessed my true identity. Although...' She hesitated, glancing guiltily at the enamelled casket gleaming in the lamplight. Ash had not liked it when she had asked for the return of the jewel chest, he had definitely been angry then. He had been angry on board ship when her message to the Princess had been intercepted and he had confined her to the pavilion, but never, not once, had he threatened her with violence...

As she stared at the shiny casket something clicked in her mind. *I hurt him! My lack of trust cuts him to the quick.*

'He made no threats, I am sure,' Hrodric murmured. 'That is not his way.'

'No, he would never threaten.' *How my father would bluster in his place. But not Ash, Hrodric is right, that is not his way.* 'He was most anxious to get back to his men. When he returns, I shall pray he forgives me.'

'Naturally, he will forgive you, he asked you to marry him.'

'That was b-because—' her cheeks scorched '—because...'

Hrodric grinned. 'Because you spent several hours together in that bedchamber?'

'His wretched sense of honour made him ask me to

marry him.' She lowered her eyes. 'It motivates his every action.'

'His *every* action? Katerina, there you are wrong, very wrong. Ashfirth is on fire to marry you. To have you for himself.'

She stared at Hrodric, shaking her head. 'He thought I was a lady-in-waiting when he proposed marriage, he did not realise I was a potter's daughter from Crete.'

'I am sorry if you think that would make a difference to him. Ashfirth wants you.'

There was still much she could not say. *The Commander of the Varangian Guard does not know I was enslaved, he does not know what I was forced to do to survive.* 'Ashfirth's father was an Anglo-Saxon thane, he cannot marry me.'

'He does not wish to be parted from you.'

Nor I from him. Perhaps, if Ashfirth can find it in his heart to forgive me, I shall ask him to consider taking me as his lover...

Hrodric picked up a blanket, folded it several times to make a wad and set it on the flagstones.

'That should keep off most of the chill,' he said. 'Here, Katerina, please be seated. We may have a long wait.'

In the dank cellars of the Imperial Treasury there was no way of marking the passage of the hours, it was eternal night. Sunlight never inched across these cold flagstones; instead, the yellow tongue of the torch must lick the walls to leave a sooty shadow on the vaulted roof. The quiet was unnatural. Deep in the bowels of the earth, there was no chattering of sparrows from nearby gardens; these tunnels never rang with the shrieks of the seagulls. The air was never freshened by a salty wind, nor laden with the mouth-watering smell of baking bread. She and Hrodric were locked in with the Imperial treasures, locked in with the mildew and must.

'Hrodric?'

'Katerina?'

'This place is like a labyrinth.'

Hrodric grunted and, drawing a blanket about his shoulders, settled down beside her. 'Aye, that it is, a damp and cheerless labyrinth.'

'I never imagined the Treasury to be like this. It is hard to believe the wealth of the Empire is mouldering in such a grim place. One might lose one's way in the passages and—'

'Here, take another blanket and try to think of more pleasant things—of dolphins playing in a sunlit sea, of what you might do when we leave this place.'

Katerina accepted the blanket and wrapped it round her. 'You are right, of course. But I have had the most lowering of thoughts, and it will not leave me.'

'Yes?'

'If Ash does not come for us, we will be immured here for ever.'

A kindly hand patted her clumsily on the arm. 'He will come.'

'If he lives. But, Hrodric, what if—?'

'He will come. As to the labyrinth, push that thought from your mind. In any case, I have found that most labyrinths are of our own making.'

She stared blankly at him. 'What on earth can you mean?'

Hrodric smiled and shook his head and refused to elaborate.

They had been in the vaults beneath the Palace so long that Katerina took refuge in daydreams.

She was walking along the beach of her home village of

Loutro, and her sandals were dangling from her fingers. It was summer and the sea was as smooth and shiny as blue glass. White sand blinded her eyes, it was warm between her toes. The beloved child of a nobleman, Katerina was wearing a silken gown like one of Princess Theodora's. She had never been enslaved; she was a lady, a pure and innocent lady. When she turned to look at the hillside behind her, Ashfirth was making his way along the winding path through the olive groves. He was wearing a long court tunic, in burgundy brocade. He was smiling at her. With his turquoise eyes and raven-black hair he was so handsome it hurt to look at him. His gold arm-ring flashed as he held out his hand out to her...

A metallic chink broke the dream. Ashfirth and the Cretan olive groves were gone. In the blink of an eye, the treasury walls closed in.

'Hrodric, did you hear that?'

Hrodric was at the mouth of the vault, peering into the corridor. 'Someone is coming.'

She heard the groaning of a little-used hinge, the scraping of a door being forced open...hasty footsteps.

Hrodric turned, relief large on his face. 'It's the Commander!'

He's alive! The chill forgotten, she threw the blanket aside and rushed to the corridor.

It was indeed the Commander, but if it had not been for the brightness of those turquoise eyes, she would not have known the man behind that metal noseguard. With his helmet on and in full armour, that fierce foreign warrior was back. His shield was slung over his shoulder and the scabbard of his sword scraped the passage wall as he came towards her.

'Ash...Ashfirth?' But Ashfirth Saxon had been transported, he was a thousand miles away. This man was invincible; he no longer answered to the Emperor, he answered only to Ares, the god of war. Instinctively backing away, Katerina finally understood why so many Imperial soldiers had the head of the Medusa engraved on their sword. They hoped to turn their enemies to stone.

This man was a stranger.

His eyes—bright as jewels—found hers. His smile was grim, the crescent edge of his battle-axe flashed. He looked indomitable.

Where is Ashfirth? This man, this Commander, has devoured him.

She snatched at Hrodric's arm.

Hrodric grinned down at her, unperturbed. 'It is Ashfirth, and judging by the look on his face, he has come to claim his rights.'

'H-his rights?'

Hrodric's grin widened. Stepping back into the vault, he picked up the enamelled casket. 'Take this. Whatever happens, don't lose it.' He lobbed it across.

Somehow she caught it. 'His rights? *Hrodric?*'

There was no time for more because the Commander—*Ashfirth*—had reached her. He allowed Hrodric to take his shield and swept her into his arms. Her heart jumped about in her breast.

'Come on, Doe Eyes,' Ashfirth said.

Juggling the casket, grabbing at his leather chest-strap, Katerina looked into his eyes and fear was forgotten.

'Ashfirth,' she murmured. 'You came!'

His mouth remained grim, his jaw was set, but his eyes were warm. 'O ye of little faith. Yes, I came.'

Leaning in, she whispered, 'I did have faith, ask Hrodric. I knew you would come if you could.'

'You did?' He stared at her a moment and his mouth relaxed into a smile.

'Ash, you are unharmed?'

Nodding at Hrodric, arms tightening about her like steels bands, Ashfirth stepped back into the passage. 'Yes.'

He might be unharmed, but she sensed anger in him. Was it directed against her? Or at whatever had happened above?

He strode towards the tunnel and the winding stairs beyond. 'Hrodric, we only have minutes. I shall take her straight to the house. Follow us.'

'Yes, sir.'

'The house? Ash?'

'There is no time for explanations. First, I will have you out of here.'

There was a small cut on his cheek, it had not been there before. Forcing herself to release her grip on his leather chest-strap, she reached up to touch his cheekbone and felt warm human flesh and the roughness of a masculine cheek badly in need of a shave. A lock of dark hair curled out from under his helmet, she managed to touch that too. She wanted to touch, to kiss…

Dear Lord, let him keep me as his lover.

She was trying to plant a kiss on his chin when the casket began to slip from her hold. *I will make him take me as his lover.*

Frowning, he came to an abrupt halt. 'Careful, Katerina. You almost lost your treasure. I cannot carry it if I am carrying you.'

She tightened her grip on the casket and managed to place a swift kiss on his chin. 'I can walk, you know.'

Shaking his head, mouth a thin line, he settled her in his arms and set off again.

They passed the first door, then the next. There was muffled noise ahead. A shout. A loud thud. A wild laugh. *Has someone broken into the Treasury?*

'Ashfirth, what is happening?'

'Never mind, you are safe with me.'

'You should not be carrying me—what about your leg? Put me down.'

His mouth firmed as they ducked under another doorway. 'My leg is healed, and I will carry you.'

They were at the point where tunnels ran off to right and left. Doors were hanging askew, and they passed a vault which was empty save for a torch sputtering on the ground.

In the next cell a large chest was bolted to the flagstones with iron bands; a Varangian was prising it free with a metal bar. As Ash hurried past, grim-faced, the iron band gave way with a groan. The Guard let out a whoop and hefted the chest on to his shoulder.

Katerina's jaw dropped. 'That trooper, he...he's stealing...'

Blue eyes briefly met hers, and then the man was pounding past them, beating them to the spiral stairs. 'Not stealing. It is his right.'

Her breath froze in her lungs. All those tales of the Varangian Guard and their right to pillage...they must be true! The hairs rose on the back of her neck.

'Emperor Nikephoros has been killed?'

His nostrils flared. 'Not killed, he has abdicated. We only have moments.'

'Moments? For what? I don't understand.'

But Ash was not listening. He leaned his back against the wall at the bottom of the stairs, chest heaving.

'Ash, please put me down, I am far too heavy...'

'Don't argue.' Lurching forwards, he started up the stairs.

Katerina gave a muffled shriek, pressed her head against him and clung to his neck and shoulder-strap. Even so, she was slipping, it was not comfortable being carried like this.

'Ash—'

'Later,' he gasped. 'For pity's sake.'

She subsided against his chest, listened to his laboured breathing and prayed that his leg should not give way.

She could hear other Varangians, odd crashes and bangs, exultant shouts. Men intent on stripping the vaults of as much as they could carry. Yes, she remembered, they may only take what they can carry.

Her heart stopped. *Ash is carrying me! Me.*

What had he said? *We only have moments.*

Moments before…what?

The answer came in a flash.

There can only be moments before he swears to the new Emperor, to Alexios Komnenos, moments during which this right to pillage may be exercised.

After that the doors of the Treasury would be locked, the Guard would resume their positions and the wealth of the Empire would once more be secure.

Of course the pillaging had to take place in a very short time. Otherwise, the Treasury would be totally ransacked!

She bit her lip as she absorbed the implications of what he was doing. Ash only had moments, the wealth of the Empire was at his disposal, and he was carrying her…

He is choosing me.

A warm glow made itself felt in her chest.

He is choosing me!

You fool! He is choosing you, but do not delude yourself that he loves you. He might have learned your true origins, but he does not know you were enslaved. The best that you can hope for is that his punishment is not too severe; the best you can hope for is that he never learns that you were forced to barter your body during the time of your slavery. For then, if you are lucky, he might make you his lover for a time.

Chest heaving, Ash took the last stair and stumbled out
at the top. The main door was just ahead, Katerina could
smell the sea. And then he was standing in a courtyard that
was grey with mist. She sucked in fresh air. Brightness in
the east told her that dawn was breaking.

'We were in there all night?' she asked, as Hrodric
emerged with Ash's shield on his shoulder.

Ash was breathing hard. Nodding, he renewed his grip
on her and set off towards one of the gates.

'Surely you can put me down now?'

'In a moment.' His noseguard hid his expression, but he
sounded preoccupied. 'I realise the Princess herself commanded you to take her place, and it is most likely you will
not be punished, but just to be certain, I thought it best to
claim you.'

'To claim me?'

'No one will think to punish you if you are mine.'

'I am yours?'

*Ash owned her? He had carried her from the Treasury
and because of this he owned her?*

'No!'

*She had used her precious freedom to repay the Prin-
cess, and this was to be her reward? Ash owned her?*

Katerina did not know what to think. Of all the men in
the world, Ash was perhaps the only one she might accept
as master...but...

'No!'

He was avoiding her gaze. 'For now. Do not misunder-
stand. It is...a temporary measure.'

Her tension eased. *He does not intend to own me. I will
not be his slave.* 'A temporary measure? So no one will
punish me?'

'Exactly.'

'And what about you?'

His gaze was blank. 'Me?'

'I deceived you. Your reputation…will it suffer because I…because…?'

'My reputation is quite safe, I assure you.' His mouth gave a wry smile. 'In any case, the Emperor who summoned Princess Theodora to Constantinople has abdicated. My failure to see through your deception has become irrelevant.'

He fell silent as they reached the gate. The sentry saluted and he hurried through. When he gained the street, he set her on her feet.

'Finally!' Katerina gave him a tentative smile while he caught his breath. Shame lay heavy on her heart. *I should have told him about my time as a slave.* But she had missed her chance. She would simply have to tell him later, and pray he was not revolted by what she had had to do.

'Come.' He was extending his hand to her in exactly the same way as he had done in her daydream. 'The house is not far, it is just off the Mese.'

She looked blankly at him. 'The Mese?'

Ash made an exasperated sound. 'The Princess really should have asked someone with a better knowledge of the city to take her place. The Mese—Middle Street—is the main street. Because of your fear of horses, we shall walk.'

Katerina nodded agreement. Inside she was aching for the impossible—she wanted him to know her full story, and then she wanted him to smile at her in the same way that he had done in her imaginings.

Chapter Sixteen

The squares and avenues were filling with people, news of the coup had already reached the streets. Katerina could sense the excitement; everyone seemed to be smiling— serious fighting had not broken out. The feeling of relief was palpable, yet she felt oddly apart, unable to share in everyone's happiness.

She stepped into the gutter to make way for a woman energetically attacking a broken amphora with a broom. Others were clearing up, too. One man was tossing snapped-off tree branches into a cart; another was replanting an uprooted shrub. Protective planking was being prised off shop fronts; troops were tramping this way and that; there was bustle and laughter. The handcarts had reappeared— the citizens of Constantinople had obviously decided it was safe to bring their chattels out of hiding and return home.

'Look at that.' Making her voice bright, she pointed to a house where a Persian carpet was hanging from a balcony, all colour and swirling patterns. The bright tone was to cover up the fact that she felt hollow inside. This was the day when she must reveal the rest of her past to him. She could no longer put it off, and while she had learned that Ash was not an intemperate man, he himself was so strong he could not help but be shocked by her enslavement. And as for what had happened with Vukan—an honourable man like Ash would surely be repelled by her relations with Vukan…

'They are celebrating,' Ash said, waving at other houses that were displaying their approval of Alexios Komnenos in a similar fashion. Bright carpets and vivid tapestries adorned the street, like rows of flags.

'General Alexios is a popular choice.' A sick dread had her in its grip. *Today, I shall tell him today. The longer I deceive him, the less respect he will have for me when he does find out.*

'Yes, the people hate uncertainty. General Alexios is a strong man, they expect to prosper under his leadership.'

Katerina glanced over her shoulder. She had her confessions to make, but she was afraid, she was a coward. Besides, what she had to say was too personal, she could hardly discuss it out here in the street! Particularly not when Hrodric was walking a few paces behind with a small escort of Varangians. With a jolt, Katerina realised that the Guard was there for her benefit. For her—a village girl! It came to her that when the moment came to part from Ashfirth Saxon she would miss the care he took of her.

'The city will be put to rights,' Ash was saying. 'Alexios Komnenos is mortified by the damage done by his troops, he will have to make amends. There is talk of penances.'

'Will the new Emperor bear a grudge against you for having served the old one?'

Ash shook his head. 'Not if my men and I swear allegiance to him, which we will.'

'It is as simple as that?'

'Yes. When Emperor Nikephoros abdicated, our contract

with him was ended. Within the hour I must pledge my loyalty to Alexios Komnenos.'

'Within the hour?' *Heavens.*

'Yes. He will be enthroned on Easter Day.'

Katerina nodded. *The townsfolk are not alone in their delight with the new Emperor; Ash is delighted, too. And since I am undecided about whether to confess quite yet, I shall follow his lead, we shall talk about the new Emperor.* 'Tell me more about General Alexios, you obviously admire him.'

Ash nodded. 'He has a quick mind and a good grasp of politics—his whole family have been bred to it. He has support inside the Great Palace, and with the army and navy behind him, the borders of the Empire may at last be strengthened. General Alexios has always commanded my admiration, I confess I am glad we did not have to fight him face-to-face.'

'And you must meet him within the hour?'

'Yes.'

His turquoise eyes were lit with happiness. *Ash is delighted with today's outcome.* 'I heard some talk at the Palace,' she said. 'Emperor Nikephoros was not universally admired.'

Ash gave her a penetrating look. 'Certainly, many spoke out against him.'

Her lips curved. 'Ash, you are too loyal, he sounded to be a very imperfect Emperor.'

'He...let us say he had his difficulties.'

Yes, it has been hard for Ash to emerge from this with honour, but he has succeeded. This is a great day for him, and I must not mar it.

He placed his hand over hers and gave it a gentle squeeze. 'I have to admit, it will be a relief to offer my report on

Norman troop movements in Apulia to someone who will understand the implications and take action.'

They had come to a stop in front of a wall with a set of double doors in it.

'Where are we?'

'Katerina, welcome to my home.'

'Your home!' The doors opened and Katerina found herself in a courtyard.

The house had three stories and was framed by tall cypresses; steps led to a columned portico and another set of double doors. Through these doors she glimpsed a tiled floor, an arched arcade, a flight of stairs…

'It's a palace!'

'Hardly.'

She stared at him. 'I thought you lived in the barracks.'

His expression was enigmatic. 'Not all of the time. I have made this my home, I am glad you like it.'

'It is lovely.' Ash must have built it with prize money he had earned over the years, Katerina realised, prize money and pay. She had known that some of the Varangian Guard were wealthy, but until this moment she had no idea of the riches that could be made by commanding the company.

The entrance hall was wide, the tiles marble. Daylight was coming through an arch in a central courtyard; she could see a slight flickering. It was a moment before she realised what it was. 'There's a fountain!'

A servant ran up, and it was then that Katerina noticed a knot of people in one of the doorways. Here were more pleased smiles and, she thought, some curiosity. As she stepped nervously inside, she received the distinct impression that these people had passed the last few hours as anxiously as she had done.

'Welcome back, Commander.' The servant—or was he

a slave?—took Ash's helmet and arms with a smile that spoke loudly of his affection for his master.

'I see the good news has arrived before us,' Ash said.

'Yes, sir. I have taken the liberty of laying out your dress uniform upstairs.'

'Thank you, Manuel.'

Clearly delighted at the night's outcome, Manuel bowed and carried Ash's arms up the stairs.

Hrodric came in and went straight to the audience in the doorway. 'Don't you have work to do? Hera, is breakfast prepared? There will be extra mouths to feed, two children are arriving here shortly. And you, Michael, get back to the stables, there will be a parade later. The harness needed mending the last time I looked.'

'Children?' Katerina touched Ash's hand. 'You have sent for Daphne and Paula?'

Ash gave a careless shrug, but he was anything but careless, he was watching for her reaction, skin darkening. 'Thought there would be no peace unless I did. Come, if we hurry, I may show you around.' He drew her hand through his arm, so her fingers rested on the sleeve of the tunic showing beneath his mail coat. Outwardly she was calm, inwardly her mind was a seething froth of questions.

Why has he brought me here? And the children? He is a kind man and he has brought the children to please me—on what terms does he expect me to stay?

After giving Katerina a brief glimpse of a well-ordered household, Ash escorted her to a spacious bedchamber at the top of the first flight of stairs. From a corner, a brazier threw out a warm glow. The walls were painted with a frieze of a distinctly masculine nature; there were chariots and—she might have known it!—horses. Black horses, greys, chestnuts—their tails and manes flying as they galloped round the walls. The shutters and window hangings were open, sparrows were chattering in a nearby plane tree, wheels rumbled out in the street.

There is no need for Ash to tell me to whom this chamber belongs.

In the centre of the bed lay the red dress uniform of the Commander of the Varangian Guard; the gold braiding was as elaborate as any she had seen at the Palace. A jewelled cloak fastener winked up at her from a circular cloak.

On a side table, a bronze basin was waiting next to a steaming ewer of water and a neat pile of drying cloths. Katerina set her enamelled casket next to the ewer and went to look out of the window.

'The mist has almost gone, I can see the Palace quite clearly from here. Ash, those stables alongside the villa, are they yours?'

He came to stand next to her in the window, winding an arm about her waist. 'Yes.'

She leaned against him and pulled a face. 'I thought Caesar was your only horse.'

'Actually—' he kissed the side of her head '—I have several.'

'Several!' She glanced at the frieze and shuddered.

'I like to race.'

'Didn't you say that was how you injured your leg? Hasn't it put you off?'

'Not a bit of it, I love horses.'

'I cannot like them.'

'Katerina…' Ash stared at her profile, at the long lashes framing those beautiful eyes. He knew, beyond shadow of a doubt, that she still had her secrets, and he wanted—no, he needed her to reveal them. Her lack of trust was more than merely galling, it had become a chill in his chest, a cold dread in his guts. Would she never trust him? If she could not learn to trust him, they had no future together. If that was the case, he must accept it and move on. The thought made him sick at heart. 'Tell me your thoughts.'

She laughed and avoided his gaze. 'I was thinking how different we are, in so many ways. I shall never like horses.'

'I promised you riding lessons,' he murmured, maintaining a neutral expression to cover a shocking and not altogether welcome realisation. *I love her!* He cleared his throat. 'I am certain if you learned to ride, your confidence would grow and you would come to love horses as I do.'

'You promised a Princess riding lessons,' she said, in a small voice. 'I am not a Princess. In any case, I doubt that even you will be able to help me overcome my fears.'

Ash found himself wondering what they were really talking about. *Tread warily, Ash, or you may lose her.* 'I want to try. Won't you let me help you? Katerina?'

Ash pulled her round to face him. A small hand came to rest on his chest, he enfolded it in his. Desperate need was clawing at his insides, but he must conceal it from her, she must not feel coerced in any way. She was so tiny, she barely reached his shoulder. *Take care, Ash, take care. Lord, I love her. I cannot let her go!*

'Ashfirth, I must thank you for sending for the children.'

'It is my pleasure.'

She glanced frowningly at the horses racing along the frieze, completely unaware that at some point during their journey from the Treasury, her veil had slipped. Beneath it her hair was unwinding in glossy silken tangles. She had a smudge on her chin, a tear in her gown and…she had never looked more beautiful.

His heart constricted. *I want her. For ever. I cannot let her go. I will find a way to keep her.*

Smoothing a strand of hair from her brow, he took a steadying breath. Sometimes, when she looked at him…he was not altogether certain that the real prize was beyond his reach. *Never consider defeat...*

'Katerina, there is something I would ask of you.'

She gazed up at him, eyes shadowed. 'Yes?'

'I have asked it before, you will have to forgive me, but I but I must ask again. Will you marry me?'

She jerked her head to stare fixedly out of the window, gently he brought it round to face him—he had to see the slightest shift in her expression.

Her eyes were glassy with tears. 'I cannot.'

'You are married?'

'No.'

'Will you not tell me why you will not marry me?'

'I...I...it would not be fitting.'

Ash didn't understand. *Not fitting?* 'Is your refusal in some way connected to the Princess? Are you protecting her?'

'It does not concern the Princess. Please, Ash, I cannot marry you.'

'You are decided on that?'

'It would not be...fitting.'

'Very well, I shall accept that answer, for now. But this I will ask.' He gripped her hands. 'This is my home, and if you are prepared to consider a less...orthodox arrangement, I was hoping you might care to share it with me.'

A tear slipped out and rolled down her cheek. Carefully, he wiped it away.

'As...as your lover?' Her mouth trembled.

'If you please. The barracks are not the best place when a man and a woman—' Ash pressed his body more firmly against hers and searched for the green flecks in her eyes '—have a...warm liking for each other.'

She sniffed.

He hid a grin. It was a most unladylike sniff, but she

was considering his proposal. Her brows were drawn, but, yes, she was considering it.

'A warm liking, Ash?' she murmured.

His smile wavered. 'You don't agree?'

She shook her head, her veil slipped a little further and her lips began to curve. 'Not a warm liking, Ash. A *hot* one.' Her words were bold, but the eyes looking up from under those lashes were disarmingly shy. She lifted her mouth to his.

'Scorching,' he muttered.

And then he was kissing her, pressing his lips to hers. He wanted to taste her, he *must* taste her...it was a struggle not to devour her because she was pushing that slight body against his, and then at last she was opening her mouth so their tongues might begin their slow, seductive dance.

Relief raced through him, mixed with the most intense rush of lust Ash had ever felt. With the scent of musk and roses filling his head, and the taste of her on his tongue, it was hard to stay standing. He gave her lower lip a last soft bite and raised his head. 'We are agreed, then—you will stay here as my lover?'

'For a time.'

For a time—what the hell does that mean? Before Ash could demand an explanation, she was speaking again.

'Ash, there is one condition...'

'Oh?'

'The horses will have to go.'

'The horses?' He drew his head back. 'You can't mean—not Caesar!'

She was shaking, and for a heart-stopping moment Ash thought he had lost her. Then he heard a smothered laugh; she was pointing at the frieze running round the bedchamber.

'The frieze?' He relaxed. 'That can easily be changed.

You may have flowers, vines, whatever you wish.' He slid his hand round her neck and pulled her close, so he could rest his forehead against hers and look deep into her eyes. 'Lord, I thought I was in real trouble, I thought you meant Caesar must go.'

'Would I dare? But I would like that wall painting reworked, I do not find it restful.'

The green flecks in her eyes were very bright, her pupils were black as night, and if Ash had not delayed too much already—his negotiations with General Alexios were imminent!—he would tear off her clothes. He wanted to seal their agreement in bed. Later he would persuade her to become his wife. *Never consider defeat.*

'Your expression was priceless, Ash, priceless.'

He kissed her nose. 'As are you to me. My love, you are a woman above price.'

Her eyes slid away.

Now what have I said? Just as I begin to make headway, she is shying away. What is the problem? It concerned her dark past, and whatever it was, he must get it out of her before she decided her time with him had come to an end. It would be proof of her trust in him and if he could not win her trust, he would have the devil of a job getting her to marry him.

Pushing her veil aside, he nuzzled her ear and cupped a perfect breast with his palm. He groaned. In the meantime there was this…this heat between them. If only he had more than a few moments. His blood was hot, he ached to lose himself inside her. The thought of those small limbs wrapping themselves around him, clinging to him… *Damnation! How does one woo a woman when you are in chainmail and you have run out of time?*

He was manoeuvring her towards the bed before he realised what he was doing.

General Alexios!

Lord, how was a man to think with Katerina in his arms?

'Ash?'

'Mmm?'

'Did you see anything of Lady Anna or William?'

He lifted his head, determined to quell the desire pulsing through him. 'Not since I saw them by the Milion. I have made enquiries, but there has been no trace of them.' He hesitated to say more, he did not want to worry her.

'Ash, what is it?' Importunate fingers tugged at his sleeve.

'It is possible the Frank has run away.'

'Oh, no.' Her voice was confident. 'That will not have happened.'

'You think not? If I were in his shoes, I would use the chance to escape.'

'William won't do that, he will keep Anna safe.'

Shaking his head, Ash finally managed to tear himself from her. Unbuckling his sword belt, he dropped it on to the bed.

'Help me off with my chainmail, will you? I have to change quickly. Unless you would rather I called for Hrodric?'

'No, I should like to try.'

Ash bent almost double and stretched out his arms. 'It is rather awkward, but if you take hold of the mail by the shoulders and yank like fury, we should manage it.'

She grunted and heaved, and Ash backed away, and between them the chainmail clattered onto the floor. 'Saints, that's heavy!' she said.

Shrugging out of his leather gambeson and tunic, Ash moved to the ewer, poured some water and began to wash.

She followed him, and out of the corner of his eye he saw her frowning at her jewel box. 'Ash...I would like to go to the slave market again. When everything is back to normal, will you accompany me?'

'If you wish.' He splashed water on his face, she handed him a towel.

'Ash, do you own slaves?'

'No.'

Her face relaxed. No, it was more than that, she looked like someone from whom a great weight had been lifted.

Slaves, her secret shame is in some way connected with slavery.

Just then, she slid her hand down his arm—it was a caress, a definite caress. A caress which prompted a heartening thought. *Katerina is not a girl who gives her caresses lightly.* Ash felt a tightening in his groin. In truth, this was the first gesture of affection he could recall that she had initiated.

Progress.

When she leaned towards him and kissed his biceps, blood flooded to his loins. Her veil tickled his chest. 'That is as it should be,' she murmured.

Gripping the towel, Ash stared down at her. He had gone hard as a rock. Her nearness, the scent of roses, that tentative gesture, the warmth in her dark eyes—the effect was all too inevitable. Lust was clouding his senses, but beneath the confusion there was a glimmer of understanding...

Slaves. Katerina is...there is some connection with slavery.

The world seemed to tilt.

Could it be that she was once a slave? Princess Theodora's slave?

Katerina was once a slave! As he looked at her, he realised that at last he knew her secret. *She had been a slave.*

'I wonder how many slaves this will free?' she was

saying. Opening the casket, she drew out a golden collar adorned with lapis lazuli. 'Ash, how much do you think this collar will fetch?'

He covered her hand with his, and the collar rattled back into the casket as her fingers twined with his. 'You are an extraordinary woman, do you know that?'

'What, for wishing to help slaves? I suppose you think I am ridiculous.' She attempted to pull free, but he tightened his grip.

'Not at all, love, on the contrary.'

Perhaps she still is a slave! Think, Ash, think. You first saw her in a convent for fallen women. Is she a fallen woman? She had certainly been no innocent when he had bedded her among those mulberry sheets.

'Katerina, does the Princess own you?'

Katerina choked—his soft question had turned her blood to ice.

He knows!

His thumb was slowly moving across the centre of her palm and he raised an eyebrow, looking at her through turquoise eyes that pierced her to her core.

'I think you heard me, my love, your cheeks have gone white as bone. Does the Princess own you? Are you a slave?'

His smile was understanding. Katerina's heart began to hammer. She had begun to shake her head, but something in his quiet watchfulness gave her pause. It made her watchful, too; it helped her to see him with new eyes.

Ash seemed startled by his realisation, but he didn't look the least bit shocked. Nor did he look revolted. The idea that he had set a slave up as mistress of his household did not appear to appal him, his thumb had not stopped calmly caressing her palm.

She had come to know his expressions and his expression

at this moment was…enquiring. Slightly surprised. Full of compassion. She looked down at their linked hands, at the slow and easy movement of his thumb on her skin. His hands…so gentle…always gentle.

Ash looked as though he was interested in her response—behind that there was something else, something Katerina dared not identify, something that she hoped she had not misunderstood.

I have found a man I might trust. Holy Virgin, do not let my resolve fail.

'I was a slave.' She stared at the floor, her lips so stiff, she had to push out the words. 'Princess Theodora bought me.' Suddenly, it was as though a great barrier had fallen and the words poured out. 'I was a child when my father sold me. Some years into my slavery, Princess Theodora bought me. She freed me at once, and trained me as her maidservant.'

Strong fingers gripped like a vice. 'Your *father* sold you?'

Now he did sound appalled. She lifted her gaze to his. His brow was deeply furrowed, he was white about the mouth.

Taking her by the waist, he dragged her to him. 'Your *father*, Katerina?'

'Yes.' *Ash is angry, but not with me, he is angry with Father…!*

Heart lifting, she put her hands on his shoulders. She was absurdly conscious of the strong muscles in his arms and chest, of the sprinkling of dark hair arrowing downwards. She could smell his scent, the masculine scent that was Ash was mixed with the scent of rosemary in the soap.

Careful fingertips were tracing patterns on her cheek. 'Dear God, no wonder you have a mistrust of men—your *father* sold you into slavery!' He traced the outline of her

lower lip with a finger before ducking his head to give her
the softest of kisses.

She gripped the wide shoulders and let her body relax
against his. 'Ashfirth, there is more. Perhaps after your
ceremony, I might tell you.'

'Tell me now.'

'During the time of my slavery, before the Princess
bought me, I was kept in a compound with the other slaves.
More than one of them...wanted me.' Ash caught his breath
and she rubbed her cheek against his chest, feeling the
slight abrasion of his chest hair. 'Ash it is all right, I was
not raped. It was just that I...I had to give myself to the
strongest of the slaves. It was the best way, the *only* way,
to keep the others at bay.'

'Not rape?' He spoke through clenched teeth. 'It sounds
very like. Was he your choice?'

'No, not exactly—'

'Did you miss him when the Princess bought you? Did
you love him?'

'Love him? Never.' Raising her eyes to his, she went up
on her toes and kissed him. 'You are the man I love. Ash,
I love you.'

He caught her to him, eyes darkening. His lips curved.
'You do?'

'With all my heart.' Inhaling the scent of him, she kissed
his chest. He was caressing her cheek, lifting her by the
chin to kiss her again.

'Finally you have told me your story,' he murmured
against her mouth, before drawing back with a scowl. 'But
your father...no wonder it took so long to open up to me!
And that slave—his behaviour was shameful, shameful.
Katerina, the shame is theirs, not yours. You do see that?'

'I...I think so.'

'I *know* so. Lord, you have suffered so many betrayals...

and your lost years as a slave…when we are at leisure, you shall tell me *everything.*'

Flushing, she looked away. 'Ash, I am sorry. I hated deceiving you. I wanted to tell you the truth long ago, but much of it was not my truth to tell. I feared your reaction.'

'The shame is not yours.' He put his arms on her shoulders to hold her slightly at a distance. 'You remind me of a warrior I know.'

'Oh?'

'His name is Palaiologos, he is a great and honourable man. When his son broke his oath to the Emperor, Palaiologos felt great shame.'

'But he cannot be responsible for the actions of his son!'

Triumph flared in the turquoise eyes. 'Just so, and that is exactly what I said to him. Palaiologos need feel no shame for what his son chose to do, any more than you must bear the shame of those who betrayed and used you.'

'I…see.'

'Yes. Finally, I think that you do. You are free in the true sense of the word—you may leave your dark past behind.'

'Yes, I am free.'

His hands slid round her waist, holding her loosely. 'Free to stay here, I hope, for ever, if you wish.'

Katerina frowned. *For ever?* 'I will stay until you tire of me.'

'Tire of you?' He laughed, hands squeezing hers. 'That day will never dawn. Katerina, I want you to have my children, I want you as my wife.'

He is still speaking of marriage? Tears stung the back of her throat. 'But…but…I am not a court lady.'

'Thank God for that. Katerina, from the moment I saw you through that convent gate, I have had no peace. No, don't look away, I like looking at your eyes.' His voice warmed, his hands were moving up and down her ribcage, gently caressing. Heat pooled in her groin, her breasts tingled. 'There you stood, a small girl with eyes like those of a doe. A mysterious girl, a girl I desired on sight, but thought I could never have because she turned out to be the Princess Theodora.'

'Ash, I—'

Firm fingers pressed her lips into silence. 'Hush.' He cleared his throat. 'Allow me to tell you that I love you. Allow me to tell you that when I am with you I am content, with you at my side, I am come home. For the first time in years it no longer matters that England is lost to me. Katerina, you are my home. I need you. I love you. Katerina, marry me.'

'B-but you cannot want to marry me, you need a noble-woman to bear your children. Your father was an Anglo-Saxon thane, while I…I am nobody.'

His eyes were warm. 'You are my love.'

'But, Ash…a potter's daughter?'

'So?' He shrugged. 'I love a potter's daughter.'

'How can you? I was a slave!'

He gave a suggestive grin. 'Even better—slaves are so biddable.'

He really means to marry me! Dizzy with happiness, Katerina thumped her fist against his chest. 'Wretch!'

'In truth, it is I whom you have enslaved. I would give you the world if I could.' His expression darkened. 'Except for one thing—never ask me to meet your father, I could not answer for my actions. You are my love. We shall be married as soon as may be arranged, after the General's enthronement. Agreed?'

Head whirling, Katerina looked mistily up at him.

'Katerina, you will become my wife? After Easter?'

'Yes.' Her voice was thick with emotion. 'I love you.'

They came together in a clumsy rush and toppled on

to the bed. With a smile, Katerina fingered the ties of his chausses. 'Do you really have to leave?'

His face fell. 'Hell, the General!' He eased her away. 'I am afraid so, my love. We shall have to celebrate our betrothal later.'

His dark hair was tangled and needed combing, he was only half-dressed and he ought to be on his way to meet his new Emperor, but his eyes were dark with desire. *The same desire that is turning my limbs to water.*

She tugged determinedly at the fastenings at his waist. 'Why do you have to wear this barbaric clothing?'

He grinned. 'Because I am a barbarian?' His hands closed over hers. 'Love, I am sorry, but there really is not much time before I have to be at that ceremony.'

'I can be quick.'

His gaze became speculative. 'Quick? How quick?'

She bent and kissed his chest. 'Very, *very* quick. Just this once.'

'I think—' Ash whipped off her veil even as she was easing him out of his chausses '—we should put this to the test.'

A foot kicked his dress uniform to the floor...

* * * * *